W9-ARF-765

1/3/13

ANGEL WITH
A BULLET

OTHER WORKS BY THE AUTHOR

Writing as Grant McKenzie:
Switch (Bantam UK, 2009)
No Cry for Help (Bantam UK, 2010)
K.A.R.M.A. (e-book, 2011)

Writing as M. C. Grant:
Underbelly, an e-book short story
(Midnight Ink, 2012)

m. c. grant

A Dixie Flynn Mystery

ANGEL WITH A BULLET

LUDINGTON
PUBLIC LIBRARY & INFORMATION CENTER
5 S. BRYN MAWR AVENUE
BRYN MAWR, PA 19010-3406

MIDNIGHT INK
WOODBURY, MINNESOTA

Angel with a Bullet: A Dixie Flynn Mystery © 2012 by M. C. Grant. All rights reserved. No part of this book may be used or reproduced in any manner whatsoever, including Internet usage, without written permission from Midnight Ink, except in the case of brief quotations embodied in critical articles and reviews.

FIRST EDITION
First Printing, 2012

Book design and format by Donna Burch
Cover design by Ellen Lawson
Cover images: Background: iStockphoto.com/Juan Facundo Mora Soria
          Golden gate bridge: iStockphoto.com/Andrew Zarivny
Editing by Nicole Edman

Midnight Ink, an imprint of Llewellyn Worldwide Ltd.

This is a work of fiction. Names, characters, places, and incidents are either the product of the author's imagination or are used fictitiously, and any resemblance to actual persons living or dead, business establishments, events, or locales is entirely coincidental.

Library of Congress Cataloging-in-Publication Data
Grant, M. C., 1963–
 Angel with a bullet : a Dixie Flynn mystery / M. C. Grant. — 1st ed.
    p. cm.
  ISBN 978-0-7387-3415-6
1. Women journalists—Fiction. 2. Art forgers—Fiction. 3. San Francisco (Calif.)—Fiction. I. Title.
 PS3607.R362953A83 2012
 813'.6—dc23

                                                        2012010694

Midnight Ink
Llewellyn Worldwide Ltd.
2143 Wooddale Drive
Woodbury, MN 55125-2989
www.midnightinkbooks.com

Printed in the United States of America

DEDICATION

This one is for the HrtBrkrs,
dreamers and believers.
If we told our younger selves
how bumpy the road ahead,
would we still walk it?
Damn right, we would.

And for Kailey and Karen,
always and forever.

PROLOGUE

Before the blood, the raw canvas cost twenty dollars. With the squeeze of a trigger, the artist would make it priceless. Quite an achievement for a bronzed urchin who first spoke his heart on the only canvas available: cave walls, tree bark, the flaking curves of abandoned cars, and sun-bleached walls of cursed and neglected huts.

In rural New Mexico, a sable brush was as foreign as indoor plumbing, reliable electricity, or parental rules. His tools came from the earth: shards of mottled flint, stone edges as thin and sharp as any knife. His paint palette surrounded him: charcoal from communal fires; solid bands of red and yellow ochre from ravaged hills, the pigments crushed in the same manner as his ancestors, by brutal force; crumbling yellow-white sulfur in pockets near the natural hot springs where he once saw an alabaster angel, naked and laughing with ripe cherry nipples atop vanilla cream; and the color that dominated most of his work: the rich orange-brown rust that grew over everything, thick as despair.

Some days he became so carried away, scratching his marks deep into charred wood or oxidized metal, he could ignore the pain. A hundred tiny cuts caused blood to dribble from his fingers and fill the grooves and swirls with living color. He became the paint; nature, his canvas.

Nothing since had ever truly recaptured that level of intimacy.

The art was forgotten.

The artist lifted a Remington .12-gauge shotgun. He stroked the warm varnished stock and cold blue-black steel, the pure esthetic practicality of the thing. Hands trembling, he positioned the weapon—aptly named "thunder stick," a foreboding tool of destruction.

It snaked between legs, unsettlingly phallic, the weight of it resting on stomach and chest, its rubberized, slip-resistant butt firmly anchored to the floor.

The weapon's terrifying black hole slid between soft, dry lips, teeth reluctantly parting as the barrel dug just a little deeper. The artist felt warm tears flowing down ruddy cheeks as he hooked a bare toe through the curved metal guard and settled it on the well-oiled trigger.

He took a deep, calming breath and whispered a final prayer to his neglectful creator.

The trigger squeezed so easily.

ONE

SOME PEOPLE LIKE TO count sheep; I prefer ex-boyfriends. Bare-chested, tight boy shorts and strong thighs flexing at my command.

I usually have them leap over the bed. I enjoy the perspective. They tense muscles to my left, leap and fly over my prone form in a variety of ways, and land somewhere to my right.

I don't watch the landings, for I hate to see them strut. Few men realize it's not the finish that makes it worthwhile, but rather the anticipation and flight in between.

Poor Andrew, a boy I met backpacking along the border between Germany and France, loved his beer. And when he leaps over my bed, his soft belly jiggles and his freckled skin glows. But he had the gentlest eyes and the softest touch.

Diego likes to show off. His body is athletic, bronzed, and trim, but his eyes are anything but gentle. He needs to dominate, his inner flame bright and hot and ... captivating. Perhaps we were too much alike.

Brian was a virgin in every way. He fell in love too easily at a time when love was not what I needed. It ended badly, and he averts his gaze now when he soars.

Johnny was a hockey player, and he grins with bloody teeth as he glides. He was all about speed and danger and taking everything to its limit. There were times I couldn't get enough and times I felt fear.

Salvador ...

Brrring.

The phone makes Salvador vanish in midflight.

It rings again as I open my eyes.

———

Dixie's Tips #1: *When a phone rings in the middle of the night, it's never good news.*

Trust me. It's not Ryan Gosling, Hugh Jackman, or Joseph Gordon-Levitt (young, but yummy) making a late-night booty call and getting your number by mistake. If anything, it's some married schmuck who thinks a few slurred overtures on how he can't stop thinking about the dimples on your ass will get him through the door—again.

And if not the schmuck, it's your mother calling about one of her seven sisters who tripped over a rug or slipped in the bathtub and "isn't that terrible, just think, it could have been me."

But it wasn't, Ma.

"But it could just as easily and who would be here to find me? Why, I could be lying in my own ..."

However, there are always exceptions to Dixie's tips. The main one being that if you're Dixie, you tend not to follow your own

4

advice, no matter how sage. Plus, if instead of getting some badly needed beauty sleep you find yourself counting seven lads a-leaping, almost any distraction is welcome.

Which brings us to **Dixie's Tips #2**: *If you don't have the self-control to follow Tip #1, unplug the damn thing before going to bed. Remember, it's never good news.*

I pick up on the fifth ring and use my huskiest phone-sex voice to say, "I can't believe it's not butter."

Obviously I grew up as a latchkey kid with the TV as my babysitter because my other favorite commercial slogans that, taken out of context, sound just plain dirty are "Where's the beef?," "Melts in your mouth, not in your hands," "It's Finger Lickin' Good," and my go-to line when people are pissing me off, "Don't hate me because I'm beautiful."

Unfortunately, the person on the other end of the line doesn't share my fondness for advertising nostalgia. Mostly that's because she's the one who allowed network broadcasters to brainwash her susceptible child.

"Do you know what he's doing?" the caller asks. "Right this minute?"

"Mom!" I exhale noisily. "It's polite to say hello before beginning a tirade."

She ignores me.

"He's on a date. At his age! And you'll never guess who with."

"With whom."

"Don't correct me," she snaps. "I'm your mother, not Jane Austen."

"OK. With whom is dearest papa out courting?"

"Thelma. She must be in her eighties."

"Thelma Carson?" I ask. "Your former best friend before the infamous pastrami incident?"

"Thelma Carson *Gonzales*. She's been married twice, you know."

"I know. You attended both weddings. And you're the same age, so she isn't eighty."

She harrumphs. "Well, you don't see me buying secondhand tits off the Internet, do you?"

"Secondhand—"

"That's what Marcy says. Pamela Anderson, that bouncy Playmate from *Baywatch*, auctioned her old implants, the extra-large ones, on eBay. Thelma bought them."

"I doubt that's true."

"That's what Marcy says."

"Marcy's your friend. It's twisted, but she's trying to be supportive."

"Unlike some people I could—"

"Don't start, mother. I've told you before I'm not getting in between you and Dad. It's better that I stay out of the way until you decide what you're going to do."

"You've always loved your father more."

"You know that's not true."

"Do I?" She begins to sob.

"Of course you do," I say gently. "You're just tired. It's after midnight. You should be sleeping."

"How can I sleep when he's—"

"You don't know what Dad is doing, and letting your imagination get the better of you won't help. Why don't you hang up the phone and get some sleep?"

"You just want rid of me."

"No, Mom. I want you to—"

"Fine! I know when I'm not wanted."

The phone goes dead in my ear.

And that's why it's wise to follow my own incredibly astute advice culled from years of life experience. I've worked horrible jobs, dated selfish men (and enough good ones to have hope there are still a few out there), and eaten dinner with annoying relatives whose photographic memories retain the most embarrassing moments of my tender thirty-six years.

It's this accumulated experience that confirms I don't need to answer the phone to know there's nothing like a guilt trip from your mother to make impossible the sleep of angels.

———

I am still tossing and turning when the phone rings again.

Remember Dixie's #1 Tip?

I answer.

"Apology accepted," I say wearily. "Now can you let me sleep?"

"Dix?" The voice has a wheezy, high-pitched squeak that could easily belong to a laughable cartoon pervert. It is that type of cruel observation, however, that if voiced aloud could make paying the rent difficult. And affordable rent in San Francisco is difficult enough even *with* a job.

"Hmmm, depends," I say with tongue lodged comfortably in my cheek. "You don't sound like Ryan or Hugh or—"

"This is why I hate calling you, Dix. I get a headache every damn time."

"Hi, boss."

"Don't get cute."

"Too late."

"You're giving me a migraine."

"Ahh, but what have you given me lately?"

"How about a job? I even pay you a wage. But that can all end, Dix. Should I get someone else to work on next week's cover?"

"Cover?"

"I don't like to repeat myself."

"Could you say that again?"

"You want me to hang up?"

"I'm all ears, boss."

"No, you're all lip. You ever hear of Diego Chino?"

All the moisture leaves my mouth. "The artist?"

"Yeah, I guess that's what you'd call him. I can't get my head around that abstract stuff."

"I know him." The memory of him leaping over my bed shimmers and fades. "He does nice work, but it's been marketed to death. He signed a seven-figure deal with Ralph Lauren last year for a line of art-inspired sweaters and a new fragrance. I don't recall if either has made it to market yet, but the success certainly changed him."

"He's dead."

I wince. "Jeez, boss, don't pull any punches."

"What are you talking about? It's a story. I need you—"

"I said I know—knew—argh!" I'm flustered, but my lips keep moving. "We were close. Kinda. We dated. God!"

A heavy sigh drifts over the phone line.

"Oh," he says. "Sorry, I'll get—"

"Don't even think about it," I snarl and suck in a deep, cleansing breath. "I want it."

"If you were close maybe it's not—"

"The operative word is *were*." My game face is on and I'm back in control of my lips. "I haven't talked to him in over a year. I want the story. He became a big deal in this town. His death will leave a mark."

The boss sighs again. "You sure? I just received the tip. The body's fresh. No details, except it's messy."

"Isn't that sweet." The sarcasm drips off my tongue like venom. "You hear *messy* and think of me."

Another heavy sigh that sounds more like a wheezy death rattle. "Forget it."

"Give me the address?"

"No, this isn't a good idea. You'll go in guns blazing and piss off everybody."

"So?"

"So? You know how tough it is to mend fences once you've plowed them over? The police commissioner and the publisher are golfing buddies."

"The commish doesn't advertise."

"So?"

"So our publisher only gives a crap about the people who buy ads, and one of the reasons they buy ads is because they know I don't play favorites."

"Is that so?"

"Yeah."

"It's got nothing to with the other reporters, editors, and photogs, or the calls I make in the newsroom every day?"

"OK," I relent, sensing he's feeling a touch sensitive. "You make me look good, but you know it's me they're dying to read."

"I don't know any such thing."

"Flatterer."

"What?"

"You know what I always say?"

"Yeah, don't hate you because you're beautiful."

I laugh. "Give me the address. I can handle it."

His voice softens. "You really sure?"

"I really am."

He gives me the address.

———

I hang up and stare into the fishbowl that rests on top of the dresser facing the bed. Bubbles, the world's oldest goldfish, having survived now for ninety-two days, turns her back to me in a disturbing show of indifference.

I hit speed dial on the speakerphone and pull on some clothes. Fortunately, I keep my natural copper hair in a frenetic, just-got-out-of-bed-and-couldn't-give-a-damn cut so that when I get out of bed, I look like I don't give a damn.

"Dispatch."

"I need a ride, Mo."

"Dixie, baby, I've been thinking about you." Mo's guttural Bronx accent usually sounds like he has a mouth full of marbles, but tonight it's more like he crunched up a few and gargled the broken shards.

"You sound rough, Mo. The clean air getting to you?"

"Doc says I need to give up the smokes."

"You should listen."

"The man puffs more than I do."

"Then listen to me: Give up the cigs."

"Yeah, yeah, I've heard it before, but …" He hesitates, a sudden loss for words, which is unusual.

"What aren't you telling me?" I ask.

"Ahh, it'll be nothing. Just the doc did a biopsy. Left my throat sore, you know?"

"A biopsy? For cancer?"

Mo snorts. "Nah, because of my fabulous singing voice, he wants to see what carat gold my tonsils are made of."

I don't laugh. "Jeez, Mo. Cancer."

"It ain't for certain," he says gruffly. "We're waiting on results."

I exhale noisily. "You need anything you call, OK?"

Mo chuckles. "What you gonna do, hire a cab to drive me somewhere?"

"No, but I'm a good listener."

"Don't be sweet, you'll ruin both our reputations." He sniffs, sucking in a lungful of air through his nose. "Now what you got?"

Back to business.

"Dead body."

"Juicy?"

I wince, but try not to let it show in my voice.

"An artist. High profile."

"Ooh! How did he snuff it? Paint up the nostrils, a brush down his—"

"Don't know yet," I interrupt, sharper than intended. "That's why I need a cab."

11

"Relax. Dispatched one as soon as I saw your number. He'll be there in two."

"You're a doll, Mo." I try to insert a little levity. "We should run away together."

"Forget it. Non-smokers make lousy lovers. After sex, they want to talk, talk, talk."

"I'm hurt."

Mo laughs the throaty cackle of a Shakespearean witch. "Go get your cab, Dix. My boys hate to wait."

———

The taxi pulls up as I exit the front door of the postcard-pretty, three-story Painted Lady where I lease one of six apartments. King William of Orange—who along with his human, Mrs. Pennell, owns the building—stretches full out on the kitchen windowsill of his main-floor domain like an African lion spied through the wrong end of binoculars. When he hears me leaving, he opens one eye and winks approval.

I am dressed for battle: notepad and pen tucked in the back pocket of slim-fitting jeans; a point-and-shoot camera and digital voice recorder neatly stowed in the pockets of a vintage tea-brown leather bomber. For emergencies, I also carry Lily, a small, pearl-handled switchblade that slips into a moleskin pocket sewn inside a pair of russet biker boots. The scuffed and scarred leather boots are secondhand, the knife a don't-tell-your-mother present from an over-protective (though rarely present) father.

My one concession to the chilly San Francisco night is the addition of a gray lamb's wool scarf that curls around my neck with the warmth and comfort of a purring kitten.

I give the driver the address where I expect to find the dead body of my former lover.

"You're Dixie Flynn of *NOW*, right?" he asks once I'm ensconced in the back seat.

I nod and glance at his registration: Charlie Parker.

"Cool name, Charlie. You play?"

"Nah! No lungs, no talent. Only one Yardbird in this world and he already made his mark." He grins. "I read your stuff though. How come it only lands once a week?"

I grin. "That's the trouble with weekly news magazines."

Charlie nods. "You ever think of moving to the *Chronicle* or *Examiner*?"

"Tried that once, but they wanted to pay me too much. Plus, they have a dress code: No shirt, no shoes, no paycheck."

Charlie laughs. "Man, I never expected you to be funny. I mean, you write about all the dark stuff in this town. Sometimes after I read one of your columns, I need to go for a drink. Mo loves it, says you're the best, but, man, you depress me sometimes. No offense."

"None taken," I lie.

———

Charlie drops me in front of the restored, seven-hundred-seat Metro Theater on Union Street with a cheery, "Catch you on the remix."

The street is lit by moonlight and yellow sodium-vapor fireflies trapped under glass. The theater's neon 1920s-era marquee is dark, while heavy shutters hide the enticing window displays of neighboring boutiques, art galleries, and gem merchants from the great

13

unwashed. This is a street that prides itself on iron bars and quick response from private armed security—unattractive qualities to those who hunt at night.

The payoff for its vigilance is an eerie silence. San Francisco isn't a town that sleeps, and it's unusual to find a pocket that has learned how to catch a few Zzzs.

Some inner-city dwellers panic when shut off from the constant rumble of cars, buses, junkies, and sirens, but I haven't spent all my life cocooned in concrete. There was a time when I also sought silence as a refuge.

Diego's place is easy to spot: a third-floor penthouse with curtains pulled back, its interior ablaze in cool white light. Two officers in inky blue uniforms pace restlessly inside. Thankfully, there isn't enough manpower on scene yet to keep the curious away with crime scene tape and an extra body on the door.

I cross the street and stroll into the open lobby like I belong. Inside, thick carpet the color of a frothy cappuccino and a smooth oak handrail lead the way upstairs. As I climb, I brush my hand along the light-mocha wall, drawn by its unusual texture. Instead of paint, the walls are covered in a soft fabric that probably cost more than my best cotton sheets.

Diego has moved up in the world since the last time we made art together.

On the first landing, a lazy three-quarter moon is framed by a large half-circle of leaded glass, the clarity of which would make that bald Mr. Clean beam with pride. I feel at the neck of my charcoal blouse, suddenly wondering if I should have worn a dress and heels—or at least a bra.

There are three apartment condos on each of the first and second levels, the occupants secure behind heavy, solid-core doors and tamper-proof hardware.

On the top floor, the door to Diego's penthouse stands open, exposing the scene within.

Messy doesn't do it justice.

Dixie's Tips #3: *Vomiting at a crime scene, although oftentimes warranted, is not recommended.* You only have to blow chunks once to be forever looked upon as a girly sidekick to the "real" journalists. If necessary, swallow.

Beyond the door waits a headless body, pale and oozing atop polished hardwood floors.

Jeez.

I brace myself against the doorjamb as my legs unexpectedly tremble.

Surrounding the body is a sticky carpet of burnt crimson edged in black. The ruby carpet also grows on walls, glistening in the light like a human lung—alive and breathing.

I look away, digging deep within myself to unearth roots for my bravado. I'm no stranger to blood. What woman is? But on my beat, death is rarely gentle, and one's first and most human reaction is often to flee.

As part of the night crew—reporters, police officers, firefighters, hookers, junkies, paramedics, undertakers, pimps, dealers, coroners, nurses, and bartenders—I learned how to survive by detaching from the humanity of the dead. I trained myself to look at death as the introduction to a story, with the body serving as merely the hook beneath my all-important byline.

It sounds morbid, but it's surprising how oddly automatic it becomes. Then again, I usually don't know the corpse on an intimate level. And, truth be told, most of us on the night crew also drink too damn much.

Pulling my gaze from the body, I scan the room. Diego has come a long way from the one-bedroom he rented in the building I still call home. He lived directly above me, except for a brief three weeks when he shared my bed. We lived a year in those twenty-one days and parted on difficult terms. We didn't hate each other per se; we just couldn't stand the sight of ourselves in the other's presence.

Beyond the lake of blood, two uniformed officers—one saggy in the seat, the other bakery fresh—stand with their backs to me. Their focus is a large picture window and the empty street below. The slump of shoulders and heavy air of silence say all they want is for a detective to show so they can report what precious little they know and book off.

Careful not to disturb them, I check the main door. It proves even more sophisticated than I first guessed. A steel bar hidden in the core of the door could slide into brass-finished iron plates on the floor and ceiling, making it practically impenetrable when locked. Try to kick that sucker in and you would end up flat on your ass with a broken ankle.

When ready, I inhale deeply and return to the meat of the matter.

The corpse is male, shirtless, with a firm, muscular stomach. *I kissed that stomach.* Not now, but then. My fingers traced sharp, square-cut muscles. Diego hated to be tickled, the loss of control. Naturally, that made it impossible to resist.

The bloodless skin still holds a bronze pigment, and I have to dam a sudden dampness in my eyes.

Focus, focus. Come on, Dix. It's been a year. Do your job.

There are no tattoos, which surprises me. Even though Diego didn't sport any when we were together, I always suspected he was just itching to ink his own skin. The body is bent awkwardly over two large cushions, legs splayed wide with bare feet pointing in opposite directions. A single-barreled shotgun is laying a few feet away with something small, red, and meaty stuck in its trigger guard.

OK, stop. Don't look.

I have to. Jesus, I have to.

The head, or what is left of it, is a burst melon—everything from the mouth up, gone.

The thought that immediately enters my head is that I miss his eyes. The light that was Diego had glistened within those eyes like an erupting volcano. The orbs were so bright that I often wondered if he could see in the dark.

No point taking a photo, I tell myself. *It would never make it into print. Can't have our readers gagging on their Sunday morning cornflakes.*

The skull's jellied contents are what carpets the walls, but there is also an abnormally symmetrical shape at its epicenter. Stepping closer, I stifle a gasp as the shape takes three-dimensional form.

Positioned directly in the path of the volcanic spatter stands a large, rectangular canvas.

The stretched canvas, anchored firmly to a heavy easel, is covered in tiny fragments of shattered bone, pummeled brain matter, and at least a bucket of congealing blood. Within the gore, however,

Diego has painted an intricate pattern in what I can only guess is some form of clear wax.

While the raw canvas soaks in the blood, the pattern repels it. Without the wax, the canvas would have been just another mess to clean up, and without the blood, the pattern would never have been revealed.

I move closer, mesmerized. As my eyes relax, shapes flicker within the pattern, but the blood has yet to set and the final message eludes me.

Once you look past the gore—which I assume will be an easier chore once the canvas is removed from the scene and allowed to dry—the power of the piece is palpable.

Unexpectedly, almost spiritually, I feel this could become Diego's greatest creative achievement: a complete and personal sacrifice to art and a single-barreled *Fuck You* to the world.

But that is also what bothers me. The Diego I had known was far too narcissistic to conceive of something so self-sacrificing.

To me, it looks more like murder.

TWO

"Hey! Get the hell away from there."

I snap a photo of the bloodied canvas and turn to see cute buns looking both stunned and surprised to find an extra person in the room.

I flash him my most promising smile, since my décolletage gene—necessary to distract all men from all things—sputtered and died shortly after puberty, and I still haven't managed to master the art of fluttering my eyelashes in a way that doesn't look like I'm having a seizure.

Time to work.

"Dixie Flynn, *NOW*. Who found the body?"

Saggy pants turns to display a face not dissimilar to a Shar Pei chewing a wasp. "How'd she get in here?"

The flash of anger that steels his younger partner's eyes shows he doesn't appreciate the inference.

I nod toward the door. "It was open. I was in the neighborhood."

I flash the smile again, playing innocent and coy, like butter wouldn't melt.

"You're the gal who writes the columns, right?" asks the first cop. "Sergeant Fury's girlfriend."

The older cop laughs. "Fury doesn't have friends, never mind a—"

The look—trained at the knee of my mother, and her mother before her—stops him short, but it doesn't seem to penetrate his partner's Kevlar vest.

"He likes this one," the younger cop says as his eyes scan my body for fingerprints. "Word in the locker room is he adopted her as some kind of charity case after she wrote a fluff piece when his wife was killed a few years back."

"Who called this in?" I ask, the words practically cutting my tongue. "Or is Detective Fury the only cop worth quoting?"

The partners exchange a look as if sharing a telepathic secret. The senior one shrugs.

"Neighbor," says junior.

"They find the body or did you?"

"We did," he continues. "Neighbor called in a report of gunfire but didn't breach the scene."

"How did you get in? That's quite the lock."

He shrugs. "Neighbor had a spare key."

"Neighborly."

"Yep."

"So the door was locked?"

"That's why we needed the key."

I nod at the body. "Messy."

"Very."

Junior puffs up his chest to show if there is any extraneous vomit on the floor, it doesn't belong to him. This was his way of impressing upon me that if I ever needed any spiders killed or leaking bodies removed, I would know whom to call.

With some effort, I manage not to shudder. His cuteness factor has dropped so far below my minimum, it's no longer on the radar. It's a pity sometimes when they open their mouths.

"You I.D. the victim?" I ask.

"Mailbox says Mr. Diego Chino. Neighbor said he lived alone, some kind of famous artist."

"That what made you tip off my editor?"

Silence.

I move on. "Neighbor sure it's him?"

The young officer winks at his partner. "She didn't feel up to helping us look for his face."

———

Detective Sergeant Frank Fury storms into the apartment with trench coat flapping and bare hands curled into fists the size of boiled hams. He is ready for a challenge and appears mildly disappointed when the two officers merely gawp and retreat.

"Ah, crap," he grumbles while looking at the body. "What a bloody mess."

The two uniformed officers physically shrink as Frank's glare falls upon them. Then he spots me.

"How in hell did you get here?"

"Cab," I say dryly. "Driver's name was Charlie Parker, but he claims not to be musical. Not sure I believed him."

Frank rubs the knot between his eyes. "I've got two boys downstairs with strict orders to keep the jackals out of my hair."

"Not much left to get tangled in."

He scowls.

I show my teeth.

It's how we work best.

Frank and I prowl the same beat, but he doesn't have the luxury of typing -30- (a nostalgic journalistic holdover from the days of the telegraph that means, quite literally, "No More") at the end of each story before sending it to press and starting the next. He tends to hold on to the idea of justice too tightly until the frustration oozes from his pores like musk. That fervency has bled into a craggy face with a W. C. Fields nose and shovel-sharp chin, and left its mark most prominently in a pair of predatory, steel-gray eyes.

His wardrobe does nothing to help, with baggy brown Kmart pants, wrinkled cotton dress shirt, a skinny tie the color of a coffee stain, and a knot so tight you know he never unties it. He wraps it all in a shapeless trench coat that barely envelops his solid 240-pound frame.

Next to Frank, I look like a juvenile delinquent. He stands eight inches taller than my five-six-in-heels, which means if there's a moonroof in his severe salt-and-pepper flat top, I can't tell.

I move carefully around the edge of the room to stand beside him. I've only been on the scene a short time, but already I've managed to distance myself. The body on the floor has become more of a puzzle piece than flesh and blood. Perhaps that cold detachment is one reason I have trouble getting second dates.

"His name is Diego Chino," I volunteer. "He's an artist."

"Never heard of him."

"He's big if you move in the right circles."

"I get dizzy easy."

We both smirk.

"Looks like suicide," I say.

Frank nods.

"But might not be," I add.

Frank flares his nostrils. "Go on."

"Notice the canvas?"

"The one covered in blood?"

"Yup."

"What about it?"

"It's brilliant."

"Come again."

"The raw power of it," I explain. "That piece is going to be worth a fortune."

"Once you clean the blood off?"

"No. The blood *is* the paint. The positioning of the canvas and direction of the gun blast was intentional. It's a modern masterpiece."

"You're one sick pup."

"Wait and see. I won't be surprised if Diego's agent has a buyer by morning."

Frank holds up one hand. From heel to tip, it is larger than my entire face.

"OK," he says. "Let's say this painting is valuable. Why does that rule out suicide?"

"Diego was a publicity machine. He courted celebrity and gained a following, but his star was fading. Hollywood's *nouveau riche* are a fickle bunch. One week you're a must-have, the next, not so much. In another year, he could easily be forgotten, re-placed by the next great discovery. Bottom line, he was too self-centered to let that happen. I don't believe he would check out without a fight. His ego wouldn't let him."

"Maybe he ran out of ideas," Frank reasons. "And legends are born when they die young."

"Could be, but the indefinable thing that makes a true artist is soul. Peel back the layers and you find an unquenchable desire to leave a mark, create a kind of immortality."

"You're making a strong case for suicide," Frank says.

I shake my head. "There's also the ego factor. Making a mark is important but totally pointless if you're not around to bask in the glory. Diego didn't want to be Van Gogh, dying a pauper with nothing but rejection to show for a life's work. He wanted to be Picasso, Dali, Warhol—worshipped while he walked the earth. That's why his limited-edition prints were practically limitless. And that's why he was letting his art be used on ties for rich busi-nessmen and on print ads for perfume. Pretty soon he would be doing Converse shoes and Christmas wrap."

"Everyone's a critic." Frank rubs his temples.

"True, but I know what I'm talking about. We used to argue into the small hours—"

"What a minute," Frank says. "You know the victim?"

I'm not big into kissing and telling to friends who happen to be colleagues. Or colleagues who happen to be friends. Whatever.

"Before he became a name."

Frank has the kind of disapproving smile that makes children cry.

He sighs heavily. "OK. Let's suppose you're right. If it's not suicide, what's the motive for murder?"

"Beats the hell out of me."

Frank guffaws so loudly that the two officers turn to stare.

"Excuse me, then," he says. "While I look for a note."

———

"Please don't touch that," cries a nasally voice from the doorway.

Frank looks up from the bloodied canvas as a smartly dressed man, a gaily colored ascot swirling wildly around his throat, trots in from the hall.

"Stop right where you are!" Frank yells, a finger the size of a small truncheon stabbing the air.

The magic finger seems to do the trick as the man stops stock still, every part of him frozen except for rapidly blinking eyes and a creepy caterpillar moustache that squirms beneath a long, hooked nose.

A silver-haired officer with a face the color of boiled beets and a gut the size of a vodka-infused watermelon arrives close behind. His lungs are expanding and contracting so rapidly he looks about to have a coronary.

"If you're going to die, do it outside," Frank warns the officer. "My crime scene is busy enough."

Ascot man chances a look over his shoulder at the gasping officer.

"Who are you?" Frank demands.

The man's neck snaps back around so quickly, I imagine chiropractors wincing in their sleep.

"My name is unimportant, but I implore you not to touch that painting." The man lifts a white handkerchief to cover his nose and mouth.

Until the handkerchief raises the issue, I can't say I noticed an unpleasant smell. Some crime scenes are nasty, especially if the bodies have been lying around for a while or the victims really went to town on a greasy last meal. But this one isn't bad at all, which makes me wonder why.

"Your name," Frank growls. "And how'd you get up here?"

This last question is directed at the officer in the hallway who is still a noticeably unhealthy color.

The thin man stiffens, but one hand still manages to snake into a jacket pocket to produce a plain white business card with raised gold ink. He holds it out proudly as though it is a double-0 license signed by M herself.

Frank storms forward, using his height to all its intimidating advantage, glances at the card, and snorts.

"Are you saying the officers allowed you up here because you own a damn art gallery?"

The man sniffs. "I don't *own* the gallery."

Frank shoots me a look that says I better swallow the sarcastic comment rising in my throat.

The man puffs out his bird-like chest indignantly. "I happen to represent a very influential art collector in our city. And I am here to take possession of Mr. Chino's final work before something unforeseen happens."

"You mean like me taking a knife to it?" Frank asks as he produces a small whittling knife from his pocket.

"Please, sir. I beg you not to deface that painting. It's so …" His voice is full of wonder. "Incredible. Perhaps his finest work."

Frank waves the knife lazily in the air, a two-inch blade rising from the handle at the flick of a gnarled thumbnail. "And you knew this bloody thing would be here, how?"

"Mr. Chino left instructions via text message, which detailed when I was to arrive at this location and take possession of his latest work."

"A suicide note?" Frank asks. "By text?"

"I suppose so, although I did not know that at the time."

"And yet, you don't seem too surprised at finding a body on the floor and its head used as a friggin' paint pot!"

The man shivers like a frightened rabbit, but I have to give him props for not backing down.

He sniffs again. "Mr. Chino has been depressed of late, and he has always had a flair for the dramatic. So although I was hopeful for a …" He pauses to consider his words. "Less messy affair, I cannot say that I am completely shocked."

"Well, that makes one of us, Mister—Hey, you never did tell me your Goddamn name."

"It's written on the card."

Frank stares at him like a hungry grizzly on a salmon run.

"It's Blymouth," says the man. "Casper Blymouth."

"And who's the collector?"

"I don't see the need—"

The man freezes as Frank moves back to the painting and begins scraping some of the blood from the bottom, right-hand corner.

"Kingston!" he blurts. "I represent Sir Roger Kingston."

Frank lets out a low whistle. "I'm impressed. You can't blurt a name much bigger than that." Frank scrapes more of the blood.

Blymouth gasps. "Please." His voice drops to a whine, and his eyes actually begin to fill with frightened tears.

Frank stops scraping and turns to catch my attention. His grin can now frighten serial killers.

"I'll be damned," he says. "This bloody thing is signed."

"Of course it's signed," Blymouth sniffs. "It would be worthless otherwise, and Mr. Chino would not—"

"You don't find that twisted?" Frank returns to his full height, wincing slightly as both knees crack. "I understand texting the suicide note, that's human nature. I can even see blowing your brains over a canvas. Why not? But signing it first? That's whacked."

"Whacked?" I pipe in.

Frank's mouth twitches.

Blymouth sighs loudly. "If you two are quite done, I would like to take possession of the painting and leave. The smell is really quite dread—"

"Air conditioning," I blurt.

Frank cocks one of his thick barbed-wire eyebrows.

"That's why it doesn't smell," I explain. "I didn't take off my jacket, and with the front door open it's less noticeable, but the air conditioning is on."

"Yeah, the place was real cold when we first entered," agrees saggy pants.

"To keep the scene fresh," Frank muses.

"Also makes time of death more difficult to pinpoint," I suggest too quickly.

Frank's mouth twitches again. "Waking the neighbor with a shotgun blast might help with that."

"Mr. Chino was no fool," Blymouth pipes up irritably. "The cool air naturally helps to preserve his work. And if you do not possess the olfactory senses to—"

"Christ!" Frank snaps. "This is why I post officers on the God-damn door."

Blymouth gulps.

"Did Chino's note say how he wanted the canvas cured?" I ask quickly.

Blymouth nods. "Air dried and then sealed with several coats of high-grade, matte lacquer. I have several artists available who can do the job."

"They'll need to wait." Frank's face turns hard. "Right now it's evidence, and I need you out of here while I do my job."

"I must protest! I have—"

"Protest all you like. Just do it outside."

The beet-faced officer rushes forward in an effort to redeem himself. He clamps a firm hand on Blymouth's shoulder and yanks him roughly out of the apartment.

"And Colin," Frank yells at the retreating officer.

The officer turns around, his seasoned face stoic as he holds onto the squirming man.

"Sir?"

"Bag his cell phone," Frank says. "I want to see that text."

Blymouth opens his mouth to protest, but Colin isn't going to mess up twice. He drags the art dealer down the stairs.

"You, too, Dix." Frank releases an audible sigh. "You've seen enough."

"Well, that's whacked," I say cheekily but quickly take the hint when Frank's mouth fails to twitch.

THREE

I SHOULD HAVE HEADED straight home and crawled back into bed. It was late, I was tired, and Bubbles was likely pining. But that's one of the troubles with the night crew: we're not too bright.

The Dog House is a cramped dungeon of a pub two blocks from the Hall of Justice on Bryant Street. Originally built as a coal cellar and storage for a turn-of-the-century boardinghouse, it was converted into a speakeasy during Prohibition and became an unorthodox street church for hippies in the Sixties.

Abandoned for decades, it was quietly reopened in the late Eighties as a place for cops and scoundrels to hide from prying eyes. The owner, bouncer, bartender, and occasional bookie is an ex-wrestler who had a slippery headlock on fame in the Seventies as the Biting Bulgarian Bulldog. In the newspaper archives, he was regaled as every wide-eyed kid's favorite Friday-night villain.

Ask him about it now and he'll tell you his loyal fans cheered the loudest when he regularly bit off his opponent's ear and spat it at the ineffective referee.

"Kids back then were less cynical," he told me once. "None of them questioned how the wrestlers all magically grew their ears back for the next match."

When boxer Mike Tyson did it for real in a heavyweight bout against Evander Holyfield, Bulldog shook his head and muttered, "Where's the magic? Dumb prick."

Nowadays Bulldog goes by Bill, but his eyes still dance when an old fan recognizes him and asks for an autograph. He even has a Hasbro action figure of himself in full costume perched on the till.

After wiping hairy hands on a black apron with the angry green face of the Hulk silk-screened across the front, Bill hands me a sweaty bottle of Warthog Ale and a shot of tequila, slice of lime hanging off the rim. I use the beer to connect a few wet rings on the scarred mahogany of the L-shaped bar before taking a sip.

"You OK, Dix?" Bill asks. "Kinda quiet."

"Tough gal like me? Couldn't be better."

"Got a story?"

"Dead artist," I explain. "Old friend, actually. Blew his fool head off with a shotgun."

"Ah, the Hemingway solution. Grim."

"You have no idea."

I pick up the lime wedge, squeeze its juice into the shot glass, and watch the tequila turn cloudy.

"Frank there?" Bill asks.

I nod and take a small sip of tequila.

Bill waits, his hands continually busy drying glasses or refilling marquee bottles from bar-brand gallon jugs.

"You think there's something wrong with me, Bill?" I ask after another sip.

"Let me think." His voice is the steady rumble of a subway train. "It's one in the morning; you're alone in a dingy bar, drinking tequila and courting advice from a mug so ugly he would give your mother palpitations." He pauses. "Nah, you're doing just fine."

"Thanks," I say dryly. "You're a sweetheart."

Bill grins. "Don't let that out, I have a reputation to uphold."

"You too, huh?"

Bill walks to the far side of the bar to serve his only other patrons, two arguing retirees with matching ill-fitting dentures who look like they can barely afford to split a beer between them.

From my stool, I have a clear view of the entire room. Eight feet to my left is the lone washroom that breaks every health regulation in the book and makes me determined to learn levitation; two feet to my right is the bricked-up doorway that once led to a boardinghouse of ill-repute above; and sixteen feet directly behind me is a steel door complete with Prohibition-era peephole that, contrary to fire regulations, is the only way in or out if you don't know about the trapdoor behind the bar that leads to a dank cellar and a maze of forgotten tunnels that are said to cover most of the block. If you put thirty people in the room, it's five too many.

Frank usually sits to my left and, as a house courtesy, the wooden stool to my right is reserved for Al Capone, the dead Chicago mobster.

According to local legend, Capone was known to be a regular of the speakeasy whenever he ventured west on business. The bar had a waitress back then whom Bill claims was Capone's one true love. When she mysteriously disappeared one day, Capone made a decree that no one was to be hired to replace her. And to this day, no one has.

To be fair though, with the way cops and reporters tip, it wouldn't be a job anyone would clamor for either.

After Capone was convicted of tax evasion, he requested to serve his time in Alcatraz, where (Bill claims) he would sit in his cell, look across the water, and dream about this place and his missing sweetheart. Of course, Bill also claims Capone still visits regularly, which is why the stool is reserved.

Personally, I have yet to meet the man's ghost, but it'll be a hell of a story when I do.

The door swings open behind me and I hear Frank's heavy feet slap the concrete floor. I glance in the mirror behind the bar to see his usual bravado lost between hunched shoulders and a slouched back. He slides onto the stool beside me and runs thick fingers through thinning hair.

Bill pours a tall mug of O'Doul's Amber—a dealcoholized draft made by Anheuser-Busch with a caramel color, malt taste, and thin head—and slides it to him. Frank sighs with pleasure as he takes a long, slow pull.

"To the blue," Frank says, lifting his glass to the ceiling.

"May the good Lord watch our backs," answer the two old-timers.

Frank nods at Bill to pour two fresh mugs of draught and deliver them to the far side of the bar.

———

Frank stopped drinking regular beer two weeks after his wife died. The fortnight in between was a time he's only talked about once, and for some reason, I was the one he trusted to tell it to.

Despite rumors that the public outpouring garnered by my story saved Frank's career, I didn't pull any punches. Frank was falling down drunk the night his wife was murdered. That's a weight only he can carry, but anyone who follows the daily news knows *anyone*—drunk or sober—can be absent when needed the most.

The medical examiner confessed it took a long time for her to die, the murder weapon being a wire brush like you would use to clean cast-iron pots or a greasy barbecue grill. The killer used it to scrape away her skin until the blood loss, pain, and terror became too much for her heart. Evidence at the scene pointed to a "person known to police" with a record reaching back to junior high and a hard-on for Frank.

Ten days after the murder, the suspect was climbing out the window of a second-story apartment (a laptop emblazoned with a Hello Kitty sticker under one arm, and his pockets stuffed with cheap jewelry and a pink Swarovski-crystal iPod) when a bullet punched through his kidney and dropped him to the alley below. Several witnesses said they were sure he was still screaming after he hit the ground, but the M.E. was unable to determine if immediate medical attention would have saved his life.

When the squad cars arrived, they found Frank leaning against the alley wall, sipping from a flask, smoking gun dangling from his fingers. More witnesses said he refused anyone entry to the alley while he silently watched the man bubble and froth, drowning in his own blood.

A well-oiled snub .38 was discovered nearby with the corpse's prints on its trigger and grip.

Rumor naturally said Frank planted the gun, but there was never any evidence to back it up.

The daily newspapers and broadcast news delivered the facts plain and true, but that's not what I'm paid to do.

Instead, I told a story about a young woman from Kansas who loved to bake apple pies with a brown sugar crust, volunteered at the library teaching adults how to read, and married a handsome, young cowboy who took her on a journey to the craziest city in America.

The killer's background, unfortunately, was tougher to unravel; despite knocking on doors in his neighborhood, talking to social workers and parole officers, and making a hundred phone calls, I couldn't find a single person with a kind word to say. His father probably summed it up best when he told me, "That boy was born dead."

A month after the story ran, Frank moved to the stool on my left and Bill began carrying O'Doul's.

———

"We found something weird in the artist's place after you left," Frank says, tipping back his glass.

"After I was kicked out, you mean?"

Frank downs the beer, places the mug on the bar, and picks up a freshly poured second. A skin of ice slides down the glass.

I wait.

Nothing.

I roll my eyes, hating when he refuses to play.

"OK. What's so weird?"

Frank digs in the pocket of his coat and pulls out a Polaroid. The snapshot shows a colorful abstract painting that invokes the cold romance of the Northern Lights dancing above Arctic tundra, but as viewed through a child's kaleidoscope.

"We found that painting between the box spring and mattress in the bedroom," Frank says. "It's signed 'Adamsky'."

"Huh. Weird place to keep a painting." I study the photo closely. "Was Diego trying to hide it?"

Frank shrugs. "If anybody knew it was in the apartment, that's about the first place they'd look. It's the only piece of furniture large enough to hide something like that. Place was practically bare."

Bill moves in and plucks the photo out of my hand. "Maybe he hated it," he says before tossing it back onto the bar.

Frank and I look up, twin frowns knitting our brows.

"Huh?" I say with my usual intellectual wit.

"It was something Al said."

"Capone was in?" I ask.

"Yesterday."

"Damn, I keep missing him."

Bill continues. "Al was telling me how he liked to put pictures of all the women who ever crossed him under his mattress. He said it was fun to screw other broads right there on top of them." He begins to chuckle. "Then he would sleep on his back so they had to look at his hairy ass all night."

Bill cracks up and wanders away, wiping tears of laughter from his eyes.

With a smile, I turn to Frank. "So what do you think of Capone's theory?"

"You never know," Frank says seriously. "Maybe fat, old ghosts know more than fat, old cops." He stares off into space for a moment. "After all, he's in a better position to ask the guy."

I pick up the Polaroid.

"I've seen this artist's work mentioned on the international wires. He's European, I think, and bigger than Diego. Most of his stuff sells in the fifty- to hundred-thousand range."

"*Dollars?*"

"Euros." I grin. "Art is big business."

Frank snorts. "Who sticks fifty-plus grand under a mattress?"

"Could be a motive for murder," I suggest.

Frank's mouth twitches. "An art thief breaks into Chino's place, goes to all the trouble of staging a suicide, and then forgets to take the painting?"

"Well, when you put it like that."

"Best leave detecting to the professionals, Dix."

"Yeah, yeah."

I finish the tequila in one shot—the glass nearly colliding with my pouting lower lip—and chase it with a swallow from the bottle of ale.

"By the way." I attempt to stifle a yawn. "What was that pink thing stuck in the shotgun's trigger guard?"

"A toe. Kickback must have sliced it off."

"Is the body missing one?"

Frank's twitch blossoms into a grin.

"Yeah, Dix. It is."

FOUR

THE ARTIST CRAWLS ACROSS burgundy carpet to dip ghost-white fingers into a pool of shimmering blood. His fingers are searching. When his hand emerges, it clutches a flap of skin with no recognizable shape. Using both hands, the artist stretches the skin over the shotgun hole where his face had been.

Flesh mask in place, he tries to grin. A white rip opens where the mouth should be to reveal pink tongue and sharp, pearly whites. Clenched between his teeth is a silky sable brush.

Wake up, Dix.

The artist dips the brush into the empty socket of his left eye, coating the bristles with crimson sap.

Gross. Wake up!

He paints ruby lips around the torn slit of his mouth as a deep bass drum begins to beat. Its pulse grows stronger, pulling...

I open my eyes with a groan.

On the nightstand, the neon display shining through the worn seat of my tartan pajama bottoms—where I must have tossed them in frustration after being unable to untie the knotted drawstring—shows it is only 7 a.m.

I have been asleep barely five hours.

"Get the door, will you," I croak to Bubbles who is merrily swimming around in her bowl despite an advanced age of ninety-three days.

She ignores me.

The incessant pounding continues.

"If I ask nicely?"

Bubbles turns her back and flicks her tail before I can finish my appeal.

"Hold on," I call as I throw off covers and head into the bathroom.

There, I splash cold water on my face, gargle with mint Listerine, and take care of necessary business. I am pleased to note that I had the presence of mind to sleep in my favorite green football jersey. A gift from a college boyfriend whose name I am no longer sure about, the over-washed shirt falls to my knees, has more holes in it than episodic television, and sports a frayed collar stretched so wide it barely holds on to my shoulders. It's like being wrapped in a hug.

I open the door to be greeted by…

"Ugh," say the two women in unison.

"'Ugh'? You wake me at seven for 'ugh'?"

"No," Kristy blurts. "It's just that you…you look kind of—"

"Ugh?" I volunteer.

"Yeah." Kristy's smile brightens her already cherubically fresh face.

In a deliberate attempt to make me feel older than my years, Kristy is wearing her honey-blonde hair in a pink-bow ponytail and—though the sun has yet to burn off the morning fog—is dressed for a summer's day. Even standing still, she gives the illusion of dancing in an ink black, pleated skirt that shows off shapely legs in multi-striped knee-high socks. She tops this with a translucent silk blouse that reveals a nipple-proud pink tank top to match her bow. If she were to walk by a junior high school, every boy would spontaneously combust into puberty—acne and awkward hair growth everywhere.

Kristy's partner, Sam, goes casual in white sweatpants with the word BUM stenciled in soft gray across her seat, and an oversized T-shirt that reads, "Dip me in honey and feed me to the lesbians."

She resembles Eighties Irish singer Sinéad O'Connor, only with a spiky black buzz cut, at least a half dozen piercings in each ear—one of which is a thin steel bar that cuts across the top of her left ear and contains five letter beads that she can rearrange at a whim. Today, it reads: BITCH. She is also fond of LEZBO, CRUEL, and FUCKU. A ruby stud sparkles in one nostril.

———

Kristy and Sam share the apartment directly across the hall on the middle floor of our eclectic Painted Lady. Our other neighbors, Derek and Shahnaz (she writes cookbooks and has a perfume collection that attracts men faster than the incredible food she cooks), split the top floor with Ben and Saffron (no stranger to exotic scents himself), while Mr. French and his parakeet, Baccarat, have the misfortune to live beneath Kristy and her morning jazzercise. Mrs. Pennell and King William live below me.

"Did you at least bring coffee?" I ask.

"Um, no," says Kristy with little hint of apology. "We like the way you make it in that bubbly pot."

"Perfect." I don't mean for it to sound as bitchy as it does, but lack of sleep will do that to anyone.

I head for the kitchen. There's no point inviting them in; they'll enter anyway.

Kristy and Sam close the door behind them and head for the mismatched couch and loveseat that take up most of the room. The only other furniture is a wooden rolltop desk stuck in the corner by the window.

The desk—a former resident of the post office and rescued from a yard sale for $20—doubles as my dining-room table and home office. It houses a widescreen iMac computer with TV tuner and an ancient printer whose only saving grace is that it consumes cheap, generic ink.

There are two pieces of art on the walls. Both are original mixed-media works, worthless and signed by the artist: me. Like all journalists, I often claim to be writing a novel. But when you spend every day working with words, it can be the last thing you want to do in your spare time.

Painting helps me relax. I'm just not much good at it.

As Kristy and Sam sit, I pull three oatmeal-chocolate-chip muffins from a box in the freezer and pop them in the microwave.

As soon as the soothing gurgle of the stovetop percolator begins, I return to the bedroom and slip into pajama bottoms and Godzilla slippers that, if the batteries haven't worn out, roar when I walk. I also manage to pull a stiff brush through my hair to offer the illusion there is a possibility that I give a bit of a damn.

Back in the kitchen, I place the warm muffins on individual plates and add a slice of aged white cheddar on the side.

"I was out late," I call from behind the waist-high island that divides the galley kitchen from the adjoining room. "A friend was killed. An artist."

"Oh, my goodness," says Kristy "Are you OK?"

I shrug. "Yeah. We weren't close anymore, but still."

"That's awful."

"Anyone we know?" Sam asks.

"Diego Chino? He used to live upstairs."

"Before our time. Not a friend of Dorothy, then?"

"No. He was straight." I pause. "At least he was when I knew him."

"We meet lots of artists at the charity events and gay fundraisers that Sam drags me to," says Kristy.

"I don't drag you," Sam protests. "You love an excuse to get dressed up."

Kristy giggles.

"Of course she loves it." I re-enter the room laden with muffins. "It's just difficult to be the center of attention with all that competition."

Kristy opens her mouth in protest. "I don't need to be the center of attention."

Sam and I exchange glances.

"I don't!" Kristy squeals. "It's just depressing sometimes when the most glamorous women in the room all have Adam's apples."

I chuckle as I hand out muffins and return to get the coffee.

I pour each of us a large mug of No Sweat Peruvian brew with cream and no sugar and carry them into the living room.

The women used to take their coffee different ways, but my mind was always too scattered in the morning to remember. Now, they drink it the same way I do. It makes life easier.

"So why the wake-up call?" I lift the mug to my lips and swallow a large, fully caffeinated mouthful. It tastes all the better for knowing I'm not exploiting Third World bean pickers.

"Two things," Kristy says. "One good, one bad."

"Give me the good. I'm feeling delicate."

Kristy beams. "Sam and I have come to a very important decision about our future."

"Let me guess. You're moving to Montana and becoming gay cowboys?"

"No!" Kristy's eyes flash with irritation. "We're going to have a baby."

Muffin-coffee goop sprays from my mouth, making Kristy shriek as she dodges the shrapnel.

"Dixie!"

"Sorry, sorry. It's just … OK, which one of you has been hiding the penis?"

Sam snorts and has to cover her mouth.

"There's no penis." Kristy blots her splattered blouse with a tissue.

"Ahh, immaculate conception. Good choice. All the best people do it."

"Be serious, Dix," Kristy warns, her strawberry lips begin to swell into a pout.

"OK, I'm sorry," I say gently. "Who's the father?"

"We don't know."

I furrow my brow. "You didn't catch his name?"

"No. We haven't chosen anyone yet."

"Ah." The morning fog clears from my brain. "You're not *actually* pregnant."

"Well, not yet," admits Kristy. "But once we find the right man, we will be."

"So congratulations here would be a touch premature."

Sam snickers but stops quickly under Kristy's stormy glare.

"This is an important decision." Kristy pouts and folds her arms across her pert bosom. Nothing wrong with her décolletage gene, and if I didn't love her so much, I might even be jealous.

I place my coffee mug and muffin plate on the carpet and cross to the couch.

"You're absolutely right." I wrap my arms around her neck to offer a hug. "It's a very important decision, and I am thrilled for you guys."

"Really?" Kristy asks.

"Really. I couldn't be happier."

"Thanks, Dix. I knew you'd understand."

I return to my chair and pick up my coffee.

"So who are the candidates?"

"We thought you could help us there," Sam says.

"Sorry, I left my penis in my other pants."

"No, I mean you have way more experience with men than we do. There's always someone coming or go—"

"Let me stop you there," I interrupt, trying not to show my discomfort. "While I certainly know some horny bastards, I've yet to find Mr. Right, or as I like to think of him, Sir Right."

"A horny bastard is OK," says Kristy brightly. "So long as he has good teeth and a clean medical record."

"Why horny?" Sam asks. "You're not sleeping with him."

"I know." Kristy rolls her eyes. "But with hands like mine, I could get a donation lickety-split."

Sam shudders and I must admit I feel a little queasy myself.

"What about finding someone who would be excited about being a father?" I ask.

Sam shakes her head. "We don't want a man involved beyond the donation."

"We certainly don't need one," Kristy agrees. "Sam has a good job with the trolleys—"

"Cable cars," interjects Sam.

"And I do most of my research from home—"

"Which reminds me," I interrupt, recalling a strange incident from two nights before. "Who are you researching those awful chastity belts for?"

"You know I can't disclose that. Author-researcher confidentiality."

"It was Janet Evanovich, right?"

"Not even close."

"Robert Crais?"

"Quit it."

"Karin Slaughter? Sean Black? Tess Gerritsen? Matt Hilton? Lee Child? Come on, give me a hint?"

Kristy giggles. "We're changing the topic."

"To what?"

"The bad news."

"You might not know this about me, Kristy, but I'm not a fan of bad news."

"Then you're really not going to like this."

I sigh. "Hit me."

"Mrs. Pennell received a threatening letter this morning."

"She what?" I blurt. "From who?"

"We don't know, but she seemed quite upset. Sam met her in the lobby when she was getting the mail."

"Post," Sam interrupts. "We're not calling it *mail* anymore, remember? *Mail, male.*"

"I'll pop in and see her after my shower," I say. "Threaten one of us and you threaten us all."

Kristy beams and leaps to her feet to give me a big hug. She smells like fresh daisies in the rain.

FIVE

Half an hour later, I knock on Mrs. Pennell's door.

When she opens it, her eyes are puffy and red, while her creased and pallid complexion is a feeble complement to her professionally coiffed platinum hair.

"The girls told me about the note," I say.

She opens the door wider.

"Cup of tea?" she asks.

"Lovely."

I step inside and close the door. Instantly, King William brushes against the back of my legs and begins to walk figure eights around my feet. It is the same shape as handcuffs and just as effective. When I bend to pet him, he plops onto his side and rolls over to expose a furry and very generous stomach.

I scratch belly and chest, working my way up to ears and chin as his appreciative purr shakes the walls.

"Oh, come now, William," Mrs. Pennell scolds affectionately. "At least let our guest in the door."

King William winks, rolls back onto his feet, and pads down the hallway. I follow.

In the kitchen, Mrs. Pennell pours boiling water into a large brown teapot. Her shoulders are slumped within a flower-patterned housecoat that has large white buttons dotting the front. Indoors, you rarely see her without the housecoat over her clothes, and from the amount of cat dander I find coating my hand, I understand why.

I wash my hands in the sink and ask, "Can I see it? The note."

Mrs. Pennell produces a small envelope—the size one normally associates with thank-you cards and invitations—from her pocket and hands it over.

The paper feels old, as though it has been sitting in a drawer for a long time without being used. I open the envelope and read the note. The handwriting is neat, but overly cursive and decidedly feminine.

It reads:

> I know it was you.
> Do not believe for a moment you can simply walk away from your responsibility in this matter.
> —Pearl

I return the note to the envelope.

"Who's Pearl?"

Mrs. Pennell shrugs. "I have been trying to think, but I do not believe I know anyone with that name."

"Someone in your past?"

"Not that I can recall."

"Is there a responsibility you've been neglecting? Something that would spark—"

She shakes her head dismissively. "I'm sure it is just nonsense."

"If it was, you wouldn't look so worried."

She sighs. "I have lived a quiet, genteel life for more than a quarter century now. Apart from taking a broom to an occasional creepy crawly, I don't believe I have done anything to warrant such attention. It is obviously a case of mistaken identity."

I start to respond, to ask what type of life she lived prior to her quarter-century mark of gentility, but she holds up a firm hand.

"Now, would you like a cookie with your tea?"

I have to admire her.

"Sure," I say softly, "that would be nice."

Mrs. Pennell places a small plate of cookies on a tray, adds a sugar bowl and tiny jug of cream, two china cups on saucers, and the brown teapot.

"Let me carry that," I say, lifting the tray and following her into the living room. I place the tray on a coffee table in front of the television set. The TV is broadcasting a morning talk show with the volume turned low.

"Would you like me to look into it?" I ask, pouring the strong brew into the delicate cups. "Just to clear up any misunderstanding?"

Mrs. Pennell raises her shoulders very slightly in a noncommittal gesture.

"If I don't," I continue, "I'm afraid Kristy may drag Sam down here to sleep on your doorstep."

Mrs. Pennell flashes a lipless smile as she accepts the tea and a chocolate-coated finger cookie.

"Do you remember the artist, Diego?" she asks, changing the subject. "The gentleman who lived above you before Derek and Shahnaz."

I nod. "Was it on the news?"

"Yes. You know then?"

"I was called to the scene last night."

"They say he killed himself."

I nod again.

Mrs. Pennell sighs wearily. "He didn't seem the type."

I have to agree.

———

After tea, I cross the hall to Mr. French's apartment and knock.

"And who could that be, Baccarat?" I hear him say as he clomps his way to the door. "Are we expecting company?"

Mr. French opens the door and beams up at me. He is an old man in a child's body. Standing at three feet, ten inches, Mr. French is dressed impeccably in tweed pants, white golf shirt, lamb's wool cardigan with wooden buttons, and a pair of comfortable Acorn-brand slippers. Clutched in his hand is a burl pipe carved in the shape of a bulldog's head, and the smoke rising from its bowl smells wonderfully of warm chocolate cake and cherry sauce.

"Ms. Flynn," he booms. "What a wonderful surprise. Come in, come in. Baccarat will be thrilled."

"I can't stay long."

"Of course, of course, but you must say hello to Baccarat or I'll never hear the end of it."

I follow him into the main room and make appropriate kissing/cooing noises to his pet parakeet, which as far as I can tell seems to pay me about as much attention as Bubbles does.

Mr. French claps his hands together in delight.

"Oh, she likes that." He beams. "Yes, indeed."

I smile and remove Mrs. Pennell's letter from my pocket as I sit on the loveseat.

"I need your help with a puzzle," I say.

"Ah, bravo. Let me get my tools."

When he returns from the bedroom, he's holding a slim velvet wallet. He moves to the coffee table and props his pipe in an electronic ashtray that sucks the smoke from the air and filters most of it away. Mr. French notices my gaze.

"Baccarat doesn't approve of me smoking," he explains. "But I grew tired of going outside every time I wanted a puff." He tilts his chin to a metal box in the corner that resembled an air conditioner. "The HEPA air purifier takes care of the big job, but this little guy also helps."

He lifts his pipe to take another puff and then unrolls the wallet like a mat, exposing a series of stainless-steel tools, each in its own velvet sleeve.

I hand him the envelope as he slips on a pair of thin, white gloves and places a magnifying loupe against his eye. Mr. French stands at the coffee table, which is at counter height for him.

"It doesn't have a stamp," I say.

"Oh?" He looks up, puzzled.

"It's the paper," I explain. "I was wondering if you could trace where it was sold and who might have bought it."

"Ahh."

"It feels old," I continue. "Not antique. Just…" I can't find the word.

"Let me take a look."

Mr. French places the envelope on the velvet mat, pulls out two pairs of long, very thin tweezers, and expertly removes the note without using fingers. After reading it, he lifts it to his nose and inhales.

"You're right," he says. "Not actually old, but stale, musty. Remainder stock most likely."

"Remainder stock?"

"Stock the vendor couldn't sell. It usually gets shoved to the back of the store until its price is discounted enough for its quality to no longer matter to the purchaser."

"Do you think you could track it?"

He looks up at me with furrowed brow. "We will have to assume several factors."

"Such as?"

"The sender lives nearby, which is why the envelope didn't require postage."

"Delivered by hand."

"Exactly. The second assumption is perhaps the larger leap. We have to assume the paper, although old, was purchased recently and hasn't been sitting for years in the sender's desk drawer."

I nod. "I know this isn't your usual area of expertise."

"Nonsense." Mr. French beams again. "Although some see philatelists as mere stamp collectors, if anything, we adore a good mystery. The story behind the stamp is often worth more than the stamp itself. For example, would you believe that I have stamps licked by Albert Einstein, Charlie Chaplin, Elizabeth Taylor, Winston

Churchill, *and* Richard Nixon? A fellow philatelist that I know has more exotic tastes. He has stamps licked by Mussolini, Stalin, Adolph Hitler, and Eva Braun. So let's give this the old college try."

I lean down and hug him.

"I'll be in touch," I say, making my retreat in such good humor that I even wave goodbye to Baccarat.

She doesn't appear to notice.

SIX

I NEVER GROW TIRED of riding cable cars. Crammed in a rickety metal box with three dozen tourists, weaving and bobbing to avoid being smacked in elbow, breast, or face by swinging cameras at every bend is the highlight of going to my office.

The bus is cheaper and drops me closer, but regular working people don't amuse me as much. Only on the cable cars can you watch model-thin women shiver violently because they thought San Francisco was going to be as warm as L.A.; or laugh at the pot-bellied men with bulging billfolds and garish T-shirts adorned with double entendres that make one groan; or wonder at the wide-eyed children dangling precariously from side rails, limbs inches from injury.

The offices for *NOW* are housed in the top three floors of a squat four-story brownstone, one block west of Alta Plaza. The ground floor, painted blue and white, contains a tasty little Greek restaurant named for the mythical flying horse, Pegasus.

The trouble with working above a Greek restaurant is the tantalizing aroma. The big buildup to lunch often makes it difficult to concentrate and results in inappropriate adjectives creeping into my work, such as the time I referred to a local politician as *succulent*. Fortunately for both my editor and my waistline, I do most of my work from home.

As usual, my mouth begins to water the moment I enter the stairwell to climb the three flights to the newsroom. The higher I climb, however, the fainter grow the smells of feta cheese, garlic tzatziki sauce, and the house specialty of fresh oven-baked pita finished with a light spray of olive oil and sprinkles of tarragon and cracked sea salt.

My stomach stops grumbling when I spot my paycheck lying alone in the dark notch of my mail slot. I snap it up and carry it to my desk, wondering hopefully if the deposit stub inside feels just a little fatter.

The spacious newsroom has the potential to be filled with natural light, since windows dot three sides, but because everyone sits in front of computer screens, the blinds are drawn tight to cut down on glare.

When I first started in this business, the newsroom was a continual hive of excitement. The pounding of keyboards, the chatter of police scanners, and the still-functioning though archaic brass bell that rang whenever the production department sent a page proof through the vacuum tube delivery system. It was a cacophonic combination that fired a surge of adrenaline directly into my bloodstream.

The reporters were noisier, the editors more belligerent, and a bottle of whiskey could usually be found in someone's desk drawer when deadline pressure made your temples throb. Back then a rookie still started at the bottom and clawed her way up, trying to stay sober and smart and unmolested along the way.

Today, the noise is gone and with it a lot of the energy. The rookies hold degrees in English, political science, economics, and psychology; their haircuts cost more than I used to earn in a day; they're healthier and smarter and duller than you can imagine.

The blinds stay closed. Welcome to the Word Factory.

My desk sits in a corner, piles of books and paper making it look like an abandoned hovel for the resident troll. My antique wooden chair, which I refused to let them replace with some modern ergonomic contraption, awaits me, but looks bare. Someone has stolen my cushion.

With a muttered curse, I sit on the hard seat, put my feet on the desk, and rip open the familiar aqua-blue envelope. The direct-deposit statement inside shows I am still being underpaid, and after a quick calculation of my outstanding bills, I come to the conclusion that a raise would be welcomed.

From across the room, a bloated giant watches my mental gymnastics before lifting himself out of his chair.

Edward Stoogan plods across the room like a Beluga whale that has suddenly sprouted legs, the strain of the exercise reddening his flour-white face. He stops halfway to catch his breath, disguising the fact by looking over a reporter's shoulder and pointing out the obvious question she has failed to ask during an interview. The reporter blushes slightly before picking up the phone.

When he reaches my desk, Stoogan pushes a large pile of paper from the edge and rests half his ass on the clearing. He is puffing slightly from the short walk and he peers down at me through moist salmon-pink eyes.

Stoogan is senior news editor. An albino with shock-white hair, he is the kind of man you can't help staring at. He tips the scales at around three hundred and his ghostly complexion makes my ancestral Celtic pigment appear as a healthy glow.

In one puffy hand, Stoogan clutches a miniature extending telescope that he needs to read the small type on the computer screen. It is a handicap that hasn't stopped him from being a master of his craft.

Most of us in the newsroom have a hard time admitting that a man who wears purple socks with brown pants can bring such life to our prose. But he always does.

"Have you seen my cushion, boss?" I ask cheerily.

"I've got it," he replies in a windy, high-pitched squeak. "I figure you're such a pain in the ass you owe me something to rest my sore cheeks on."

I grin as his face turns serious.

"Sorry about wasting your time last night," he continues. "I heard it was suicide."

I shrug. "Maybe, but I think there's still a solid story there."

"Don't play with me, Dix. I'm too frail."

"No, I'm serious. The human-interest angle alone is terrific. Talented but unfulfilled artist makes a final, drastic statement, ironically creating his greatest work. And there's even the possibility—"

"The dailies didn't bother re-plating for it," he interrupts. "I thought the *Chronicle* might have tried to slip something in for second edition, but it's a dead story to them now."

"The dailies are idiots; I'm not."

Stoogan massages his temples in small, circular strokes. "I received a call this morning from the police commissioner."

"Does he miss staring at my ass, the letch?"

Dixie's Tips #4: *Short skirts and windy crime scenes don't mix.*

Stoogan sighs. "He heard you were at the artist's apartment and harassing two of his officers. He claims you were trying to get them on record even though you're well aware it's departmental policy not to comment on suicides."

"Hmmm, sounds like I was doing my job." I reach over my shoulder and pat my back. "Good for me."

"He also wanted to assure us the story wasn't worth our attention."

"Prick! What's he covering up?"

Stoogan smirks. "Nice to see you're not getting paranoid in your—"

"Don't say it," I warn. "Besides, when do we allow bureaucrats to dictate what's newsworthy?"

"We don't."

"Exactly. So you trust me on this?"

"No."

I tut. "Come on. Why not?"

"Because you're the one who keeps trying to sell me on the 'ghost of Al Capone' story."

"Hey, I'm still researching that. It'll be a hell of a story once I track down who the mystery waitress was. Maybe I can reunite their ghosts."

"See. That's what I mean." Stoogan sighs again. "There are days when I don't know what to do with you, Dix," he says despairingly. "And I'm not just saying that."

"Our love has always been a one-way street," I say soothingly, while flashing a cheeky grin. "Just think of it. The daily buffoons will bury this story because Commissioner Gordon Vanmoore tells them it's nothing. But we'll hit the stands in five days with a cover story that at its worst will explore the human tragedy of a sensitive artist driven over the edge by his need to succeed in a too-competitive commercial world."

"And at its best?"

"Murder." I lock on to his watery eyes. "You didn't see the body, boss. There was nothing left of his head except what was splattered on the walls and canvas. It was a plea, signed in blood, too powerful to be made by accident."

Stoogan studies me intently. "Is this personal?"

I shake off the suggestion. "We hadn't talked in over a year. Old news. Diego was living the dream he always talked about. He'd quote-unquote 'made it,' so why throw it all away? That's the hook."

Stoogan holds up two fat, pink, baby-soft fingers. "Two days," he says. "If you can't show me you've got the makings of something meaty by then, I'm assigning you to work on a lifestyles piece with Clooney."

I glance over at the petite Barbie doll three desks down who is fast-tracking an Eighties fashion revival by leading the charge to bring back big hair and shoulder pads. Without a care, she applies a fresh coat of scarlet lipstick to collagen-plump lips and blows a kiss at her reflection in a desktop mirror.

Mary Jane Clooney's last opus was headlined "The Twelve Secret Erogenous Zones You May Not Know You Have."

Stoogan follows my gaze and grins.

I shudder.

———

After two hours on the phone, I've only found one gallery in the entire Bay Area, the Gimcrack, that specializes in Diego's work. Unfortunately, the owner is at a showing on the white sandy beaches of Carmel and isn't expected back until tomorrow.

I scratch my head, not wanting to admit Diego's death is looking less artistic and more self-pitying than I hoped. I try one more.

"Avenida Gallery, how may we help you?" The voice is smooth, gentlemanly and instantly likable.

"Dixie Flynn of *NOW* calling," I reply, just as friendly. "Is the owner in?"

"Speaking."

"And your name?"

"Jonathan Smithwick, Jr."

"Any relation to the British beer maker?"

"None."

"Pity, it's a nice brew, especially poured slow into a frosted mug."

He laughs. "You're not wrong."

"I was wondering if you could answer a few questions for me?"

"About art?"

"Or imported beer. Unless you're an expert in other areas that'll make for a good story."

He laughs again, sealing our friendship and dulling his natural defenses.

"How may I help you? Dixie, was it?"

As a reporter, I'm used to people not wanting to talk. The trick is to come across like an old friend or sympathetic relative. Whatever makes them forget you're a single-minded bloodsucker whose only interest is in the inches of gray matter below your byline.

If they laugh, they're yours.

"I understand you carry Diego Chino's work?" I begin.

"Not any longer, I'm afraid. Diego really hasn't produced anything of interest in the last six months or so."

"I understood he was very popular."

"That was last season. I'm afraid his work has become rather …" He hesitates, searching for the right word. "Stale."

"Do you know of anyone who still carries him?"

"I believe the Gimcrack on Union Street does."

This is the same story I heard from the other galleries.

I switch topics. "Do you carry Adamsky?"

"Certainly. He is very popular."

"Do you have any in stock?"

"Originals or prints?"

"Originals."

"Not at the moment, but we are expecting a shipment of new works to arrive this week, and I'm planning to get my hands on several choice pieces."

"Where does the shipment go when it lands?"

"Stellar Galleries is Adamsky's North American agent. But several galleries, including my own, have an agreement to purchase works directly from them."

I scratch my head again. "Why doesn't Stellar keep all the paintings?"

Smithwick Jr. chuckles softly. "Adamsky is quite prolific and Stellar doesn't have the space to show all his work. Plus, it can be rather overwhelming for the client to make a decision when facing an entire gallery full of work from a single artist. It's easier to find a favorite piece when there are fewer options. Under our agreement with Stellar, we purchase the paintings at an agreed price. Everyone benefits."

"How many galleries are involved?"

"There are ten of us within the city. Stellar also opened a new gallery in Carmel recently that is attracting buyers from L.A."

"Does Stellar have originals for sale?"

"Yes, I believe they do." His voice drops to a conspiratorial whisper as he adds, "However, if you are interested in purchasing, might I add that the paintings I choose become some of his most sought after."

"You have a good eye?"

"One of the best. It keeps me ahead of the pack."

"I'll keep that in mind, Jonathan. Thanks." I add a touch of feminine laughter to cement our secret pact.

After hanging up, I flip through the Yellow Pages and discover Stellar Galleries has a high-rent showroom in Ghirardelli Square overlooking San Francisco Bay. A quick fumble through the reverse directory tells me the owner is one Declan Stellar.

I dial.

"Stellar Galleries, Casper Blymouth speaking."

The nasally voice is familiar, and I instantly have a mental picture of the annoying little man who wanted to remove the blood painting from Diego's apartment before it even had time to dry.

"Is Mr. Stellar available?" I ask, using my most polished voice. No, not the phone-sex one.

"He is presently having lunch at the Hyatt. May I take a message?"

He emphasizes Hyatt, just to let me know that if I can't afford to eat there, I am wasting his time.

"No, that's all right. I was planning to stop by. Do you know what time he'll be returning?"

"Two o'clock. Can I leave your name?"

"Just tell him Dixie called."

He sniffs as if the plainness of the name annoys him and then hangs up without a goodbye.

I stretch my arms above my head, feeling a vertebra in my spine pop back into place, and rub my ear. I've never liked the phone, and I have a bad habit of holding it too tight. But in this economy, the paper frowns on taxi fares to a dozen galleries for background into a story based on a hunch.

I glance over at the sunlight trying to squeeze through the cracks of the closed blinds and sigh. The SPF 15 in my daily moisturizer isn't doing me any good if I'm stuck indoors.

I still have one more call to make.

The Hall of Justice line goes dead twice during call transfers before I finally connect with Frank.

"Homicide. Fury here."

"Do you know that if you added a second *r* to your name, you would be Detective Sergeant Furry?"

"You're like one of those stray dogs, Dix. The kind that never goes away."

"Shouldn't have fed me."

"I didn't."

"It must have been the ear rubs, then."

"How would you like to play a game of catch off the Golden Gate?"

"Cruel, Frank. Very cruel."

"What do you want?"

"Greek food, but I hate to eat alone."

"Fine. One condition."

"I'm not bringing my mother."

Frank sighs. "We don't talk about the stiff."

"What stiff?"

Frank sighs again. "I mean it, Dix. I've had it up to here with paperwork on that headless..." He mumbles to himself but doesn't finish the thought.

"Is the autopsy done?"

"No and don't bother interrogating me right now either. I'm still in the middle of transferring the file over to Northern. Their chief has been on my ass all day, you'd think he didn't have anything better to do."

"When is the autopsy planned?"

"Possibly later today, or maybe tonight, or maybe never. Nobody's exactly screaming for it."

"If you attend, are you allowed to bring a date?"

"Jesus, Dix."

"Come on. I've got a feeling about this one."

"Right now you're the only one."

"Way I like it."

A rumble enters Frank's voice that can almost be mistaken for a chuckle. "See you at lunch and remember what I said."

"We're playing catch after?"

Frank hangs up. Noisily.

SEVEN

After slipping into my coat, I stop at the paper's morgue to convince the lone librarian that I need clipping files on Chino and Adamsky.

"When do you need them?" Lulu Lovejoy's lips form into a quivering kiss as she sucks the end of a yellow pencil.

"This afternoon will be fine."

"Will you come back for it, or do you want me to ..." Lulu works the dramatic pause by pushing her shoulders back and crossing her legs, flashing more meaty thigh than is appropriate for a bordello, never mind a morgue, "deliver?"

I shake my head, trying not to laugh.

"You know, Lulu, since the operation, every word out of your mouth sounds like a come-on. It was bad enough when you were—"

"I'm a very sexual person, Dixie."

"Sexual I get, but it's like you're a hormonal hand grenade ready to explode."

"Maybe I am."

I grimace. "I don't normally do this—in fact, it goes against my core beliefs—but have you ever considered porn?"

Her eyes open wide, curious.

"You know, like acting in …" My awkwardness is palpable as I attempt to stop my flushed cheeks from catching on fire. "It might give you the relief you're after until, well—"

"Know anyone?" she asks.

"No! I—I mean, how would I? Ch—check the classifieds. There must be a union office or casting agency. Hell, you're the librarian. If anyone can find …"

Lulu laughs and flattens her skirt.

"You're so cute."

"No," I blurt. "Really, I'm not."

"You want me to leave the files on your desk?"

"Yes. I would appreciate that."

"Mmmm," she moans. "How much?"

"Oh, jeez," I groan. "I'm outta here!"

———

I run down the three flights of stairs and burst outside before the sizzle of lamb souvlaki and aroma of lemon-infused potato forces me to detour. I don't slow down until I'm a block away with my nasal passages clogged with fresh traffic fumes.

Union Street is only six blocks away, and the sun has yet to rise high enough to make the walk unbearable. That's one of the troubles of being a redhead. I hate to be indoors, but my fair complexion leaves few alternatives.

Just as some women always know the location of the nearest washroom, I tend to plot where to find the next patch of cool shade. In the middle of summer, I scurry from shadow to shadow like a leper hiding her face while the beautiful bronzed people soak in the sun, sacrificing their skin in the hope Mattel will one day immortalize them in plastic.

Lately, I've found the shadows becoming more crowded as the ozone/cancer scare sinks in. It's nice to have the company, but sometimes I wish the reformed sun worshippers would leave the cool places to those of us who don't have a choice.

One of the joys of walking in the morning is the chance to watch the illusive wisps of ethereal mist that still huddle deep in the alleys. Like vampires, each tendril shrinks away from the encroaching sun, entwining with others of its kind to dance and brush lips.

Sometimes, I feel their vaporous arms challenging me to run down the silver-streaked alleyways and join them. But each time I get up the nerve to become a child, stretching my arms wide like an airplane and readying my lips to make propeller noises, they dissipate. In their place, solid forms twitch and stumble, unfocused eyes glistening within pale, skeletal masks, and the road's shiny shards of silver become broken pieces of glass.

San Francisco does that to you. It loves to tease, taunt, and flirt. If you listen close, you can hear a snicker as it forces your collar to rise against its frigid breath, then, as though forgiven, it lifts the haze and allows the sun to shine.

Of course, I could just be crazy. The city does that to you too.

In daylight, the building that houses Diego Chino's condo looks no different. It is still trendy and unsettlingly expensive.

I enter through the first set of glass doors in the lobby and press the buzzer for Mrs. M. Stewart, one of the ground floor tenants. Unlike last night, the inner set of doors is locked.

"Hello?" a woman's singsong voice calls out from the tiny wall speaker. "Who's there?"

"It's Dixie Flynn of the *NOW*. I've come about the shooting upstairs."

"Oh, come in." The woman's lilting brogue is either Irish or Scottish; if she has joined the American melting pot, she made sure to stick to the edges.

The buzzer sounds, and I push open the second set of doors. A short distance from the elegant staircase, a petite woman dressed in purple from head to toe smiles out at me. I estimate by the wrinkles in her neck that she is in her seventies, but with her gray hair perfectly coiffed and the cut of her suit giving her a lovely figure, she appears ageless.

"Oh, my," says Mrs. Stewart, "what lovely hair you have, dear. Are you no Scottish yerself?"

I laugh. "It's been a few generations."

"Aye, I thought so. You can't hide a Scot. Spot them a mile away. Two if I have my glasses on."

I laugh again. "I hope I'm not catching you on the way out, but I was wondering if I might ask a few questions?"

"I was just trying this on." She smooths the suit and reaches up to play with a large pearl and diamond bauble in her left ear that could likely pay my rent for the year. Her eyes twinkle, and she lowers her voice conspiratorially. "My son has a big function coming up at his law office and wants me to look the part. This is a Donna Karan, do yeh know her?"

I take the question to be rhetorical, but nod anyway.

"To be honest," she continues, "I'm more comfortable in housecoat and slippers, but if you look like the cleaning lady they try and lock you in a home and take away your money and the remote for the TV. As though being relaxed is the same as being addled."

I don't know what to say. Fortunately, I don't have to say anything.

"Well, don't just stand there. Come in, come in. What do you take in your tea? I'm brewing up."

Before I can reply, Mrs. Stewart is striding down the short hallway to the kitchen. I close the door and follow.

The apartment is half the size of Diego's, but more elegant with polished cherry hardwood floors, antique European furniture, and crystal fixtures that cast tiny rainbows on the walls and ceiling.

I stop at the kitchen doorway and watch Mrs. Stewart scuttle from one side of the room to the other, humming contentedly. When she spots me, she waves toward the living room.

"Sit doon, sit doon," she says. "I'll get some biscuits. And don't you fret about the furniture, a chair is just a chair no matter where it came from or what it cost."

The living room would have been large if not so crowded. An antique couch and two high-backed armchairs are covered in tartan shawls, and every flat surface is overflowing with knickknacks: tiny china teapots decorated with British town crests; a collection of clay animals with curled, ram-like horns and trumpet-shaped snouts with *MacHaggis* written on tiny brass plaques; an assortment of thimbles and spoons; a collection of well-used pipes in a wooden rack, the smell of tobacco still faint on their bowls; sets of silver coins bearing scenes of royal weddings; a framed Elvis stamp; and a waist-high bookcase packed with large-print paperbacks by Martina Cole, Ian Rankin, Stuart MacBride, Ken Follett, and Val McDermid. Sitting on top of the bookcase is a white porcelain bust of a man with unruly muttonchops.

Despite her wealth, it seems Mrs. Stewart loves to be tacky. It reminds me of something my father often said about my mother: "You can take the girl out of the trailer park, but not the trailer park out of the girl."

Of course, this was usually said just before he was banished to the couch for the night.

"Do you like Rabbie?" Mrs. Stewart asks as she clears a space on the coffee table to set down a wooden tray. On the tray is a stoneware teapot, two large mugs, a bowl of sugar, a little container of milk, and a plate of chocolate-covered cookies.

"Rabbie?" I ask.

"You were just admiring him." She indicates the porcelain bust. "Rabbie Burns. He's a grand poet. Bit of a lad, they say, but better that than a poofter like most of the English lot."

I smile across at her, not sure what she is talking about, as she busily fusses with the teapot to make sure everything is just right. Her bony hands look frail, the skin paper thin, and yet she moves around without a hint of arthritic pain. I wonder what her secret is.

She pours the tea.

"Bet you drive the lads wild with that hair of yours, don't you?" She chuckles. "When I was a lass, my hair was nearly as bright, like the sun it was. Oh, the boys used to fight over me something rotten." She giggles. "I was thinking I should dye it again. Redheads really shouldn't go gray, should we?"

I shake my head, which makes her smile.

"Right, that's settled. I'll make an appointment and get it done before my son's big do. Won't he be shocked? Now, how do you take your tea?"

"Just cream, thanks, Mrs. Stewart."

"Och, call me Millie."

I sip the tea, smile gratefully, and accept a chocolate cookie. I notice Millie doesn't take one herself. I dunk the cookie into my tea, lick the melted chocolate off the crispy base, and then pop the whole thing into my mouth. Delicious.

I accept another one.

Millie smiles, sipping her own tea, as she watches me.

After a few sips, she says, "Now, what do you want to ask me about?"

"Diego Chino."

Her eyes turn sad. "Such a nice young man," she says softly. "And talented too. He can't have been much older than you, dear. Such a waste."

"Did you notice if he had any visitors last night?"

"No, I was watching ma shows on the TV. The Mystery channel has been showing some great reruns lately: *Wire in the Blood* with Robson Green, that scruffy Inspector Rebus, and Inspectors Morse and Frost, of course. Do you like them?"

"I don't watch much TV anymore. Had my fill when I was younger."

"Och, they say it'll rot your brain, but I love a good mystery. *Coronation Street*, too, though it's English. But it's the North, so that's OK. You watch *Corrie*?"

I shake my head.

"It's very good," she continues. "My son says I'm addicted, but that's ridiculous. A week just wouldn't be complete without ma shows."

"But you heard the gunshot?" I ask in an attempt to get back on track.

"Aye, I did. There I was in front of the TV, feet up, wee cup of tea, enjoying myself, like you do, when I heard this awful clatter upstairs. It was as if the four horsemen had arrived and discovered no beer in the fridge. Well, I thought to myself that was odd since it's normally very quiet here. And then," she claps her hands together, "Bang! Well, I've watched enough police shows to know a gun when I hear one. I have that surround-sound thingy on my TV, you know? The woofs and tweets. My son set it up. He's very clever that way, not like his father at all, rest his soul. If it wasn't about trains, he wasn't interested—"

"You called the police?" I say.

"Oh, yes. Talked to this nice woman, very efficient but already divorced, which surprised me because she was very pleasant and has a good job there. Anyways, I told her what I heard, and she said she would send somebody right over. Well, these two nice big policeboys arrived, looking very smart in their uniforms, and went about investigating. I keep keys for everyone since I don't go out much, so I let them in. And oh my, I didn't linger when I caught a peek of the mess inside."

I press on. "And you didn't notice if Mr. Chino seemed depressed or angry over the last few days?"

"No, he seemed his usual self. Quiet, you know? I don't think he had many friends, poor dear. I kept inviting him for tea, but he was always working on a painting."

I wasn't getting anywhere. "Would you mind if I looked at the apartment?"

Millie wrinkles her nose. "It's an awful tip up there…"

"That's OK," I assure her. "I was here with the police last night." She nods. "Let me get ma key."

———

At the door to Diego's apartment, Millie hands over the key.

"I hope you don't mind," she says, "but it's too sad to look at. Would you just lock up when you're through? I'll go down and re-fill the kettle."

I nod, feeling a twinge inside as Millie wipes a tear from her powdered cheek before retreating.

With no crime scene tape or other official encumbrance to bar the way, I unlock the apartment and enter.

The smell of death is strong; air, musty and stale, warmed by sunlight streaming through the large picture windows. If Diego had ever felt like catching a movie, all he had to do was take a few steps to the window and read the Metro's marquee across the street to discover what was playing.

The apartment is empty—eerily so. No paintings or partially finished canvasses; no television or radio; no dining room table or even a comfortable couch. The only pieces of furniture are an antique armchair with Queen Anne legs and oak arms, plus a matching coffee table that appears too delicate to be of much use.

It's a home made for a ghost to glide through, and the thought sends a shiver down my spine. I glance over at the blood-spattered wall with its ominous clean rectangle where the canvas had blocked the spray and will myself to ignore the movement of shadow in the play of light.

I pace the room, aware of every footfall, trying to get a feel for the hollow space. *Suicide? Murder?* I can't help but think of the last moment's of Diego's life in this room. Was he afraid? If so, was he afraid of *someone*?

If Diego, or his ghost, popped out now to shout "Boo," I expect the whole city would be deafened by my scream.

Repressing my unhelpful imagination, I focus on the search for clues to the story behind Diego's death and find a small tin case in one of the corners, abandoned and forgotten. I pry it open with a thumbnail to find eight tiny tubes of used earth-tone oils and a thin sable brush, its tip hardened into a stiff point from years of use. It's the kind of beginner's paint set that one buys for a child.

For a reason I can't explain, I close the lid again and slip the tin into my pocket.

With a sigh, I survey the desolate space again.

Strange. This isn't like any artist I've ever met. In my admittedly limited experience, an artist's home is usually cluttered with half-realized ideas, rough sketches of beginning works and failed experiments; magazine clippings of shapes and colors that took their fancy; paint splatters from late-night trials in shade and texture; pencils, paper, charcoal, pastels, anything that will leave a mark on paper, cardboard, or canvas. Inspiration is fleeting—no artist ever wants an idea to leave without trying to capture its essence.

Diego may have lived here, but it doesn't seem like he ever actually worked here.

I return to the window. The view is a yuppie's dream: cappuccino bars, art galleries, wine boutiques, all mixed with a scattering of cozy, ethnic restaurants that serve mostly white, wealthy professionals. If you climbed to the roof and stretched your neck, you may even be able to see the Golden Gate Bridge. Who could ask for more?

Millie's tea is starting to weigh on my bladder. I head into the bathroom and poke through the medicine cabinet before sitting. The usual contents are accounted for: toothpaste, toothbrush, deodorant (both stick and unscented powder), electric shaver, cologne (the same brand I remember), and mouthwash. There is also a small inhaler with a prescription label on the side showing it's for asthma. There are no other drugs on the glass shelves, not even a bottle of Tylenol or aspirin.

The absence of painkillers annoys me. *Who doesn't get headaches?* If this was a woman's medicine chest ... well, I better not get started on how blatantly unfair it is to be a member of the fairer sex.

After washing my hands, I head into the bedroom to poke through the closet and a chest-high, four-drawer dresser. Diego's clothes look perfectly normal, although better quality than I remember. No paint stains on the crisp dry-cleaned shirts, and the feel of a silk-blend suit jacket is expensive. Even the two pairs of jeans (one black, one blue) have been ironed. I sniff the closet, hoping to catch his scent, but the only odor is of dry-cleaning fluid.

There are no condoms in the nightstand and no dirty magazines under the bed. In fact, there are no magazines, newspapers, or books anywhere.

Remembering the painting that Frank found sandwiched in the bed, I lift one side of the mattress and look down at the box spring. It looks no different from any other box spring I've ever had the pleasure of eyeballing; even the *Do Not Remove New Material Only* tag is still attached.

I let the mattress drop, the motion causing the tucked sheets to spill out. When I bend to tuck them back in, I notice they are lightly stained with splotches of paint. I lift the mattress again, but this time I look up. More splotches of dried paint dot the underside of the mattress.

The only explanation I have, unless Diego often hid paintings under his mattress, was the paint came from the Adamsky. But according to the gallery owners, Adamsky lived in Portugal.

Why would an artist ship a painting before the oils had completely dried? It makes about as much sense as Diego hiding one under his mattress in the first place.

The only other thing of note is located outside the bedroom window. A black metal staircase descends at a sharp angle, stopping at a landing in front of each apartment below. Also, a simple metal ladder attached firmly to the outside wall ascends to the roof. The window exit is locked from the inside and a small security sticker indicates it is alarmed.

Feeling none the wiser but unaccountably sad, I leave the apartment and head back downstairs.

———

Millie's singsong voice calls me inside when I knock on her door. She clicks off the TV and immediately pours a fresh cup of tea when I join her in the living room to hand back the key.

"It's such a shame, isn't it?" Millie says, raising her eyes to the ceiling.

I agree it is and take a sip of tea. The strength of it makes my eyelids flutter.

"Do you mind if I ask a few more questions?"

"Not at all." Millie offers the plate of cookies. "Have another biscuit. A growing lass like yerself needs her energy."

I accept, even though the only growing I would find acceptable at this point in my life is perhaps an enhanced bosom. And even that idea lost some of its luster after I stumbled into my thirties.

"Do you know if Diego has a workshop anywhere?" I begin.

"I believe he does," Millie replies. "He never spends much time at home. An ideal neighbor really."

"Do you know where it is?"

"No, Mr. Chino isn't—wasn't—much of a bletherer at all. Very quiet."

"Blether?"

Millie laughs. "Forgive ma Scots. A bletherer is someone who likes to talk. Get a couple of bletherers together, and it becomes a right natter." She touches a finger to the side of her nose and winks. "I just love a good natter." She giggles. "Do you read that Mary Jane Clooney in your paper? She's a rare gossip. I wouldn't mind having lunch with her one day. The stories she must know. All those celebrities, and she's certainly one to kiss and tell." Millie slaps her knee and crunches her face into a pincushion as she chuckles.

I try to keep the grimace off my face.

"Do you think it would be OK to speak to your other neighbors?" I ask.

"I don't see why not, but they won't be in right now. If you come back around suppertime, you'll have a better chance of catching one of them home. Such busy professionals, you know? Everyone trying so hard to make a good life, they don't realize it's passing them right by."

I take a second, smaller sip of tea to be polite and thank Millie for her time.

She walks me to the door. When I open it, I feel the heat of the day filling the hallway. It reminds me of how much colder Diego's apartment had been last night compared to today.

"Did you turn the air conditioner off upstairs after the police left?" I ask.

"No, wasn't me," Millie answers. "I'm just so happy it's working again. It was broken for nearly two weeks, but that handsome repairman—George, I think his name was—came just yesterday or the day before." She sighs, disheartened. "It's sad though, Diego won't be able to enjoy it."

EIGHT

FRANK ENTERS THE RESTAURANT just as I am scooping out a large dollop of yogurt-garlic tzatziki sauce with a thick wedge of warm pita. I quickly stuff it in my mouth and wash it down with a swallow of chilled Domestica.

He strolls over to the table in his lopsided gait, thin tie askew, the knot looking tighter than usual, and his sleeves shoved up to expose thick, hairy arms.

Above his left wrist, the words *Nasty Habit* are tattooed in blue ink around the black outline of a broken horseshoe.

The first time I saw the tattoo, I asked Frank for the story, but he shrugged me off. Naturally, this only made me more tenacious. It had taken a little digging to discover a young cowboy from Butte Creek, Montana, had ended his burgeoning saddle-bronc career going full-bore for a million-dollar payday at the Calgary Stampede.

According to the newspaper story, Frank's chute jammed as he sat upon the ornery steed, and before the cowhands could get the gate free, Nasty Habit bucked Frank onto the steel rails with his hand still wrapped to the leather saddle horn on the horse's back. Both cowboy and horse fought to get free, and both came off for the worse. Frank went to the hospital to have his shoulder shoved back in its socket, his broken nose realigned, a steel rod inserted in his left leg, a cast put on his wrist, and enough stitches sewn on him to make Frankenstein envious.

Nasty Habit wasn't so fortunate.

Frank turned in his spurs soon after, and his next news mention was a short notice in the *Spokane Review* when he graduated from the police academy with a special mention for being top marksman.

Before Frank reaches his chair, I order the house specialty combination platter for two, another glass of Greek wine, and an O'Doul's.

Frank sits with a weary sigh.

I open with, "So what can you tell me about the late Mr. Chino?"

Frank growls.

"Easy, Frank. If we don't talk business, I can't write this off."

"You're buying?"

I find the incredulity in his voice surprisingly hurtful. I may not be wealthy, but I try not to be cheap. Then again, my skin is normally much thicker. I blame lack of sleep.

"If you're talking," I volley back, just a touch off my usual pace.

"Off the record?"

"Mostly. The public doesn't care about your opinions, but if you hand me some useful facts, I'll use 'em."

He nods and places a red cloth napkin on his lap, tucking one corner into his waistband.

"There isn't much to tell. The apartment was clean."

"Clean?"

"Clean, clean. No signs of a struggle, no signs of a break-in, front door was locked when the officers arrived, and there's nothing to indicate anyone but the victim was ever there."

"Sounds too clean," I say.

Frank's mouth twitches. "OK, for a single guy living alone, the apartment did appear a little too spotless. But before you jump to any conclusions, he had a maid in once a week. Yesterday was her regular day. She was there just a few hours before he ventilated his skull."

Frank stops as the waitress brings our drinks.

I hand her my empty glass and take a generous sip from the fresh one. It is sharp, cold, and pleasantly bitter, though sadly not as good as the first glass. It never is.

"Why kill himself after the maid left?" I ask. "Wouldn't it make more sense to kill yourself the night before? That way, your body gets discovered when the maid arrives and you're not rotting around for a week. I mean really, yech, nobody likes to leave an ugly corpse, right?"

"The guy was checking out, what does he care who finds him?"

"Suicide tends not to be spontaneous. You know that. Depressed people plan their deaths, often meticulously."

"Exactly." Frank's grin widens. "And you don't get any more meticulous than spraying your brains over a signed canvas and sending a suicide note to your art dealer, do you?" He snaps his fingers. "See! He arranged it so the art clown would be first on the scene. He wanted to make sure no one messed with his grisly work of art, especially not a maid."

Frank dumps his bottled beer into a tall, frosted glass. Not being a connoisseur, he doesn't tip the glass for a smooth pour. I sip my wine, feeling depressed.

"By the way," Frank adds, "I didn't want to tell you because I knew you'd be upset, but since you're already there—"

"You're leaving me for another?" I quip dryly.

Frank rolls his eyes. "No, they did the autopsy earlier this morning."

"Shit, Frank. I asked you to get me an invite."

"Yeah, yeah, I know. But by the time I found out, the coroner was nearly done."

"I thought you had to be there to witness it."

"Usually the investigating officer is notified, but because this isn't looking suspicious, no one saw the need."

I grunt my displeasure. "Did they find anything?"

"I haven't seen the report yet, and the screens are still in progress, but I'm told there were minute traces of cocaine under his right index finger and in his nasal passage."

"Nasal passage!" I say loudly. "How in hell did they find a nasal passage? His face was splattered from floor to ceiling."

Frank chokes on his O'Doul's, the splutter making people at nearby tables turn to stare.

"People are trying to eat, Dix," Frank wheezes when he gets his breath back.

"Well … it's a legitimate question."

Frank's eyes dance with mirth. "The coroner is a woman of many talents, kid. One of which is identifying chunks of flesh and telling us what they used to be. In fact, she's probably the only one on the force who can actually tell her ass from a hole in the ground."

"Sounds like love."

"Fuck you."

I laugh as the indignant and slightly embarrassed look on Frank's leathered face brings me out of my doldrums. Methinks the coroner has definitely caught Frank's eye.

"Can your lady friend tell if a person had asthma?" I ask.

"Probably, why?"

"Diego may have been asthmatic."

"So?"

"If he had asthma, why would he snort cocaine? Wouldn't a drug like that cause an attack?"

"If you were going to blow your brains out, would you worry about an asthma attack?"

He has a point.

"Besides," Frank continues, "how do you know he had asthma?"

"I found an inhaler in his medicine cabinet."

"You went back to his apartment?" His tone is disapproving.

"Sure," I reply. "The police don't consider it a crime scene. It's a nice apartment in a nice neighborhood."

"One you can't afford."

I stab myself in the heart with an invisible knife. "That hurts, Frank. Really."

The lunch platter arrives loaded with moussaka, dolmades, spanakopita, calamari, souvlaki, and Greek meatballs. We immediately split it onto our oven-warmed plates and begin to devour the feast. Before the waitress leaves us alone, I order another glass of wine and a second O'Doul's.

"When do you think you'll see the autopsy report?" I mumble, my mouth stuffed with béchamel cream and savory ground lamb.

Frank shrugs. "Depends on the drug screens. The morgue is a busy place."

He turns his attention to the shoulder chop in his hand and busily scrapes the blackened fat onto his tongue with eager teeth.

"Did you interview any of Diego's neighbors?" I continue.

"Just the woman on the ground floor."

"Millie?"

Frank cocks an eyebrow, but lets it go.

"You planning to go back?" I ask.

"Haven't you been listening? The case is closed. Hell, it's not even my case anymore. The Commish told me to forward the paperwork to Northern and let them tie a bow on it. I've got other cases."

"Since when does Vanmoore do you favors?"

Frank shrugs again.

"You think there's something there he didn't want you finding out?" I ask.

"Christ!" Frank drops his chop and his hand snakes out to grab my drinking arm, spilling a spoonful of wine onto the white tablecloth. "OK, I don't like people telling me how to handle an investigation, Dix, but this one is cut and dry. Northern is welcome to it. Let it go."

He releases my arm.

"Fair enough," I say. "New topic."

The waitress returns with our drinks. I down the rest of my wine and hand her the empty glass. When she leaves, I lift my fresh glass and sip, enjoying the sensation of chilled grape mingling with warm garlic in my mouth.

"So what do you think about the signature on the blood painting?" I ask. "Genuine or forged?"

Despite himself, Frank chuckles. "You're as stubborn as a Brahma bull I used to know."

We eat the rest of our lunch with chitchat about the 'Niners, Sharks, and Giants. When the bill comes, I pay. Just as we're getting ready to leave, another thought creeps into my head and immediately escapes my mouth.

"Do you know who turned the air conditioner off in the apartment?" I ask.

Frank sighs. "It was on when I left. The only people still there were Vanmoore and McInty, the chief from Northern. They probably switched it off when they left."

"How green of them," I say.

Frank chuckles. "Yeah, a right pair of toads."

NINE

FRANK DROPS ME AT the block-long Ghirardelli sign with its white neon letters dancing above the open-air plaza. Ghirardelli Square is your typical tourist trap with a gorgeous view of San Francisco Bay. But unlike some others, the bright boutiques, galleries, strolling minstrels, and fresh-seafood restaurants add a touch of class to the clutter of tacky T-shirt and postcard booths.

With a few minutes to spare until my two o'clock "appointment," I drop into the landmark chocolate factory to buy a small square of Ghirardelli peppermint dark. It's the closest thing they have to a breath mint and tastes deliciously decadent, even if it can't quite disguise my garlicky Greek lunch.

The entrance to Stellar Gallery is all stainless steel and clean glass with Adamsky originals on display behind virtually every pane. The plaza's unobtrusive coral stone pathways and bleached sand walls heighten the art's whimsical abstract designs and iridescent colors.

I dig out the Polaroid that Frank had given me and hold it up to the paintings in the window. It's tough to tell from the small image, but the one Diego hid under his mattress seems more brooding, with thicker brush strokes and darker tones than the ones on display.

I've discovered from numerous interviews over the years that a lot of creative people dance around the edges of mental illness. Periods of mania when they produce some of their brightest and most colorful work are often followed by tortured bouts of dark depression. The most famous artists, writers, poets, and musicians also tend to be the ones who, often at their peak, slip off the edge and plummet into the bottomless depths of the illness.

I wonder if that is what Diego was trying to hide under his mattress, something only another artist might notice: Adamsky's encroaching dark side. But if so, why? What's his connection to the reclusive Portuguese artist?

I return the snapshot to my pocket and push through the oversized glass doors to the gallery. Inside, the showroom is alive with art. The explosion of color, shape, and form combine with an icy blast of conditioned air to make me feel disconnected from my body for a second. That third glass of wine doesn't help either. I usually know to limit myself to two at lunch, but visiting Diego's shook me up more than I care to admit.

I find myself suddenly afraid to make a sound as I glide across the gallery's polished marble floor like a cat burglar. The eclectic collection surrounding me is both remarkable and completely unaffordable.

For all I know, automatic sensors have scanned my wallet and are already doing a credit check. If that's the case, it shouldn't take long before two burly linebackers burst through a hidden doorway to toss my impoverished ass out on the street.

I decide to look around before that happens.

In one small room to my left a Sixties Warhol stares through silk-screened eyes in seeming disdain at a lone Mark Kostabi on the far wall. Dominating another wall is a disturbing, and almost life size, tar-and-oil scene by Attila Richard Lukacs showing naked skinheads in a Berlin slaughterhouse. Countering that it is a stunning seascape by Frederick J. Waugh, plus a tranquil nude by Eric Fischl.

Another room, defined only by a transparent barrier, contains a well-chosen collection of modern stone sculpture. I recognize the clean lines and elemental shapes of Kazutaka Uchida but find myself immediately drawn to a collection of exquisite jade carvings by Canada's Deborah Wilson.

I reach out to stroke the smooth, feminine green stone of a naked torso. Immediately, a thin figure scurries forward, a lemon-yellow scarf wound around his throat like an overly affectionate ferret. He makes clicking noises with his tongue.

"We meet again, Casper," I say, before turning around to lock on to his beady eyes.

He is surprised that I know his name, but it doesn't stop his advance.

"Please don't touch," he sniffs, his feeble mustache clinging desperately to his sweaty upper lip.

I grin cruelly at flesh-colored pimple cream on the end of his nose.

"Isn't that what sculpture is for?" I challenge. "To please one's sense of touch as well as sight?"

"I—I wouldn't—I just—we do not like our nudes fondled." He puckers his lips into a crinkled Cheerio and attempts to unlock my stare by concentrating on the bridge of my nose.

"You really should try it." I allow my fingers to slide gently down the curve of sculpted back, slowing above viridescent buttocks before continuing around their smooth curve.

Casper glares at me, and I can tell it is pointless to continue annoying him. The poor man is in dire need of a personality transplant.

"Is there anything in particular you are interested in?" His voice has an irritating squeak that burrows beneath my skin like an invading army of ticks. If I were forced to work alongside such an annoying person, I would need to see if a few squirts of WD-40 could loosen him up.

The gleeful vision of Casper choking on a mouthful of oil makes me wonder if I might not be in the pre-alarm stages of PMS.

"Diego's suicide note. What did it say exactly?" I ask.

Casper's pale face turns even whiter.

"I'm not at liberty to discuss that," he says. "The police have a full transcript. Ask them if you're so curious."

"I will. I just hoped you could summarize it for me. Diego must have trusted that you would follow his wishes."

Casper stands a little straighter. "We had a good relationship."

"Hmmm," I muse. "And how much will you get for his blood painting?"

He gulps. "I beg your pardon?"

"It's a simple question. What's your cut?"

Casper's shoulders stiffen and I watch as several blood vessels form blue ridges in his forehead. "I'm afraid I can't talk about that either."

I stare at him for a few seconds, allowing the silence to grow awkward, before shrugging. "In that case, could you tell Mr. Stellar that Dixie Flynn is here to see him?"

Casper's sunken cheeks flush a muddy red as he scurries across the marble with a staccato click, click, click to a glass-fronted office in the far corner.

I am studying a wall of watercolors when Declan Stellar walks out from behind a large transparent glass desk and frames himself in the doorway to his office. The atrium casts a diffusion of soft white light across porcelain features and makes mid-ear-length, plum-black hair shimmer. I am instantly drawn to stormy almond eyes perfectly centered above a strong nose and kissable lips.

My heart does a little dance as I scan the rest of him: black collarless shirt tucked into cashmere pants, expertly finished with a tasteful leather belt, silver buckle, and stylish John Fluevog lace-up shoes. As he moves, the shirt tightens to hint at a muscled chest and firm stomach.

Dixie's Tips #5: *Before meeting a hunky man, discreetly check there isn't a nasty booger dangling from one of your nostrils. Otherwise, that's all you'll be thinking.*

I quickly spin around to catch my reflection in a mirrored surface. All clear.

"Ms. Flynn? Hello. Would you care to join me in my office?" invites Declan with a smile that reflects the light as though his teeth are dusted in diamonds.

"Yeah, sure." I wince upon hearing my voice, fearing I sound like a weak-kneed tweener being asked to dance at the Junior Valentine's Ball.

Declan returns to his office and I follow. Focusing on the way he walks, a silly smile creeps onto my face, and I recall the sculpted nude I had been admiring earlier. The smile would have stayed with me all the way into the office if Casper hadn't tossed a haughty harrumph in my path as he scurried out of the way.

Inside, I sit stiffly on a steel contraption that I mistake for a chair. It's as comfortable as an ice-cube tray, but a quick scan of the office doesn't reveal any alternatives.

Under the harsher lighting of the office, Declan doesn't look quite as flawless. He's still handsome, but the illusion of pampered softness has faded to reveal deeper furrows on his brow and crinkled recesses spreading around his eyes like spiderwebs.

I wonder if he has trouble sleeping in that big, empty bed of his.

"You don't look like an art critic, Ms. Flynn." Declan crosses his legs and fixes a slumped sock to purposely distract my attention while he ravishes me with his eyes.

"I'll take that as a compliment."

I try an innocent smile, but it likely comes across too much like a leer. At least I'm obeying **Dixie's Tips #6**: *Don't drool over men. Cheesecake, I understand, but never men.*

"But you *are* a journalist," he says.

"Who told you that?"

"My secretary, Mr. Blymouth. He says you're definitely not a client, but you might be a critic. He has a good eye for this sort of thing."

"Ever run a background check on him?"

"I beg your pardon?"

I lean across the desk (which is a great move if, unlike myself, you have been blessed with a bosom) and whisper, "I caught him fondling the nudes."

Declan tries to stifle a laugh, fails, and allows it to trickle forth. Instantly, he becomes less stiff with eyes relaxing into warm pools and one hand tugging absently on a nibble-worthy earlobe.

"He is a touch odd, I admit," he says. "But he's been with me since I opened and is a perfect companion for some of our more eccentric clients."

"So you're loyal?"

"Always."

I smile. Normally I avoid the drop-dead gorgeous creatures who haunt our mundane lives, but that's because they tend to avoid me too. In this case, however, Declan has laughed at one of my jokes, and everyone knows that handsome men love funny women. Of course, once again, that could be that third glass of wine talking.

"So how can I help you?" Declan asks.

Back to business.

Pity.

I slide the Polaroid across the table. "Can you tell me anything about this?"

Declan picks up the photo with slim, long-fingered hands and studies it carefully. His brow furrows as he reaches into a drawer to produce an antique, brass-handled magnifying glass. He studies the photo more intently.

"It appears to be an Adamsky," he says finally. "But I have no recollection of this particular piece."

"Wouldn't you normally see all Adamsky's work before it's parceled out?"

He shakes his head. "Not always, although I definitely try to."

"So you wouldn't know which gallery displayed or sold this one?"

"It could be any one of the ten who sell locally or one of the galleries in Canada or Mexico that also handle his work." He hands the Polaroid back. "Who's the owner?"

I notice he doesn't even consider it may be mine.

"The police have it now," I answer. "But it was in the possession of a local artist, Diego Chino."

"The one who killed himself last night?"

I nod.

"Why do the police have his painting?" He leans forward, caressing my eyes with his own in an obvious attempt to seduce.

The office is getting warm.

"Good question," I admit. "Since it doesn't look likely that there is going to be an investigation into his death, I suppose they'll return it to his next of kin."

Declan leans back in his chair and narrows his eyes in puzzlement.

"His death doesn't have anything to do with this painting, does it?"

"That's something I'm trying to find out."

"I knew you weren't an art critic."

"I still take that as a compliment."

I smile again.

This time, he smiles back.

"What can you tell me about Adamsky?" I ask.

"There isn't a lot to tell, really. He's a talented artist who didn't pick up a brush until he was in his seventies. He lives in Portugal and is simply trying to translate all the images of his mind onto canvas while he can."

"Does he ever pop over for a visit?"

"We're planning a small tour for later this summer actually."

"Is there a number where I can reach him?"

"Do you speak Portuguese?" He laughs, but when I don't join him, he continues. "Actually, Adamsky is quite impossible to reach. He is somewhat of a recluse."

"How do *you* get in touch?" I feel myself slipping into hard-nosed reporter mode.

"I'm contacted when he is ready to ship over more paintings."

"You speak Portuguese?"

The comeback catches him off guard.

"N—no … it's Adamsky's agent who gets in touch."

"I thought you were his agent?"

"I'm his North American distributor and also the largest seller of his work."

"And his agent …"

"Roger King—" The name leaves his lips before he can stop it and his eyes widen, exposing both shock and a flash of anger.

"Roger Kingston," I complete. "A man of many interests."

"Please don't disturb Sir Roger," Declan says anxiously. "He is a very important business associate and a man who places a high value on privacy. I had no right to mention his name."

He's making me feel bad, which I hate. Here I am, all pleased that I pulled some juicy information out of him, and he ruins it by reminding me why I don't get many dates. But since I've already blown it, I carry on.

"Why is such a powerful man acting as an artist's agent?"

"I couldn't say."

"Because you don't know, or—"

"Because it's not my place to comment on Sir Roger's relationships."

"He has a relationship with the artist?"

"A business relationship!" he snaps.

Let it go, Dixie. He's getting pissed.

"Of course." I use my softer voice. "How often does Adamsky ship paintings over?"

"Whenever he has enough. There are no set dates." Declan attempts to rebuild his composure by brushing invisible lint off his shirt.

"What was the time span between the last two shipments?"

"I'm not sure."

I try the coy smile. "Could you please check? It would be such a hassle to have to go through Customs to find it." Now I was being both a bully and a liar. I just hoped he didn't know it would be practically impossible to squeeze information out of the Customs office.

He reaches into another drawer and produces a ledger. He opens it with an annoyed sigh.

"The shipments were a month apart; twenty-eight days to be exact."

"How many paintings in each shipment?"

"I only have invoices for the ones I keep."

"How many was that?"

"Five."

"Was any of the paint still wet?"

"Of course not!"

"Then—"

The chirp of a clear glass phone cuts off my question. When I first saw it on the desk, I assumed it was a piece of sculpture rather than a functioning device. As it rings, its electronic innards light up in a rainbow of neon.

When Declan answers it, I take the time to notice a simple diamond stud in his left ear and the absence of a wedding ring. He tells whoever is on the line to hold a moment, and then extends his right hand across the desk.

"This is an important call," he says. "And I have a lot of work to catch up. I hope I've managed to answer all your questions, Ms. Flynn." His voice is so cold it practically has freezer burn.

I squeeze his hand, pocket the Polaroid, and head for the door.

"By the way," I say, turning around in the doorway. "What is Adamsky's first name?"

"He doesn't use one," Declan replies stonily.

I give him my best smile with just a touch of lost-girl pout. "Well, just remember mine is Dixie," I say. "Thanks for your time. You have a terrific gallery here."

He doesn't reply.

I walk into the showroom, intending to look around more, but Casper scurries up beside me.

"Are you leaving, ma'am?" he sniffs.

"Yeah, but—" I narrow my eyes, voice turning ice cold. "Did you just call me ma'am?"

"Y-yes," he stammers. "It's a sign of—"

I hold up one hand. "Just don't, OK?"

"The door is this way," he says quickly and rushes over to open it.

I scowl at him as I walk into the concentrated heat of a blistering day, sweat instantly beading on my freckled forehead. I ponder whether to further study the Adamskys in the window, but Casper's rat-like countenance looming behind the art makes me turn away.

That's when I notice a small café perched on an upper-level balcony. Its large shady umbrellas invite me to climb the short flight of stairs and indulge in an iced mochaccino.

How can I refuse?

TEN

THE CAFE HAS A magnificent view of the bay and a cheerful waitress who delivers a mochaccino on the rocks with a long straw peeking out from a fluffy cloud of whipped cream.

I enjoy the coffee and friendly smile before pulling out my notepad and jotting a few scribbles. There isn't much in there, but it's a start:

I have learned that the local expert doesn't recognize Diego's hidden Adamsky, and that the paintings are being shipped directly from Portugal. I also learned that Declan has never come across one that was still curing. What that means, I don't know, but it's worth filing away in the back of my mind.

I take another sip of cold coffee just as the sun is eclipsed by a broad-shouldered vision.

"Do you mind if I sit?" Declan asks.

I glance up. "Not at all."

I indicate the empty chair facing me, while attempting to keep the puzzled amusement off my face.

Declan smiles nervously as he sits and orders a soda and lime from the hovering waitress. It may be a trick of the light, but I could swear that both the waitress's smile and her peek-a-boo bosom swell at the sight of Declan.

"I got the impression you didn't want to spend any more time with me," I start.

"Are you always that direct?"

I shrug unapologetically, and his face melts into a mask of such boyish charm that I want to stroke his hair, coo softly in his ear, and nestle him to my chest.

"Actually," he says, "I want to apologize for my rudeness. I'm not used to reporters and didn't realize being interviewed would make me so … nervous."

He nibbles on his lower lip, and I have to resist the temptation to ask if I can join in.

"I should be the one apologizing," I say, trying to lift my eyes above his lips. "My interview style can be on the rough side. Most times I don't notice what a jerk I'm being until someone kicks me in the ass."

Declan laughs, and I join in. When his spritzer arrives, he lifts it into the air for a toast.

"To art," he says.

"To beauty," I agree and clink my mug against his glass.

The apologies done, Declan sighs contentedly, allowing his shoulders to slump as the tart soda cools his throat.

"Can I ask why you're interested in Adamsky?" Declan asks.

"I'm not, really."

"Then why the questions?"

"Curiosity. The painting is an anomaly in Diego's death."

"Anomaly? I thought it was a clear suicide."

"The cops think so too."

Declan narrows his eyes. "I don't understand?"

"Neither do I. That's why I'm looking into it."

Declan takes another sip of soda. "You don't buy that he killed himself?"

I shrug. "Makes a better story if he didn't, but apart from a few oddities, everything points to the official verdict."

Declan smiles. "You're a curious one, Ms. Flynn."

"Call me Dixie."

"OK." He smiles wider. "Will you have dinner with me tonight, Dixie?"

"Why the change of heart?"

"Change of … I don't understand."

"Earlier, you couldn't wait to get rid of me, but now you want to take me out? I know I'm charming and gorgeous, but …"

Declan's laugh is like butter sauce: smooth and dreamy.

"You intrigue me. Is that so wrong?"

"You intrigue me too."

"Does that mean you'll join me?"

"I would love to," I say. "But I don't know if I have anything in my wardrobe that costs more than the shoelaces for your Fluevogs."

Declan laughs heartily. "I play the part of the successful gallery owner, but underneath …" He pauses, and I can feel sweat trickling down the back of my neck. "Underneath I like blue jeans and T-shirts like everyone else."

My cheeks hurt from smiling.

"OK," I relent. "Pick me up at seven-thirty." I write my address and phone number on a napkin and hand it to him.

"I'll be there."

His eyes sparkle.

ELEVEN

"MY GOD, DIX," STOOGAN bellows across the newsroom as I stroll to the copy runners' desk. "Gracing us with your presence twice in one day?"

"It's always better the second time, boss," I call over my shoulder.

The baby-faced copyboy looks at me expectantly as I slide my rump onto the edge of his desk.

"What's your name?" I ask.

"John ... Underwood."

"I've got an assignment for you, John. Up for it?"

"What is it?"

"Wrong answer."

He blushes slightly. "Yes," he says. "I'm up for it."

I show him the Polaroid and explain that I want him to visit every gallery that carries Adamsky's art to see if anyone recognizes it. If they do, he is to get their contact info. Simple.

"Will I get overtime?" he asks.

"Doubt it."

He accepts the photo. "Is it for a big story?"

"Yep."

"Will I be mentioned?"

"Nope."

"But you'll know I helped?"

"Yep."

John slips on his jacket, picks up a small stack of signed taxi vouchers, and takes off.

I had been hoping for more enthusiasm, but copy runners—or editorial assistants as they've been renamed in our electronic age—are a different breed now. When I started in the news business, I was eighteen and full of cocky idealism.

My first job was running copy at the *San Francisco Chronicle*. There, I spent my days tagging and redirecting page proofs, phoning the weather office, checking the crossword puzzle, and fetching files from the morgue (news morgue, that is, not the deadbody morgue). I also had the character-building chores of getting coffee, ordering pizza, and picking up off-sales.

My first real break came courtesy of a veteran photographer who forgot the first rule of journalism: *Report the story, don't become it.* Then again, maybe he had his eye on a television career, where the mantra seems to be the exact opposite.

It was close to deadline and digital photography was still in its infancy. I was tasked with picking up film from a Rolling Stones concert in time to make first edition. That way, the photog could stay at the concert in case a better shot presented itself for the city run.

Luckily for me, a minor riot broke out and the photographer had his skull cracked open by an irate drunk swinging a bottle of

Jack Daniels. Before the paramedics rushed him to hospital, I grabbed his camera. After safely delivering the film, I talked the city editor into letting me write a few paragraphs on the incident.

It made the front page, inserted into the middle of a staff reporter's story. My byline was nowhere to be seen, but my words were mostly unchanged.

Two years later, after studying journalism at college by day and working for the paper at night, I made staff reporter. Another three years and I was making good money as a seasoned senior.

I resigned the following year, headhunted by *NOW*.

NOW was a brand-new venture with few assurances and a riskier paycheck. But they offered me something the *Chronicle* couldn't: a chance to sink my teeth into investigative reporting, where my worth would be judged on quality rather than an accountant's tally of bylines.

The timing was right. I had become disillusioned with the shrinking world of the daily press. Television and the Internet had turned the whole business into a fast-fact chain where reporters were rarely given a chance to play out a hunch. After a while, too many journalists stopped caring.

Society's watchdog had been put to sleep, and nobody seemed to give a damn.

The saddest part was the whole industry had become so infuriatingly stagnant. As media conglomerates grew, competition disappeared along with jobs, growth, and fresh ideas. This left a decade of young journalists with no opportunity to enter the closed ranks. Instead, they became trapped in small-town limbo with pathetic wages and meatless stories. Only now are the tired boomers beginning to pack their bags, but it's too late for a legion of bitter, burnt-out reporters with nothing but ashes where dreams used to burn.

And I fear the new breed of pampered and over-educated graduates won't know a time when shifty corporations and duly elected governments used to hold us in contempt. We were tenacious, fearless, honest, and brash. With hard-earned reputations that made the unscrupulous piss blood, a politician's wrath was a standing ovation.

At one time every newspaper's motto was: *Only honest men have nothing to fear.* Now, they tend to preach: *Money buys happiness—especially if you're friends with the publisher.*

———

I sit at my desk and rub my eyes. Two thin cardboard sleeves filled with photocopied newspaper clippings are sitting on top of my keyboard. A yellow sticky reads: *Slim pickings, but here's what we have. Love, Lulu.*

Although grateful for the folders, I find myself distracted by a feeling that I have missed something important. Unable to bring it into the light, I mentally retrace my steps, arrive at Diego's apartment, and begin searching again. This time, I freeze each room on the back of my eyelids. Nothing stands out. It's an empty, sterile shell. No soul, no passion, no heart.

Was it always like that?

I flip open the directory, find Millie Stewart's phone number and dial.

"Helloo," Millie sings into the phone after the second ring.

"Hi, Millie. It's Dixie Flynn, we talked this morning."

"Oh, yes, dear. How are you?"

"Fine, but I was wondering if you know the name of Mr. Chino's cleaning lady?"

"Why, of course," Millie says. "That's Sheila. Such a lovely woman, lovely skin, too, but won't share her secret. Not even with me. Originally from Africa—well not her, really, but her ancestors. They were brought here as slaves." She clucks her tongue. "Actually, we've been looking into whether her great-grandfather might have known one of my distant relatives who was sentenced to American slavery by the English for being unable to afford bread. The Sassenachs shipped out a lot of troublesome Scots that way, and who was to stop them?"

I try to interrupt, but Millie is on a roll.

"Sheila inherited some slave papers and shipping manifestos that showed my great-great-uncle listed as arriving in port on the same day as her great-grandfather. Two different ships, mind you, but it's possible they were sold to the same farm in Virginia. Isn't that something? Sheila and I usually share a pot of tea after she—" Millie gasps. "Oh, dear!"

"What's wrong?" I ask quickly.

"Now that poor Mr. Chino has, err—departed, Sheila won't be coming 'roon anymore. Won't that be a shame?"

"I'm sure she'll still visit," I say. "She must like your company as much as you enjoy hers."

"Och, I'm sure you're right. I always look forward to those wee visits."

"Would you have her phone number?" I ask.

"Oh, yes. I should give her a dingle, shouldn't I?"

"That would be fine, but would you mind giving me the number as well? There are a few questions I need to ask."

"Hold on, I have ma address book here somewhere." Millie lowers the phone and I can hear her plodding around the room. When she returns with the number, I delicately end the conversation by promising I will see her soon.

I dial the maid's number.

"If you're selling anything, don't waste my time," says a bored, raspy voice.

"Is Sheila in?" I ask.

"You talking at her."

"Sheila, I'm investigating the death of Diego Chino and would like to ask you a few questions?"

"I already talked to you lot this morning. I'm sad he's gone, but he wasn't family." She sighs noisily.

"I have just a few more questions."

"You know how many hours I work, girl? You think I'm waiting around all day for you to call and ask questions?"

"OK, Sheila. Why don't you just tell me what you told the officers?"

"You jacking me around?" Sheila snarls.

"No, I—"

"You're not a cop?"

I clear my throat and try to deliver a warm laugh. "My name is Dixie Flynn. I work for *NOW*."

"No shit! You know Mary Jane Clooney?"

"Sure, she sits a couple desks down from me."

"Love her stuff. Read it every week. Can you tell her that?"

She was turning friendly and even if I didn't like the game, I had to play ball.

"Sure, I'll tell her. Mary Jane's great."

"And the horoscope," Sheila says. "I like that too. Has a little meat to it, not like some."

"I'll pass that on. But would you mind answering a few questions about Diego?"

"No problem. Any friend of Mary Jane is a friend of mine. You tell her that too."

"Sure. I was wondering about Diego's apartment. It seemed very empty."

"Yeah, he's an odd one. Place always like nobody lives there. Suits me fine, though. He pays me to clean the whole place, but apart from dusting and sweeping, I really only had to do the bedroom and bathroom. Occasionally the kitchen was a mess, but not usually."

"Did he have a girlfriend?" I ask. "Or did you ever notice women's clothing or makeup lying around?"

"Nope, poor man, and I looked. There are too many weirdos out there, so I like to make sure I'm not working for one. Mr. Chino always struck me as ..." She struggles for a word. "Too much alone, I guess. I don't think he had a personal life at all."

I wasn't getting anywhere. I try another route. "The police found a painting hidden between the box spring and mattress of Diego's bed. Did you notice it?"

"Sure, you can't hide stuff from me."

"Had the painting been there long?"

"Nope. First time I saw it was yesterday."

So Diego had the painting in his apartment for less than a week. But what that means, I don't know.

I thank Sheila for her time and hang up.

Closing my eyes, I run the conversation over the cobbles of my brain to see if anything sticks, but it flows like muddy water. When

I reopen my lids a minute later, a giant, balloon-like face blocks my view of the ceiling.

It's amazing how adept Stoogan is at proving once again that Murphy's Law—*the boss will always appear the second you look like you've stopped working*—still holds true. He is smiling down at me through thick vanilla lips.

"We're heading across the street for a beer. You joining us or you too busy?"

I give him my patented scowl and pick up my notepad. I still have some time before Millie's neighbors are due home from work.

————

The Princess Lounge is one of those narrow, dimly lit joints with red-velvet booths and an ancient mirrored disco ball hung over a two-foot-square dance floor. Fortunately, one of the copy editors smashed the jukebox at his retirement party last month and it still hasn't been fixed.

I slide into our usual booth near the back and glance at the TV chained to the wall above the bar. There is a baseball game in progress, but it isn't the Giants. Ignoring it, I spin around to meet the perky, pinched face of Mary Jane Clooney.

Mary Jane is crunched into the corner of the booth in anticipation of Stoogan taking up the rest when he finally arrives. It always takes Stoogan five minutes longer than everyone else to walk down the stairs and cross the street.

In the hallway by the washrooms, two copy editors are starting up a game of baseball on the darts board at a dollar per inning. I prefer 301, but sometimes word junkies find the math too stressful, especially if they're being whipped by a girl.

I twist my body to lean against the wall and rest my feet on the velvet bench. Mary Jane produces an electronic cigarette from a tiny eel-skin handbag and attaches it to an ivory holder. By the time she is finished assembling it, the cigarette is about six inches long. She likes to have the glowing tip well away from her over-lacquered hair.

"What did you do to your eyebrows?" I ask.

"Nothing," she answers too quickly.

"Yeah, you did. They look different."

"You like them?"

I grin. "I don't like you, so why would I like your eyebrows?"

She scowls and takes a puff from her toy cigarette, drawing the nicotine vapor deep into her lungs.

Mary Jane and I have never been close, but the ice thickened considerably a few months back after she wrote a piece on the intelligence of a visiting supermodel. I convinced the copy editor into going with the headline: *Schiffer Brains*.

The funniest part was Mary Jane agreed it was good until someone read it aloud to her.

"So what did you do to them?" I ask again.

"If you must know, I had them made level."

"They used to be crooked?"

"Slightly, yes."

"Does your doctor work on commission?"

She scowls again. "He is a perfectionist."

"And are you perfect yet?"

"Almost." She smiles.

"What have you had done?"

She smiles wider.

It makes me nervous.

She wets her lips with her tongue.

"Let's just say that to see me naked is to faint with desire."

"I'd faint alright," I answer, "but it wouldn't have anything to do with desire."

The scowl surfaces again, and I notice that her eyebrows do look even, especially when they are hooking down toward her nose. I hold up three fingers to the bartender who begins filling two tall glasses with draught and an amaretto on the rocks.

I turn back to Mary Jane. "I met some fans of yours today," I say. "They asked me to pass on how much they like your stuff."

"That's nice," she answers in her best, bored tone. "I can't say I've ever met any fans of yours."

I growl at her as the bartender drops off the drinks and the front door bursts open. Stoogan drags himself down the length of the bar, huffing and puffing all the way before sliding into the booth next to Mary Jane.

The glass of beer doesn't stand a chance as Stoogan swallows it in one gulp. He orders another while Mary Jane and I wait in silence for him to catch his breath.

After a few minutes, the color leaves his face and he is back to breathing normally.

"How's the story coming along, Dix?" he asks, his hand still shaking as he brings the fresh beer to his lips.

"It's slow, but coming together."

I sip my beer and try not to notice the sharp smile on Mary Jane's powdered face. I'm not the greatest liar, and Mary Jane's an expert at reading body language.

"I need to track down Chino's studio and talk to some of his peers," I continue. "Get a little deeper into his background, that kinda thing."

"What angle you taking?" Stoogan asks.

I try not to mumble. "It's two-pronged. For one, I'm still not convinced it was suicide. But if it was, why does an artist who's finally attained his dream kill himself? And ..." I pause as a deliciously wicked thought suddenly breaks through the fog. "Who profits from it?"

Stoogan nods before turning to Mary Jane and asking the same question.

"It's going great, couldn't be better," she bubbles sweetly. "Everyone is so helpful. Perhaps I could give Dixie some lessons in charm."

"There's a lot of things you could give me, Mary Jane," I say. "But charm is the least of them."

"Dream on."

"What story are you working on anyway? How to get plastic surgery at bulk-rate prices?"

"For your information," she huffs. "I'm doing a very delicate and discreet piece on the new rage of masked safe-sex parties. They're proving very popular with the corporate and political elite. And the scenarios are so hot they'll raise the collective temperature of my readers by forty degrees and melt your petty little story right off the page."

"Petty?!" I sneer. "While you're wrapping yourself in latex and spermicide to frolic in a room full of horny strangers, I'm busting my balls looking into the destruction of an artistic soul. Instead of being obsessed with sticking his meat into some siliconed bimbo,

Diego wanted to share his vision with the world. And that's something we, as an increasingly self-absorbed, self-pleasuring society, desperately need."

Mary Jane's face lights up in an angry hue of crushed beet. "Why, you pig-headed, flat-chested bitch! For one thing, you don't have balls. And for another, you're delusional if you think the world sees you as some corporate-bashing crusader fighting for the soul of San Francisco. Your story's about a guy who committed suicide; it doesn't get any more self-absorbed than that."

Stoogan slaps the table with a puffy palm. It has all the effect of popping a marshmallow.

"OK, kids," he says. "Knock it off. I'm sure both your stories will be first rate …" He pauses to crack his lips into an evil smile. "Once I get through editing them of course."

Mary Jane glowers at me, and I wonder how long it will take to strangle her. I want it to be slow.

I swallow the rest of my beer in one gulp and stand up. "I still have work to do," I say and walk out.

TWELVE

THE LOBBY DOOR IS slightly ajar, hardly noticeable until you're up close, its latch having failed to properly connect.

I slip inside and up one flight of stairs to the three apartments that share the middle floor. Millie doesn't pop out from her dwelling to inquire what I am up to, which means anyone could have easily done the same thing the night Diego died.

So much for security.

On the landing, I arbitrarily select the door farthest to my left and knock.

A skinny, forty-something stockbroker type with over-gelled hair and a thin, though sporting, Clark Gable mustache opens the door. Even before his eyes scan my body and return disappointed, my first impression is *jerk*.

He's dressed in a neon yellow kimono adorned with red dragons, the front flap open slightly to reveal white silk boxers with purple yin-yang symbols. He is sucking on a hand-blown glass pipe, the smoke smelling sweetly of marijuana—medicinal, I'm sure. His feet are wedged inside Japanese slippers that look about as comfortable as two blocks of wood. My Godzilla slippers, even without batteries, could take them for breakfast.

The dissatisfied look on his face says I'm not who he is expecting.

"Sorry to disturb you," I say. "But I wanted to ask a few questions about Mr. Chino."

"Who?"

He tugs the flap of his robe closed. I try not to show my disappointment. It isn't difficult.

"Chino. Your neighbor?"

"Which one?"

I point skyward. "He was found dead early this morning."

"Damned nuisance." He is clearly undisturbed by the news as his gaze wanders over my shoulder in search of an expected guest.

"I take it you didn't know him well, then?" I ask.

"No."

"Did you hear the gunshot?"

"No."

"Were you at home?"

"None of your damn business."

I find it disturbing that when he talks, his mustache doesn't move. It's as though instead of being attached to flesh, it's a separate entity hovering in place just below his nose. It makes me want to flick it away.

"Did you notice anything unusual last night?" I try.

"No. Now will that be all?"

"Just a couple more." I ignore his impatient sigh. "Do you have trouble with the lobby door? The latch isn't fully—"

"Christ, how should I know?"

"Well, you use the door, I assume?"

"Yeah, I use the door," he snarls. "It's handy for coming and going. Great invention."

"Then you would notice if—"

"Are you done?" he interrupts.

"Almost." I try not to bare my teeth and growl. "Did you kill Mr. Chino?"

He stares at me with dead, shark-like eyes, his nose twitching above motionless mustache.

"Who the hell are you?"

"Molly the meter maid?"

I jump back as the door slams shut.

After taking a deep breath, I knock again.

The door opens.

"The Karmic police called." I glance down at his crotch. "They want their shorts back."

The door slams again.

Pleased with myself, I turn to the next apartment just as a tall, raven-haired Goth with a ghost-white face and dangerous black lipstick floats up the stairs. She is wearing the navy blue uniform of a Japanese schoolgirl, but I doubt it has ever seen the inside of a classroom. The buttoned white shirt is at least two sizes too small—or her breasts are two sizes too large—and the pleated skirt is indecently short. I like the school tie, though. Very chic.

"Your friend needs a spanking," I say as we pass.

"He usarry does," she replies dryly.

I hesitate, and then call after her. "You weren't over here last night by any chance?"

118

She stops and turns, her almond-shaped eyes narrowing with suspicion.

"Fuck off."

Kids today.

We both knock on our respective doors. Hers opens quickly, and she disappears inside with nary a giggle. After my fifth knock, a weary voice grumbles that it's coming.

A red-eyed man with a two-day growth of beard covering his creased face opens the door. He wears a wrinkled white shirt partially tucked into a pair of rumpled dark gray pants.

"What time is it?" He rubs his eyes.

I don't smell alcohol on his breath, but I can tell he hasn't gargled in a while.

"It's just after six. Sorry if I disturbed your nap."

"If it's six in the morning, I guess it was a little more than a nap." He shakes his head and is struggling to get his bearings.

"No, evening."

"Evening?" He sounds shocked. "What day is it?"

"Wednesday."

"Wednesday?"

"Yeah, caught me by surprise too. It's the one they snuck in between Tuesday and Thursday."

"Ah, crap! I've slept all day. My boss is going to flipping kill me." He tries to focus his road-mapped eyes. "Are you from the office?"

"No, I'm investigating the death upstairs."

"Death? Who died?"

"Diego Chino. He lived above you." The man leans against the door to steady himself. He looks ready to vomit. "Didn't you hear the shotgun blast?"

"Shotgun?"

I nod again.

The blood drains from his face and without warning he turns and bolts.

I hear the clang of toilet lid against porcelain before his stomach empties. I enter the apartment and close the door.

The condo is orderly and neat. No severed heads peering out from glass jars in the bedroom or dismembered bodies hanging from hooks in the kitchen. In fact, the whole place has the cozy, relaxed feel of a high-income bachelor who enjoys his solitude.

I am studying his extensive CD collection—heavy on jazz and obscure Icelandic metal—when he emerges from the bathroom. His forehead is beaded with sweat, but some color has returned to his cheeks.

"You want coffee?" he asks in a raspy voice.

"Sure."

"I'm all out of Colombian. French roast OK?"

"Sounds fine."

I follow him into the kitchen and watch as he pulls a tiny brown paper bag out of the freezer, opens it, and measures five teaspoons of finely ground coffee. He sprinkles the coffee into a flat-bottomed, cone-shaped metal basket, inserts it into a gleaming drip coffee maker, pours in water from a filter system on his tap, and switches it on.

It's all so boringly civilized.

In combination with the sparkling cleanliness of the kitchen, I figure either he's gay, hides his mom in one of the bedrooms, or is a domesticated cast-off from a ball-breaking bitch who grew bored after he bent to her will.

"What happened last night?" I ask.

"I don't know," he says. "The last thing I remember is getting settled on the couch to go over an annual report. Not the most exciting project, but ... after that, you started banging on my door and telling me I've missed a whole day." He pauses, his mind still struggling to get the gears moving. "I better call the office."

He picks up a cordless phone from the kitchen counter, hits speed dial, and waits. When someone answers, he babbles.

After hanging up, he scratches his head.

"That was Janine," he says. "Apparently, she's been calling all day. They assumed I was sick." He slumps his shoulders and drops his head into his hands.

"Go sit down," I say. "I'll get the coffee."

He nods and leaves the room. When the machine stops sighing, I pour us each a cup, add a drizzle of milk, and carry them through to the living room.

"I don't even know your name," he says, while accepting the coffee gratefully.

"Dixie Flynn. I work for *NOW*."

"I'm Paul. Paul Gibson."

"What's the last time you remember, Paul?"

"I put my feet up around nine. That was last night. Yesterday."

"Did you take any sleeping pills? A hit of E? Spoon of heroin?"

He shakes his head with a confused smile.

"Any visitors?"

"No, I was planning a quiet night."

"Did you have anything to drink?"

"A small cognac. Just the one."

I point to a bottle of Remy Martin VSOP sitting on top of an antique oak sideboard beside an unlit gas fireplace.

"Is that it?"

He nods.

I cross to it, pull the cork, and inhale. It smells fine. Wonderfully so. I splash a drop onto my finger to taste. My tongue tingles and my taste buds dance. Pete Townshend of the Who thanked Remy Martin in the liner notes of one of his albums for making the damn stuff so expensive that it prevented him from drowning himself in it.

"Do you think it's drugged?" Paul asks.

"I can't tell."

Suddenly, the absurdity of the comment makes me laugh out loud. "I don't even know why I tasted it," I say. "I'm a reporter, not a chemist. I'm sure it's fine."

Paul smiles. "And why would someone want to drug me anyway? I'm an accountant for gosh sake. Not even an important one at that. Most of my clients are funeral homes."

I feel foolish. "You should go to the hospital for a checkup. Blackouts can be caused by high blood pressure and that's a killer—especially in men."

"Yeah, you're right. My mother has been bugging me to get a physical too. I'll have a shower first, though. I feel like... well, not pleasant."

I smile and head for the door when a nagging whisper enters my brain.

"Do me a favor, Paul. Let me know what the hospital says. Just out of curiosity."

I hand him a business card.

"Sure thing." He accepts the card. "And thanks for waking me. I'd hate to be the Rip Van Winkle of San Fran."

———

There is no answer at the next apartment or either of the ones on the ground floor beside Millie's.

As I dig in my pocket for another business card to slip under the door, Millie opens hers.

"That one isn't occupied," she says, her words sounding slightly slurred. "Helen has it up for sale. She moved in with her fiancé about a month back. Handsome fellow, and Helen's no beauty, but she comes frae money. I told her to be careful, but she says it's love."

"Maybe I should rent it," I say with a smile.

"Oh, we don't rent roon here, dear. Too much chance of riff-raff."

"Ahhh."

That's me told.

"Would you like a wee martini?" Millie asks. "I use pickled onions instead of olives. Gives you a tingle in the nethers."

"Thanks," I say slowly, not quite sure I heard correctly. "But I need to get home. Date tonight."

"Oh, you girls today." Millie beams. "Is he handsome?"

"Very."

"Hmmm." She presses her lips together into a thin, wrinkled line. "Be careful, then. The handsome ones can take advantage."

I cross my fingers. "Here's hoping."

Millie opens her mouth in shock and then covers it with both hands as she has a good old-fashioned giggle fit.

When she catches her breath again, her face is flushed and her tongue is darting around dry lips.

"You sure about that martini?"

I nod. "But," I say, "what can you tell me about the Japanese prostitute with the short, short skirt? Does she visit often?"

Millie looks at me quizzically, and I'm not totally surprised when she doesn't know what I'm talking about.

THIRTEEN

THE TAXI DROPS ME at home under the protective gaze of King William. From his perch on the window ledge, William has a clear view of his kingdom and all its subjects.

I tip an invisible hat to him and am rewarded with a wink. I even hear the throaty rumble of a purr, a sure sign that I am one of his special humans.

No sooner have I entered the lobby than the apartment door to my right opens and Mr. French beckons me inside.

Despite my weariness, I oblige.

As I follow the short man down the narrow hallway, past bathroom and bedroom, puffs of smoke rise above his head like the Hogwart's Express. The puffs smell deliciously of black licorice.

When he stops at Baccarat's cage and turns to watch me greet his feathered pet, I see his latest burl pipe is a fierce Chinese dragon polished in such a vibrant shade of red it could make a Ferrari look drab. This causes a brief and disturbing image of Mr.

French in the yellow kimono with red dragons to flit through my brain.

At least it wouldn't be short on him.

"Long day, Ms. Flynn?" Mr. French asks as he settles onto the couch beside the long coffee table and pats the cushion beside him.

I nod and sit.

"Gathering the first threads of a story is always the toughest part," I say. "The fun doesn't begin until you find the right one and begin to tug."

"And then it all unravels." A smile adds delight to smooth, chubby cheeks.

"Precisely."

He claps his hangs together. "Oh, Baccarat and I enjoy that." He turns to his bird. "Don't we, Baccarat? Yes, we do."

The bird chirps in response and flutters its wings, sending several small, multicolored feathers flying through the air.

Mr. French turns to me expectantly, and I wonder if I am meant to applaud.

"Clever," I say.

Mr. French beams and two large puffs of licorice smoke erupt from his pipe before being sucked away toward the air purifier in the corner.

After a second of contemplative silence, Mr. French removes the pipe. His face turns serious.

"The paper," he says, referring to the note I dropped off that morning. "I believe I have found the initial source and departure point."

"Initial source?"

"The manufacturer," he explains. "There was a small water-mark on the paper that gave me the name of the parent company. From there I was able to uncover its West Coast distributor and with a few discreet inquiries track it to the departure point."

"Departure point?"

"The local store from whereupon it was most likely purchased."

"Ahh."

"And the news gets better."

"Go on," I encourage.

"The store owner is a fellow collector. I have made an appointment with him for the morrow. With access to both his memory and his bookkeeping, we shall soon uncover the name of the likely purchaser."

"Very impressive."

Mr. French puffs out his chest. "Baccarat was rather pleased when I told her too. She often worries about me, little dear, so these exercises assure her my mind is still sharp."

"I'm sure."

I stand to leave, but Mr. French leaps to his feet, face stricken.

"Forgive my dreadful manners, Ms. Flynn," he says. "I was so caught up in my own news that I failed to offer a pick-me-up after your laborious day. Would you care for a whiskey, a wee dram as the Scots like to say, before you go? I have a rather smoky eighteen-year-old malt from the Isle of Skye, or Isle of Mists as the locals call it, that I believe you will find most pleasing."

I waver, but only slightly, as the only Scotch I can usually afford doesn't bother announcing its age on the label.

Mr. French beams with delight when I accept his offer. He quickly busies himself pouring generous measures of barrel-aged single malt into two crystal glasses.

———

Upon returning to my apartment, I turn the faucets to fill the bathtub and set iTunes on the computer to play a soothing mix of Coldplay, Travis, Lissie, and James Morrison.

The taste of fine malt lingers on my tongue, igniting desire for another dram. However, I don't want to spoil the taste with the cheap blend I keep under the sink. Instead, I pour a cold glass of tap water, drop my clothes on the bathroom floor, and climb into the wonderfully deep clawfoot tub—the one true luxury of living in an older building.

Easing my body against the tub's curved back, I feel the grime of the day begin to soak away. A sprinkle of bath salts turns the water to liquid silk, and I close my eyes to sigh contentedly.

There is a knock on the front door.

Bloody hell.

Opening my eyes, I strain to see the clock in the other room. It's only seven. Declan is early. I begin to pull myself out of the tub.

"Dixie. Dixie, are you in there?" Kristy calls, attempting to sound sweet.

I sink back into the tub, wishing I had remembered the remote in order to crank the music.

"Dixie, I can hear your music," Kristy calls again.

I groan and cover my ears, wondering if I remembered to lock the door. I usually don't.

There is silence for a moment, and then the front door swings open and Kristy appears in the living room.

Shit!

I try to duck below the rim of the bathtub before she spots me, but I'm too slow.

With a toothy smile, Kristy skips into the bathroom, drops the toilet lid, and sits. She is barely wearing a white silk teddy, one strap dangling mischievously off her shoulder to give her the oops-one-of-my-voluptuous-breasts-is-about-to-pop-out-of-hiding-and-smack-you-in-the-eye look that could liquefy the average man in under half a second.

Before I can utter a word, she dips her fingers in my bath water.

"Feels nice," she says. "Not too hot, not too cold."

"You're not coming in."

Kristy laughs. "I wasn't hinting."

"Just so we're clear." I fold my arms across my breasts, which are not used to sharing bath time and feeling rather jealous.

Kristy laughs louder and splashes water in my face. "You know I don't fancy you, Dix."

"How do I know that?" I protest. "I'm a fantastic catch."

"You're straight, for one."

"True, but you've often said that's only because I don't know any better."

Kristy grins, her tiny pink tongue darting between her lips, enjoying the game.

"I prefer my women the same way you prefer your men: a little rough around the edges."

"Are you saying I'm too girly for you?"

Kristy nods. "And you have small tits."

129

I scream in mock horror and splash bath water high into the air. Kristy screams when the water splashes over her teddy, turning the garment transparent.

"Oooh, y-you!" she stammers. "This is silk. I'm wearing it for a reason."

"What's that? You're all out of body paint?"

"No!"

I start to giggle. "Go on then?"

Kristy's lower lip vibrates. "I wanted your opinion on if I should wear this to go upstairs."

"Upstairs?"

"Yeah, you know, to visit Derek."

"Derek—Shahnaz's husband?"

"Yeah, he looks fit and he's really nice. Good teeth, polite—"

"Hold on," I say. "You're talking about seducing Derek?"

"Sam and I want a baby. We talked about this."

"And Derek has volunteered? What did Shahnaz say?"

"Well, we haven't told her yet."

My mouth falls open in disbelief. "You're going to sleep with her husband behind her back? The cheating bastard."

"It wouldn't be sleeping," Kristy protests. "Just a one off."

"And Derek agreed to this?"

"Well, not exactly."

"What do you mean, not exactly?"

Kristy twirls a loose strand of hair around her finger. "We haven't talked about it."

I close my mouth. "Are you saying he doesn't know you're planning to bounce upstairs and jump his bones?"

"You make it sound ... mean." Kristy pouts again. "It didn't seem like that big of a deal when I thought of it. He's got it, we need it. It wouldn't *mean* anything. But ..."

"Kristy ..." I'm not sure where to begin. "You can't pounce on one of your neighbors just because you're feeling maternal. Shahnaz is a friend."

"Yes, and as a friend she should want the best for us."

"But the best for you doesn't mean sharing her husband."

"I don't want her husband."

"No," I agree. "You just want his sperm."

"Exactly." Kristy beams. "I knew you'd understand."

I sigh and bury my face in my hands. The water is becoming colder and I can feel goose pimples puckering my flesh.

"Look," I say calmly. "If you're really serious about this, then you need to go about it properly. Invite Shahnaz and Derek over for drinks and discuss in a rational, friendly manner the possibility of him becoming a sperm donor. Just be forewarned that they may be planning a family of their own some day, and he may not be comfortable sharing DNA with the neighbors."

Kristy wrinkles her nose. "Rats. That sounds more complicated than just wearing the teddy."

"I know," I say soothingly. "Adult decisions often are, but the end result is better for everyone. Now pass me the towel, this water is freezing."

After I wrap myself in the towel and step out of the tub, Kristy lunges forward to wrap her arms around me.

"You're so great, Dixie," she gushes. "Thanks for being my friend."

I laugh and kiss the top of her head.

"You're welcome, sweetie," I say. "But I really need to get dressed now."

"OK."

Kristy skips across the floor, her ethereal teddy fluttering like angel wings, and yanks open the front door.

Standing outside, just getting ready to knock, is Declan.

I stand speechless outside the bathroom door, frozen to the spot, cold water dripping from my body and towel to form puddles on the floor.

Kristy barely bats an eye as she gazes up at my date and asks, "So what's your sperm count?"

"Kristy!" I shriek.

Kristy glances over her shoulder, winks mischeiviously, and runs across the hall to her own apartment. I'm thankful Declan doesn't go chasing after her.

Dixie's Tips #7: *Never let your date see another gorgeous half-naked woman in your apartment, especially if their curves make your curves look like a kiddy ride.*

"Am I too early?" Declan asks as he steps into the apartment and closes the door. His lips are quivering with an effort not to grin.

I look down at my pale, towel-wrapped body and fight the urge to cry.

"Take your time," he adds, sensing my discomfort. "I'll wait."

I retreat to the bedroom, wondering how much worse the date can possibly get with this kind of beginning.

FOURTEEN

DESPITE MY BATH BEING interrupted before I had time to shave, I decide to brave a tight-fitting, above-the-knee black skirt that presents my ass in its best possible light. I marry it to a short heel for extra lift, black tights with a subtle swirl of green, and a jade silk blouse that shimmers like lake water and exaggerates the gentle sway of unrestrained breasts.

Unfortunately, due to tonight's cooler weather, I have to hide the sexy illusion beneath a bottle green, calf-length leather trench coat. On the plus side, I look damn good in the trench coat.

Declan is a silhouette of elegance in black Calvin Klein jeans, black T-shirt under a charcoal gray crewneck sweater, and a thigh-length, soft wool jacket that London Fog has ripped off a World War II sailor and updated in fashionable style. The *pièce de résistance*, in my opinion, would have been a pair of black crocodile cowboy boots, but Declan chose a more conservative pair of soft leather loafers.

"So where are we going?" I ask, boldly linking my arm through his.

"Chinatown," he says. "I thought it might be fun to play tourist and catch a cable car."

I smile agreeably.

"Should we drive to Market Street?" He stops beside a gleaming two-door Mercedes. The electronic key fob is already glowing in his hand.

I give him one of my patented "Do I look like a woman who's impressed by a car?" eye rolls and shake my head.

"Parking's a bitch. Let's walk."

Walking is nice. Arm in arm, the crisp evening air makes each breath puff from our mouths in tiny clouds. I show him how to blow rings—a trick my father taught me when we relaxed on the front porch after supper and he puffed on a cheap Mexican stogie.

When mom caught him giving me a puff, he told her it was the best way to make sure I never picked up the habit. He was half right. I don't smoke cheap Mexican cigars, but a Canadian boyfriend was sorry to learn that when we broke up, I took his smuggled stash of fine Cubans with me.

From Market Street, it's only another half block to the bottom of the cable-car route. The open-air station is packed with tourists, their grins locked on high beam for a pair of amateur jugglers dressed in tuxedos, top hats, and Abraham Lincoln beards. One is black, the other white.

"It would be quicker to keep walking," I reason.

"What's the rush?" Declan replies. "We're tourists."

"In that case, the ride is my treat."

I cross to the ticket machine and buy two passes before he can protest.

A soapbox preacher, his stubbled chin and sour stench failing to hide that he drank every donated penny, is stationed within spitting distance of the machine. No one is listening to his slurred version of the gospel; the jugglers are more entertaining.

The preacher catches me looking and turns his rhetoric up a notch. His arms flail and his bloodshot eyes begin to weep.

The topic is sin. Isn't it always?

A quote springs to mind as I pull a handful of change out of my pocket and drop it into the hat that lies at the foot of his salvaged pulpit.

"Forgiveness begins here," I say and point at his chest.

The preacher stops talking and stares at me like he has just been confronted by the devil.

Another saying springs to mind: *Don't feed the animals.*

I cross quickly back to Declan. Jeez, a few minutes playing tourist and I start to act like one.

"What was that about?" Declan asks.

"Nothing," I say. "He reminds me of someone. It was a long time ago."

When the cable car arrives, I spot Sam jumping off the back to help turn the vehicle around. The circle of road turns slowly until the tracks click back into place. The tourists quickly pack onto the car, leaving just enough room for us to stand at the back railing, directly beside Sam.

"Hey, Dix." Sam beams as she leaps aboard to take her post on the brake.

"Hey, Sam, busy night?"

"Always." She rings the bell in response to the driver, releases the brake and the cable car lurches forward. "Did you see Kristy at home?"

"In more ways than one."

Declan taps me on the shoulder, and I make the introductions. "Sam, this is Declan. Declan, Sam."

"We share the floor," Sam says before grinding the brake and ringing the bell again as we climb a section of hill.

"Oh, really." Declan's voice betrays too much interest. "I just met another one of Dixie's neighbors."

"Kristy," I explain.

Sam grins. "Did she do something embarrassing?"

Declan smiles back. "Ummm, well, she certainly isn't shy."

Sam laughs. "Definitely not. Did she get your medical history?"

I feel my face turn red as Declan turns to me, his face wrestling itself in eager curiosity.

"I'll tell you later," I say quickly. "If you're good."

Declan grins.

Sam grabs the large handbrake to slow the car, allowing a handful of tourists to leap off, while others leap on. Releasing the brake again, she rings the bell and we climb farther up the steep hill.

"So can he be on our short list?" Sam asks. "Nice genes, I would say."

"Oh, look. This is our stop," I say abruptly. Grabbing Declan by the hand, I pull him off the slow-moving car.

We both land safely, four blocks from our destination, the only problem being an older American town car that finds the need to suddenly change lanes and accelerate past the tram on the left-hand side.

"What was that about?" Declan asks.

"The car? I don't—"

"No, your friend."

"Oh. It's complicated."

"I have a master's."

I laugh. "You would need to have one in biology, psychology, and Audre Lorde."

"Audre Lorde? The warrior poet?"

"Very good," I say, appraising him anew.

Declan wrinkles his brow. "If you don't want to tell me, that's fine."

Dixie's Tips #8: *The male ego is more fragile than a balloon at a children's birthday party.*

I pat his arm reassuringly.

"Sam and Kristy want to have a baby."

"Ahh." Understanding dawns and his eyes widen. "So the question about my sperm count?"

"They asked for help in finding a donor."

"Hmmm." Declan's mouth begins to morph from a worried line into a hopeful grin. "Does this mean you need to take me for a test drive first?"

Laughter erupts from my throat.

"You wish!" I punch his arm. "You haven't even bought me dinner yet. I'm starving."

Declan joins in the laughter as we pick up the pace and enter the gates of Chinatown.

I don't know exactly what I was expecting from the evening, but Declan is surprising me by acting like we're on a *real* date. Despite my cynical misgivings of his true intentions, I soon discover I'm enjoying myself.

———

Arm in arm, I allow myself to be led as Declan maneuvers through the brightly lit tourist traps of Chinatown. Each store is filled with every cliché souvenir you can imagine: wisdom caps, fans, kites, chopsticks, and jade and ivory sculptures of varying size and shapes yet still looking identical, as if there is only one dragon willing to pose. I wonder if that is because she is the most beautiful or the most vain.

We also avoid all the Caucasian-filled restaurants with photos of first-, second-, and third-tier Hollywood stars that supposedly dined inside. Naturally, it never says if the celebrities actually enjoyed the food or just stuck to the booze.

Finally, Declan turns down a dark alley toward a flickering neon sign that reads: *Dragon's Wing.*

"I've never heard of this place," I say.

"It's usually quiet, and the food is fantastic."

As Declan leads the way down the unlit tunnel, I peer intently into every pitch-black doorway that dots both sides like abandoned guard posts. I've long believed you don't make it through life in a large city like San Francisco without a healthy fear of the dark.

Glancing over my shoulder, I spot a dark four-door town car gliding slowly past the mouth of the alley. Nothing unusual in it, except the driver appears to be looking at us rather than the road ahead. I open my mouth to mention it to Declan, but the thought leaves my mind as quickly as the car vanishes back into traffic.

Just before the lit entrance to the restaurant, a small sign glows in reflective paint upon a plain wooden door. It consists of an elaborate Chinese symbol and, in smaller English script beneath it, Wong Door.

I point it out to Declan. He seems slightly embarrassed when I ask what it is for.

"Superstition," he says. "Some Chinese believe it's bad luck to use the same entrance as non-Chinese."

"Charming," I say. "So they meant it to say 'Wrong Door'?"

He smiles. "No. It's named after the Wong family who first requested it. It's the owner's little joke."

Inside, the restaurant is a low-ceilinged cave with a variety of wooden tables scattered haphazardly around a cement pit. Inside the pit, a small fire crackles and spits. Hanging over it, suspended on thick iron rods, is a large black cauldron. Something bubbles inside.

"Don't tell me you're a witch," I whisper.

"Not yet," Declan whispers back. "Still have to take a few more courses. Harry Potter makes the whole broomstick thing look easy, but it's a real bitch to master."

A five-foot-zero elderly woman bows gracefully as we hang up our coats. Declan bows back and whispers something in her ear, and we are escorted to a table in the far corner where a glass-block window reflects the fire's glow.

I sit down and pick up the menu. It is written entirely in Chinese.

"Do you mind if I order for both of us?" Declan asks.

"No, go right ahead. I'm an omnivore." I glance back at the cauldron, wondering what I am getting myself in for.

When the woman reappears, Declan rattles off a list of dishes with names I don't recognize. He finishes by ordering a carafe of house wine.

"I hope you don't mind red," he says. "I know white is the usual choice with seafood, but the crispness of the air seems more suited to a heartier grape. The house red is a Cab Sav from Chile that the owner decants and serves at a perfect cellar temperature."

"You could have stopped at the color," I say with a laugh. "It sounds fine."

Declan chuckles softly. "Sorry, do I sound pompous?"

I hold thumb and finger just slightly apart.

"Would it help if I told you the name of the wine translates roughly into 'Grandma's dimpled knees'?"

I laugh again. "Now that doesn't sound pompous at all."

Declan beams wider. "I'm glad."

———

Over dinner, I begin to form a more detailed picture of this handsome man. If he's been told to charm me, he's certainly doing a good job.

It also helps that the smooth, full-bodied wine is relaxing our tongues and mellowing our inhibitions. Declan tells me he arrived in San Francisco from Portland almost two years earlier to open a gallery at the request of a friend. The friend financed the whole deal, and in return owns 40 percent of the business.

After a few glasses and a plate of squid in an inky black sauce, I learn his "friend" is Sir Roger Kingston, the same man who represents Adamsky and had sent Casper to collect Diego's blood painting.

As the night progresses, I manage to extract that Kingston disliked most gallery owners in the city because of their original refusal to carry Adamsky's work. And as a powerful businessman who never accepts the word *no*, it explains why he branched out to finance his own.

"I have complete say over what pieces I display," Declan explains, licking a dab of sauce from the tip of one finger. "Of course, I also give a large display to Adamsky, but the sales of his work give me a certain financial freedom to display lesser-known artists."

"You must also like sculpture," I say, remembering the jade nude.

He beams. "I adore it. In fact, I think it's safe to say I represent one of the best collections of stone carvers on the West Coast."

I don't doubt him, but one question nags at me. "If Kingston is angry at the other galleries, why does he let them carry Adamsky's work now that he's popular?"

Declan laughs. "Revenge, I suppose. Adamsky is the hottest artist in town these days; galleries beg Roger to carry his work. And Roger is first and foremost a businessman. He still rubs their noses in it, though, by charging them more than I pay."

"You actually buy the paintings? They're not on consignment?" I ask.

"That's the way Roger works. If you're not paying cash, he doesn't want to know you."

"Sounds like a cuddly guy."

Declan laughs, but this time his eyes lack twinkle.

The waitress returns to the table and expertly replaces the empty carafe of wine with a full one. Once our glasses are refilled, she claps her hands and a waiter rushes over with two steaming bowls the size of dinner plates. Each bowl is covered with a bamboo lid.

The waiter places a bowl in front of each of us and lifts the lids. Clouds of steam mushroom from the bowls and the decadent aroma makes my head feel light.

Declan grins. "Drunken crab," he says. "Dig in."

I look down at the large, whole crab in the bowl and the lone pair of skinny chopsticks resting off to the side.

"How do I—" I am instantly silenced as Declan wrestles one of the crab's legs free with his bare hands, leaving the chopsticks untouched.

As he snaps the steaming leg in half like a wishbone and begins slurping out the meat, he catches me staring.

"Too messy?" he asks.

"Not at all," I say. "I just wanted to make sure you were the first to throw table manners out the window."

He remains frozen, the broken crab leg dripping sauce over his hand, not sure whether I'm joking.

When I can't hold a straight face any longer, Declan relaxes and we both attack our crustaceans with zeal.

The alcohol- and spice-infused meat is absolutely delicious, and I am thrilled when the waiter returns with a basket of crusty sourdough buns to soak up the intoxicating sauce.

"Now that you know all about me," Declan says between bites, his lips glistening with sauce. "What's your story?"

I shrug. "Not much to tell. I write, I sleep, I have crazy neighbors. What else is there to know?"

Declan refills my wine glass. "What makes Dixie Flynn chase after a story?"

The hairs tingle on the back of my neck and the room does a quick 360-degree turn. It's a signal that it is time to abandon the wine. I catch the waitress's eye and order a pot of tea and a jug of ice water. The woman looks at me blankly until Declan translates my order.

"Are you OK?" Declan asks.

"I'm fine," I say, speaking slowly in an attempt not to slur my words. "The crab is making me thirsty, that's all."

"So about my question?"

"I'm curious," I say. "And I like to uncover the story that people don't want to tell. Take Diego. The police are saying he killed himself, but I don't buy it. But even if he did, that's only part of it. I want to explore his background, talk to people who really knew him and find an explanation for how and why he reached that final, drastic point. I believe every person, good or bad, is a microcosm of our society. Explaining how they lived and died is a story worth telling. And this may sound naïve or even egotistical, but I also don't buy this bullshit that a story told well can't change society. I've seen that it can. When I sharpen my pencil and shine a spotlight on someone, people pay attention. And if that makes me a nasty bitch at times, so be it."

"I didn't—"

"No." I smile and pat his hand. "No, you didn't, but that is part of who I am. Perfume and short skirts only get you so far. After a while, you need to kick a few people in the balls too."

Declan lifts his wine glass and smirks. "I'll keep that in mind."

When the water arrives, I pour myself a tall glass and down it in one long swallow. The second glass I sip more slowly until the waitress brings a pot of jasmine tea and two tiny cups to drink it with. I fill both cups.

While Declan is trying to think of something more to say, I refill my cup until my mind begins to clear. I know only time will sober me up completely, but the tea is helping clear a path through the fuzzy maze.

"What do you hope to learn?" Declan asks.

My mind flips back through time until I realize he is still asking about Diego.

After a moment's contemplation, I say, "I hope to learn that at some point he was happy."

Declan looks puzzled.

"Finding happiness is important," I continue. "It may sound silly, but I work hard and try to be there for family and friends, but when you break it down, all I really do is get through each day. I like the idea that there are people out there who have chosen a different path. We're so wrapped up in the humdrum of life that we often forget that we can change—that we can break down barriers and challenge our beliefs. We look at a field of ripe canola and think it's all the same wonderful yellow, but an artist sees a thousand shades.

"Deep inside, I'm scared that I may never do anything of importance. Something is holding me back, and I don't know what it is. And on the days when I can't stand it anymore, I go to the galleries and stare at other people's dreams. I may not have understood Diego's vision. Hell, I didn't even particularly like it, but he was living it. He wasn't hiding behind a paycheck in a one-room apartment. He was an artist. Someone or something killed that dream, and it pisses me off. I can't bring him back, but I can find out who or what destroyed him. It's a small part to play, but it's something I have to do."

Christ, I'm drunk. I feel an embarrassed flush heat my face, and I lower my eyes to the tiny cup.

I have just broken **Dixie's Tips #9:** *Don't let them know you're a nutcase.*

Declan reaches across the table to fold a hand within mine. He leans closer and his lips gently brush against mine, teasing them open. Hungrily, we lock together and his tongue, like fire, darts across the jagged barrier of my teeth.

The empty teapot rolls off the table to shatter on the hard wooden floor.

———

Declan insists on paying the bill and brushes off my attempt at paying my share. Admittedly, I don't put up much of a fight after I glimpse the total.

Arm in arm, we stroll into the cool night to breathe in the sickly stench of trapped smog and decaying garbage. In the city, we like to think of it as aromatherapy for the homeless; it curbs the appetite and stops them from realizing just how hungry they are. The "fresh" air does little to clear my mind, and I still feel off-kilter. I hope the long walk home will do me good.

The alley is a dark canyon surrounded by brick, all light blocked by tall, windowless buildings. The sky is a shimmering blanket of cloudy gray, hiding the stars and any sign of the previous night's moon.

Our only source of light is the busy street a block ahead. Its multicolored neon serves as a beacon to which we are drawn. Keeping our eyes on that light, we weave around oily puddles and the occasional lost shoe.

Oddly, it's rather romantic; a scene from *Lady and the Tramp*.

Twenty feet before we reach the main street, a black shadow enters the mouth to slice the light in half. It seems to stretch the entire width of the alley, and I can hear the impatient rumble of a powerful engine.

I wonder why the vehicle's headlights are switched off, but before the thought can sink in, four bright halogen eyes blind me. I recoil as the engine roars and tires screech.

Instinctively, I grab Declan's hand and turn to run.

"Dixie? Wha—"

"Run!" I yell.

Declan moves, but I feel him holding back in confusion as I search the alley for an escape route.

"This is sil—"

His words are cut off by the clang of metal as the car smashes into a garbage can and sends it soaring over our heads.

Declan and I both turn to see the vehicle bearing down at a reckless speed. It's American-made steel with chrome teeth and a blunt nose that shows no sign of slowing down.

With a roar of frustration, I plant my feet and shove Declan roughly to the side. I am too blind to find a doorway, but the bulge of a brick chimney offers inches of cover.

I flatten my date to the wall and suck in my breath to make my body as thin as possible.

A scream pierces the night as a sharp pain slices into my left leg, buckling it. I stumble, my leather trench coat snagging on speeding iron as a violent tug lifts me off my feet.

I scream for a second time as my body twists in the air before hitting the ground and bouncing. All the air leaves my lungs in a singular cough, leaving me gasping in panic like a dry-docked fish. My coat is still snagged. Gravel and dirt spray over me like breaking waves as I am dragged down the alley behind the speeding car. If not for the thickness and length of my leather coat, my skin would be flayed like tree bark.

It feels like forever, but it's only a second before my jacket rips free and I am tossed aside like yesterday's news. I smack the alley wall, bounce and roll back into the middle of the alley to land face down in a greasy puddle. Nearly blinded by pain, I lift my head to see four angry red eyes flaring in anger before disappearing around a corner at the far end of the alley.

I can't make out the license plate through the thin veil of blood that flows down my face.

Son of a bitch!

I roll onto my back, struggling to catch my breath, every muscle in my body screaming. I hear someone moan, but it's muffled, as though they are far away.

If the driver comes back to finish the job, I don't think I can stop him. I hear the car rumble away down the street. The car's failure to return tells me something important: This is a warning. But for what? The story on Diego? Or a story already printed and dismissed from my thoughts?

Another moan.

"Declan?" I croak, my throat burning from the effort.

There is a sharp gasp. "Dixie, are you OK?"

Sweet music.

"I think so."

I hear hurried footsteps, and Declan's face comes into focus above me. He looks a little worse for wear. Red scratch marks crisscross his handsome face from where I pushed him into the brick wall. Blood drips from a tiny gash in one cheek and another on his chin.

Despite the pain, I feel like laughing. Not because the situation is remotely funny, but because it's over and we're both alive.

"Jealous wife?" I ask.

Declan stares at me like I farted in church.

"Sorry," I say. "Occupational hazard; inappropriate humor. Help me up."

With Declan's help, I drag myself to my feet and conduct a search for broken bones. There are a number of tender cuts and bruises, but luckily my skeleton seems intact. The blood caking my face probably makes me look like Carrie at the prom, but scalp wounds always look worse than they are.

My clothes haven't been as lucky. My beautiful coat is ripped down the back and my funky tights are ruined. Something has torn through my left leg and sliced into the meat of my calf. If the prick had been a better driver, I could've lost the leg.

"Wh–why didn't he see us?" Declan is trembling. Shock.

"He did."

"What?" Declan's eyes go wide.

"When he flicked on his high beams, he couldn't help but see us. He was trying to hit us … or at least me."

"But why?"

I look up at the dark sky. As a reporter, I sometimes make enemies, but very rarely do I enrage someone enough to take it beyond a stern letter to the editor or a heated rant if they pass me on the street.

If somebody wants me to stop looking into Diego's death, they just picked the exact wrong maneuver.

"Mistaken identity?" I say. "Or perhaps your friend is sending a warning."

Declan doesn't smile. "My friend?"

"Kingston. He wants Diego's blood painting so badly he sent Casper to collect it while it was still dripping. But if I uncover evidence that Diego was murdered, the painting stays in police lockup for a long time."

Declan shakes his head. "That's the craziest thing I've ever heard. Roger wouldn't try to kill you over a lousy painting, and he certainly wouldn't try to kill me."

"Maybe I'm being paranoid, but—"

"We should call the police." Declan's voice is cold.

"And say what? I didn't get the license or make of car. Without that, there's nothing they can do."

Declan won't look at me. "But if you believe Roger was trying to kill you—"

"It's just one theory," I interrupt, feeling my temper rise. "I don't know who was in that car, but it seems damned suspicious that you invite me out for dinner and then a car pops up to turn me into a hood ornament."

"I was here, too!" Declan yells. "Why would I put myself in danger? Fuck. I wanted to have dinner with you, is that a crime?"

"Why?" I snap.

"Why did I want to have dinner?"

"With me. Yes."

Declan takes a deep breath in an attempt to calm his nerves.

"I—" he begins. "I thought you were sexy."

"Sexy?"

"Yes, sexy!"

I pause, allowing the compliment to sink in. "You said 'thought'. You don't think that anymore?"

Declan sighs. "Well, not if you think I tried to get you killed."

I reach up to stroke his battered cheek. "But you didn't?"

Declan bites back a laugh. "No, I didn't."

"OK, then." I straighten my clothes and run a hand through tangled hair. "Let's get out of here."

Declan doesn't move. "What about the police?"

I shrug. "I know cops. I know what they can do and what they'll ignore. They'll smell the alcohol on our breath and say we were hallucinating. They won't chase a phantom and, like it or not, that's what we have."

"But…"

I take Declan by the arm and press my head into his shoulder.

"I'll talk to them in the morning," I say softly. "I have a friend on the force who'll look into it."

"So we just walk away?"

"And be thankful we can."

FIFTEEN

AT MY APARTMENT, I pour two large tumblers of brandy and carry them into the bathroom.

Declan follows.

While I fill the bathtub, I help him remove his sweater and T-shirt. He has a beautiful, well-defined chest, marred after only one date with me by several red welts from impact with the wall. I prefer my men with chest hair that I can sink my fingers into, but Declan's smooth skin feels deliciously naughty.

I fill the sink with warm, soapy water and hand Declan a soft cloth. When he covers his face with the cloth to let the steam soak into his scraped skin, I undress and slip into the tub. I gasp as the water stings the gash in my leg and fresh blood flows to turn the bubbles pink. At the same time, I can feel the dirt, oil, and God knows what else being flushed from the wound.

I'm frightened to look at the rest of my body. I know it has taken a more serious beating than I want to admit. By morning,

I'll look like a piece of spoiled fruit even the dumpster divers would throw back.

Despite that, I know I made the correct call in not involving the police. When you work alongside an organization, you quickly get to know its priorities. Without a witness, you might as well not have a crime. Or if the witness has as little information to go on as I do, it amounts to the same thing.

Still gritting my teeth, I submerge beneath the skim of coral foam. Pain flares in my shoulders and scalp as more cuts protest the cleanse. When I come up for air, Declan is waiting.

The scrapes on his face are already barely noticeable and the messy nature of his hair makes him look roguish.

He sits on the edge of the tub and uses the cloth to wipe the remaining flakes of blood from my face and hairline. I close my eyes as the cloth moves in circles, gliding across wet skin, cleaning chunks of gravel from cuts and massaging aching muscle. Soon the cloth is gone and I feel soft hands take its place.

I didn't know my breasts were injured, but his touch feels wonderful all the same.

I open my eyes to find Declan stepping into the tub, naked and perfect. His nursing concern is replaced with a growing and rather glorious desire. I reach out to touch his smooth legs, stroke his balls, and draw him closer. He groans with pleasure as he stands over me and a wonderful shiver runs through his body as my hands find a firm grip on tensed buttocks.

"Oh, God," he moans.

I move my mouth and tongue to his stomach, then his chest as I slide up his body.

Standing, we kiss, his lips nearly bruising mine with a burning desire.

"This is sexy and all," I say, "but I need somewhere softer."

Declan laughs and takes my hand. Fortunately, the apartment is small and he finds the lone bedroom without difficulty.

———

Later, Declan dresses the cut on my calf and we crawl back into my unmade bed.

With my head on his shoulder, his warm breath tickling my neck, I fall into a deep, untroubled sleep.

SIXTEEN

When the phone rings, I am having such a wonderful dream that I forget Tip #1.

A familiar voice says, "Dixie, sorry, it's an emergency."

"Wrong number," I say sleepily, eyes still closed. "There's no one by that na—"

"No, listen!" The voice is squeaky and girly and—though I hate to say it—blonde. "We're desperate."

"Hoo-ray." I muster a total lack of enthusiasm. When I try to roll over, my back goes into spasms and I bite back a cry.

"Fuck sake, Kristy," grumbles a voice in the background. "I have to pee."

"Keep your panties on, Sa-man-tha." Kristy giggles. "Oops, guess we're too late for that."

I groan and open one eye. Declan isn't beside me and instinctively I know he isn't just getting a glass of water.

"What do you need?" I ask as I slowly sit up and glance at the clock. It is 2:34 a.m.

Bubbles is officially ninety-four days old. My body, however, has aged a hundred years.

Despite the pain and lack of sleep, I actually feel rather happy. Must be the endorphins. Gotta love those little suckers.

"Ummm, do you still have those handcuffs we bought you for Christmas last year?" Kristy asks.

"Yeah, somewhere."

"And the key?"

"Sure."

"Ummm, can we borrow it? Just the key, I mean. I seem to have misplaced ours, and Sam is—"

"I get the picture. I'm coming over."

"Yay, Dixie! You're our hero."

———

After slipping into pajama bottoms and a crumpled T-shirt with *San Francisco NOW—Independent and Proud* silk-screened across the front, I decide to add a green terry-cloth robe from behind the door and my Godzilla slippers.

Kristy didn't say if it was a formal emergency, but I hate to be underdressed.

The tiny steel key is in my nightstand. The thought crosses my mind that if I had used the cuffs on Declan, he would still be lying in my bed. Of course, there are probably laws about that. I'll need to ask Frank.

I retrieve the key and cross the hallway.

"Come in," Kristy calls when I knock on the door. "It's open. We're in the bedroom."

Dixie's Tips #10: *When entering the bedroom of a couple in need of a handcuff key, it's best to keep one's eyes aimed at the ceiling.* The one flaw to this tip, as I was about to find out, is when the ceiling is mirrored.

"Jeez, girls, what are you doing?"

The bedroom looks like someone has stepped on a landmine filled with dildos, and judging by the size of some, there was a reason this pair had chosen the same-sex route; no Earth-born male could hope to compete.

"Nothing," Kristy says indignantly. "It's research."

"I've really got to pee," injects Sam.

"You're naked," I say, trying to avert my eyes but finding that nearly every surface in the room contains a reflective surface.

"Naked happens," admits Sam. "What happened to you? You look like you've been boxing. And lost."

"Forget about me. You're wearing a dog mask and collar."

"Awkward but true."

"And is that a tail?"

"I have one, too," Kristy interjects excitedly as she turns around to shake her too-perfect-to-be-best-friends rear at me. "Isn't it purr-ty?"

Blonde and petite, Kristy is dressed in a red dental-floss thong, crimson leather bustier with black lace peek-a-boo windows, and a cat-ear headband made from dyed rabbit fur. She has also drawn whiskers on her cheeks and a black triangle on the tip of her nose.

I wonder what King William would think.

Sam rattles her handcuffs. "I really have to—"

"Here!"

Kristy snatches the key from my hand and frees her partner from the bedpost. Handcuffs jangling on her wrist, Sam rushes by me in such a blur she could have inspired a certain Ray Stevens's song from the Seventies.

Kristy returns the key.

"Thanks again, Dix. You're a life saver."

"Call the S.P.C.A.," I say. "Maybe they'll give me a medal."

Kristy smiles apologetically as we wander out to the living room. "Feel like some wine? We have a bottle of white in the fridge."

"As wonderful as that sounds, I just want to go back to bed."

"You OK? Sam's right, you do look like you were in a fight."

"Just stiff. But at least it'll look worse in the morning."

Kristy doesn't laugh. "He didn't hit you, did he?"

"Who?"

"Your date."

I shake my head. "No, it was a car thing. Declan was really nice, actually. He thinks I'm sexy."

Kristy smiles. "I'm glad."

When Sam emerges, she has removed the dog mask and slipped on an oversized San Francisco 49ers sixtieth-anniversary football jersey. The crimson jersey falls to around mid-thigh and shows off long, athletic legs. She is still wearing the leather collar, but it actually goes well with her buzzed black stubble and ear piercings. Until a few moments ago, I didn't know she had pierced other, more tender parts of her anatomy as well.

"You're looking ruff," I say.

"Ha, ha," Sam replies without humor.

"I thought you were barking mad there, when—"

"OK!" Sam interjects. "I get it. You're a wit. Can we drop it now?"

"Sure," I smirk. "But before I go, I'm just curious how you got the pet license. I would have thought—"

"Arrgh!" Sam stomps into the bedroom and slams the door behind her.

I turn to Kristy.

"Has she had her distemper shots?"

Kristy giggles and shows me to the door. I can hear my bed calling.

SEVENTEEN

WHEN THE PHONE RINGS again, it is barely 7 a.m.

Every muscle in my body aches as I edge my hand over to the receiver and bring it to my ear.

"Don't hate me because I'm beau—Nah, that's not true today. Hello?"

"You sound awful, kid," Frank says.

"Somebody tried to run me over last night. But apart from some cuts and bruises..."

"Jesus!" Frank's voice turns hard. "Are you OK? Did you get a plate?"

"Didn't get a damn thing or I would've called."

"Son of a bitch! Who did you piss off this time?"

"Oh, so being nearly killed is my fault? Don't yell at me, Frank, my head is delicate."

The line goes silent for a moment. "Sorry, kid. I don't like to see you get hurt."

"I'm not too fond of it myself."

159

"Any thoughts on who or why?"

"I was thinking the Diego Chino story may have stirred some people up, but I don't get the point of warning me off when at the moment it's little more than a sad profile."

Frank exhales loudly.

"What?" I ask.

"It's probably nothing."

"But?"

"I was playing cards with some of the regulars last night, and Willie from Northern said someone picked up the painting we found under Chino's bed."

My half-closed eyes snap open. "A relative?"

"I asked that, but the body is still in the morgue. Nobody has even looked at it, never mind claimed it."

"Did Willie get a name?"

"That's all he had, and I didn't want to push. Like I said, it could be nothing."

"But it's odd."

"Yeah. It is."

"I'll look into it. Thanks."

"Just be careful."

"Always." I know how hesitant I sound. "Oh, and by the way, can you check out a Paul Gibson for me? He lives in the apartment below Diego's."

"What gives?"

"I don't know yet, but he slept through the gun blast directly above him and didn't wake up until I arrived on his doorstep the next evening."

"Drop by the Dog House later, I'll see what I can dig up."

"We can compare bruises," I say cheekily.

Frank laughs. "You've got a lot of life to live before you get any-where near my score, kiddo."

After Frank hangs up, I debate getting into the shower but de-cide to take a page out of King William's book and sink under the covers for an extra catnap.

EIGHTEEN

Cowering in a corner, I struggle to breathe beneath a blanket of heavy smoke. Wood splinters and cracks. I am trapped. But where?

Suddenly, the smoke parts and he stands in front of me—the artist. His skin is deathly white, butchered lips twisting in a sneer. A waterfall of blood pours from a gaping hole in his skull where the rest of his face should be.

I shrink back, hoping to hide within folds of smoke. He moves closer and I squeeze my eyes tight like a child. Fingers of ice touch my skin to peel back eyelids. A nightmarish laugh cackles in my ears.

I try to push his face from my dreams, but I can't wake up. Hate flows from him and oozes toward me like a giant slug. It smells of bacon.

Bacon?

I sit up quickly, feel my muscles scream, and collapse back down. I am awake, my body tender, but the smell of bacon lingers.

I crawl out of bed, grab my slippers, and pad into the living room.

"Morning, Dix. Sleep well?"

Kristy is sipping a cup of coffee in front of the computer. She has clicked on the TV tuner and is watching *The View*. The guest is former host Rosie O'Donnell.

"Did you know that Rosie has four adopted kids?" Kristy asks.

"And she still has the baby fat to prove it."

"That's not nice!" Kristy's attention twitches slightly in my direction, but her eyes refuse to break contact with the screen.

"It's one of Rosie's own jokes."

"That means it's only funny when she says it."

"OK." I hold up my hands in surrender. "But do I smell bacon?"

"In the oven. A breakfast sandwich for my late-night hero."

"You're a doll. A pain in the ass, but a doll."

Kristy playfully sticks out her tongue before returning to watch the estrogen gang dish dirt and scold naughty celebrities.

I open the oven door to breathe in the warm bacon, egg, and processed cheese on a sourdough biscuit. The sandwich's wax paper wrapping has melted slightly onto the bun, but I don't think a little wax is going to do me any greater harm than the artery-clogging filling.

"Coffee?" I ask hopefully.

"Red thermos by the microwave."

The coffee is still piping hot, so I pour myself a large mug with just a splash of cream.

I have half the sandwich stuffed in my mouth when the commercials come on and Kristy turns to give me her full radiance. She reviews my swollen and discolored face.

163

"You look awful."

"I'm OK," I mumble as my tongue attempts to free itself from the processed cheese flypaper that coats the roof of my mouth.

"No, you're not. Are you sure he didn't hit you?"

"It was a car," I say as I finally swallow. "But it missed—well, it mostly missed."

"That's horrible."

"Agreed, and now I'm even more pissed if I look as bad as your expression says I do."

"Sorry. It's just … your dates are never exactly normal, are they?"

"Look who's talking. What were you doing with the dildo factory and handcuffs last night?"

Kristy twists a curl of hair with her finger. "Research," she says timidly.

"Who for this time?" I ask. "Alex Kava? Elmore Leonard? Stephen Hunter? No, I bet it was John Sandford. That Lucas Davenport character is a frisky devil."

"You know I can't say."

"Hmmm, well, some of us do our own research, and that occasionally includes the perils of dating."

Kristy smiles. "Was he nice?"

I smile back. "He was, actually."

"But he didn't stay over?"

"No."

"Did you want him to?"

"No," I lie. "A gal's got to have her independence."

Kristy smiles wider as she invades my personal space to pull me into a hug.

Quietly she whispers, "Men are bastards. Be careful."

Sometimes, she breaks my heart.

———

After dressing and attempting to cover the worst of my bruises with spackle and makeup, I stop in at Mrs. Pennell's.

She opens the door in her housecoat. King William leans against her left foot, licking one of his paws and rubbing it over his face as though trying to remove a smudge. How she isn't constantly tripping over him, I don't know.

"Ah, Dixie. We've been expecting you. Tea?"

"Not this morning, Mrs. Pennell, too much to do."

"Late night?"

I nod.

"Your male friend left around two this morning."

I nod as if it's no surprise.

"He looked in better shape than you, dear."

"There was a car."

She reaches out and gently touches my cheek. Her fingers feel like fine sandpaper.

"I worry about you. The work you do, the type of people you meet."

She removes her hand, her eyes beginning to glaze as though remembering another time, another life.

"No need to worry, Mrs. Pennell. I'm a tough cookie."

"Mmmm, sometimes tough isn't enough." Her eyes shift back into focus. "I'll get the note."

"You got another one!" I blurt.

"It arrived this morning," she says over her shoulder. "Sam knew; I thought that's why you dropped by. I'll just be a second."

While I wait, I reach down to scratch King William's ears and the bridge of his nose. Instantly, he plops onto his back, stretches to his full three-foot length, and spreads arms and legs.

"Can't scratch your belly today, I'm afraid," I tell him. "The flesh is weak … and stiff, and sore."

King William holds up his paws to imitate a sea otter, but no amount of cuteness can win me over today.

When Mrs. Pennell returns, she looks at King William and tuts.

"Have you no shame, William?"

The cat looks up at her with loving eyes and purrs louder.

I laugh again and accept the note.

Like the first, it is the size of a small invitation or gift card. I open it. The writing, to my untrained eye, looks identical.

It reads:

Abandonment of love is an acceptable loss.
Abandonment of responsibility is not.
—Pearl

Before I can ask anything, Mrs. Pennell says, "I am no more enlightened by this note than I was by the last."

"And no memory of a Pearl?" I ask.

"None."

"Abandonment of love?" I say aloud.

Mrs. Pennell shrugs. "I have no children. Nor ex-lovers, still living, who would bear me ill."

Her use of the word *lover* takes me aback. Coming from the mouth of a white-haired pensioner, did I expect her to say "gentleman caller"? And, come to think of it, how many gentlemen are named Pearl? Not only was I being ageist, but I could also be accused of sexism. Or sexual-orientationism?

So much for my being an enlightened, modern woman.

I place the note back in its plain, unaddressed envelope.

"Do you mind if I take this?"

"Not at all. Any answers you find would be appreciated."

I slip the note into my pocket, wink at King William, and turn to leave.

Mrs. Pennell gasps. "Dixie! Your coat!"

"I know."

I am wearing my green trench coat despite the large rip in the back that oozes silk lining like a weeping wound. The beautiful leather is also marred by grease, dirt, and water stains. It looks like I've been dragged down a dark alley behind a car.

"I don't have another coat for this weather," I say. "And"—it almost sounds silly—"it's my favorite."

Mrs. Pennell smiles. "I know a wonderful seamstress who works from her home. Leave it with me when you return and I'll see what can be done."

I beam. "That would be wonderful."

Mrs. Pennell laughs. "Well, King William and I cannot have our tenants looking homeless now, can we? It reflects badly on us all."

I try not to look too embarrassed as I exit the apartment.

———

Mr. French does not answer my knock, though I can hear Baccarat chirping happily in his cage. I slip the note under his door with a brief, hastily scribbled explanation.

NINETEEN

NORTHERN STATION HAS SEEN better days.

A recent attack of skinhead graffiti greets me with racist slurs and obscene gestures. A painter, his white overalls splattered in a rainbow of color, works busily with a giant roller and a bucket of industrial steel-gray. He is whistling, happy for the work, and nods to me as I walk by.

The morning mist has burned away and the first prickle of perspiration salts my wounds during the short walk from bus stop to station. Once inside, I take off my coat, drape it over my arm to hide the worst parts, and approach the desk sergeant.

The weary officer ignores me as I study the front of his desk. The wood panels are splintered as though a steel-toed boot has recently smashed through. The hole is patched from the inside with cardboard from a case of Budweiser.

I flash a cheerful smile. "Rough night?"

The name on his badge reads SGT. ROBERT WOODS.

Woods glances at me grimly before returning his attention to the computer on top of his desk. Its pale blue glow makes him look sickly.

"I'm looking for information," I try.

Woods grunts without looking up.

"Perhaps you can help?"

He sighs.

Woods is around fifty, maybe older, going bald from the crown down—like a monk, but without the serenity. He has a cheese sandwich look to him: plain, unassuming, and soft in the middle.

I hold out my laminated press card that, in truth, looks about as professional as anything an eight-year-old can create on his home computer.

"I need to find out about a painting that was claimed from evidence yesterday."

"Uh-huh." He glances up, skims the ID, tries to peek at my bosom, appears disappointed, and turns back to his computer.

My teeth grind together noisily. "Look, sergeant. Detective Sergeant Frank Fury tells me you're an upstanding guy and that you wouldn't mind helping me out."

That's a lie, but what the hell.

Woods's eyes flicker back to me. They are small and the whites have turned a pale yellow streaked with tiny rivers of red: the sign of a nicotine junkie who washes each cigarette down with a swig from a flask.

"You know Fury?"

I nod.

"Tell him he still owes me ten bucks."

He turns back to the computer before I can reach over the desk and strangle him.

I take a moment to compose myself, then fish into my pocket and pull out a twenty. My jaws ache as I hand it over.

It vanishes into Woods's puffy hand with barely a crinkle. He flashes me an ugly grin.

"What do you want again?" he asks.

"Somebody picked up a painting that originally belonged to a dead man named Diego Chino. I want to know who."

Woods punches a few keys and moves his lips silently. Finally, he says, "The chief OK'd it."

"OK'd it for whom?"

"Doesn't say."

"Give me a break. You're not going to release evidence to an unknown."

Woods shrugs. "The chief OK'd it. Who am I to argue?"

"Can I see the chief?"

Woods laughs and white spittle sprays from the side of his mouth as though laughter is something he doesn't have much experience with. He wipes the spit on his sleeve.

"You sure you want to do that?"

"Yeah, I'm sure."

"The chief is a busy man," he warns.

"Could you at least try?" My anger is barely contained.

Woods picks up the phone and jabs at the buttons. He chit-chats with someone on the other end who I assume is a secretary, and judging by the fresh drool pocketing the corner of his mouth, she's an attractive one at that.

Suddenly, his face goes pale.

"Yes, chief," he sputters. "Straight away." He practically salutes the phone before hanging up. "The chief will see you. Second floor."

"Thanks." I turn to head up the stairs and then swivel back. "By the way," I ask, "can I get change for my twenty?"

He snorts. "Dream on."

———

On the second floor, I step around a bottom-heavy cleaning lady and knock on the gold-plated plaque that adorns Chief Caleb Mc-Inty's outer office. A youthful brunette with the ripe body of a centerfold opens the door and invites me in.

She swishes back to her desk, a light spring dress dancing above the dimples on the back of her knees. The dress clings to her in all the right places and flows over the rest. I wonder how she manages to work in a testosterone-laced environment like this without wrapping herself in bulky pullovers and sweats. Cops aren't known for subtlety.

I sit on a hard chair, my eyes wandering from the sexy secretary to the closed door of the inner office. She's typing something without looking at the keyboard, which tells me she isn't just for decoration.

After five minutes, a tall, wide-shouldered man opens the inner door and grins at me with perfect teeth. His silver hair, like the portrait on the wall that bears his name, is neatly styled, while an Italian made-to-measure suit carefully disguises any flaws in his trim frame.

"Welcome, Ms. Flynn."

Chief McInty extends his hand as I haul myself up from the chair without grimacing. His fingernails have been smoothly manicured and his handshake is cool and dry.

Placing a hand lightly on my shoulder, he guides me into his office like we're fishing buddies and releases me in the direction of a leather armchair.

After I sit, I find myself having to look up at the chief's perch behind a polished cherry-wood desk. I glance down and notice his desk and chair sit on a subtly disguised four-inch platform. It reminds me of a piece of advice delivered on the silver screen from an old Errol Flynn swashbuckling movie: Never fight a man of equal strength on equal ground.

Behind the desk and through a large picture window, an American flag sags in the still morning air.

The chief beams at me from his perch like a saint getting ready to read aloud one's list of sins. I'm not impressed. I've dealt with enough egomaniacs in my time to find their power games more foolish than effective.

"I've heard good things about you, Ms. Flynn," McInty booms, his voice showing all the oratory skill of political grooming.

I give him a polite smile.

"I've even heard several of my men commenting on your columns. They have a degree of respect for you."

"I do my best."

"Good, good, we all must."

I wonder if he is going to toss me a doggie treat.

"Now, what can I do for you?" he asks.

I tell him about the painting.

"Ah, yes. The suicide."

I nod.

"I'm afraid there isn't a scoop for you here, Ms. Flynn," he beams, pleased with himself for using what he considers to be journalistic vernacular. "The rightful owner of the painting presented us with a receipt for the work and we turned it over."

"Who is the rightful owner?" I ask.

"We were asked not to make that information public."

"Why not?"

"It isn't relevant."

"It might be to me."

He pauses in order to make sure he can keep control of the conversation.

"I wish I could help you," he says, patronizing. "But I can't go against the wishes of a private citizen who hasn't committed any crime."

"Can you tell me why Mr. Chino had the painting?" I press.

McInty frowns slightly. "It appears the painting was stolen."

"Stolen? Who from?"

"From—" He stops and his voice turns to ice. "I believe you have brought our conversation to an end."

I see no reason to argue. This guy isn't going to have much of a political future if he can't handle a simple one-on-one with a tired, bruised, and—according to the reaction of the desk sergeant—cleavage-deprived journalist. I slide out of the chair. There is a noticeable drop in the quality of carpet at the doorway.

The secretary looks up through large hazelnut eyes. There is no warmth in them.

I leave the station and hail a cab, my mind muddled.

Theft of the painting gives a slim motive for murder, but it opens a whole new arena of questions. Diego obviously made a decent wage from his own art, so why steal a rival's painting? And if he did steal the Adamsky, what did he plan to do with it? Fencing stolen art is a tricky business. You can't exactly stick it on eBay.

I give the cabby the address for the Gimcrack Gallery. Since the owner is the only person still carrying Diego's work, maybe he can fill in some of the blanks.

TWENTY

THE GIMCRACK WOULD HAVE been "Cool, Man" back in the days of free love and hairy armpits, but Union Street—for better or worse—has updated its style in the last forty years. Now surrounded by architectural glass and sandblasted brick, the rustic gallery exudes all the retro appeal of a flophouse or crack den.

I climb a rickety staircase that leads to a sun-bleached porch. The state of the runners makes me nervous, and I hold tight to a gnarled, wrist-thick branch that serves as a handrail.

On the landing, a thousand cobwebs of fractured light twist off a shattered window. Someone has tried to repair it with lead piping to make it resemble stained glass absent of color.

The more I study it, the more I like it.

Directly to the left of the window is a single slab of redwood. A solid frame has been custom made to fit the door's odd shape. It opens on well-oiled hinges and if not for the large brass bell pealing my entrance, no one would have heard me enter.

The inside of the gallery is a different story. Though it retains a homely character, modern track lighting has been added to wooden rafters, each mini-spotlight focused on a painting or piece of sculpture. As I look around, I find the owner has taken great care to find the perfect frame for each work of art. Some are carved white pine, while others are stark metal, tie-dyed canvas, or painted papier-mâché. I even spot one constructed from strips of red licorice sealed in clear resin.

Bare wooden floors creak and moan as I walk from room to room. I'm fascinated by the amount of art in each space. Finally, I spot Diego's name stenciled on a piece of bleached driftwood over the entrance to a tiny alcove.

The art hanging inside the cramped space is nothing like I expect and I'm suddenly ashamed of my earlier judgment. It's apparent that Diego had grown dramatically as an artist over the last year.

Instead of the ungrounded abstracts that made his name, this collection showcases stark and stunning images of New Mexico's cliff dwellings. Brown faces peer from dark holes in impossibly high cliffs; sunlight streaks from the sky in thick, blinding strokes that possess incredible weight and power; proud ghosts of the past watch over a destitute present to reveal an intermingling of both hope and despair.

Each piece draws me further in and my imagination swirls with a force that can only be described as rebirth. Oil paints mix with red clay and ocher, crushed stone blends with ragged patches of animal fur, and tiny pieces of bone sparkle with haunting fragility. In one canvas, a rake-thin dog lies in the middle of a deserted road, and I see that Diego's suicide note may not be the first time he added real blood to his palette.

My story has a new and more powerful face, and I feel regret at the loss.

"Who were you?" I ask.

"A talented man," answers a strong baritone behind me.

I turn to stare into the face of Willie Nelson's twin: red bandanna wrapped around a taut, wrinkled face; close-cropped ashen beard; salt-and-pepper hair pulled into an impressive ponytail. He wears a tie-dyed shirt and denim vest above faded and patched jeans. He's missing the cowboy hat, and where cowboy boots should be, he sports open-toed sandals.

I also notice this face doesn't wear the strain of years battling booze. Instead, the eyes are electric, the body lean and fit. Strong teeth shine from a tanned face.

The man studies me as closely as I study him, all the while slicing into an apple with a well-honed pocketknife.

"Slice?" he asks, indicating the apple.

"No, thanks. Are you the owner?"

"That I be," he says proudly. "The name's Cahn." He holds out his hand and I shake it. His grip is firm but also sticky from the apple.

I introduce myself.

"I read your stuff," he says. "Not bad. A touch on the depressing side at times. It must drain you to dwell that deep in the dark side of human nature."

"Sometimes," I agree. "But then I get drunk and go slam-dancing to Flogging Molly or the Dropkick Murphys and everything's OK again."

He laughs. "So what can an old hippie do for you today, Ms. Flynn?"

"I'm writing about Diego Chino and was hoping you could fill me in on some background."

Cahn stops eating, places his knife and the browning core on a shelf, then sticks his juice-covered fingers into his mouth one by one before wiping them dry on his pant legs.

"He's off to a better place at least," he says finally. "A friend phoned me the news while I was in Carmel. A real shock." He pauses to look at Diego's work. "You can see for yourself that he had a vision. He finally escaped his chains and was discovering a truer path. It's a pity he never got the chance to show the world what he had inside."

"Was he suicidal?" I ask.

Cahn stares through me for a moment before shrugging.

"Who isn't nowadays? Poor people, rich people, businessmen, and whores. We're all moving so fast and in so many directions that the thought of a long nap has a creepy way of crawling into our heads. So, yeah, it's possible; but Diego struck me as too angry to go so quietly, you know?"

"Angry?"

"Yeah. He was pissed that no one wanted to buy these." He indicates the dozen paintings on the walls. "There was a lot of pressure on him to go back to the stuff that sold. I encouraged him to hang in there. That eventually the public would take off its blinders and see what a talent he was."

"You were friends?"

"I like to think so."

I pull out my notepad. "Do you mind if I take notes while we talk?"

Cahn smiles. "Sure, but I better make some tea first. Talking is mighty thirsty work."

He turns and heads deeper into the bowels of the gallery. I follow to a cozy nook in the rear that contains a circular table, an odd assortment of chairs, and basic kitchen appliances. Cahn places an old whistling kettle on a gas stove and sprinkles a chunky orange powder into a teapot that is made to resemble a large, overfed hedgehog. I sit at the table as Cahn produces a plate of square cookie bars.

"They're all natural," he says of the bars. "No processed sugar, preservatives, or gluten."

He sits across from me and bites into one.

"What type of person was Diego?" I ask, picking up a bar to munch on. It's surprisingly good.

"Quiet mostly, except when he talked about art. Then you couldn't get him to shut up. He'd rattle away in Spanglish for hours and I would struggle to keep up. If he got too carried away, he started throwing in words in his native tongue, and then I was lost."

"His native tongue?"

"Navajo."

"I didn't know he was Navajo. I mean, I knew he was Native, but not the tribe."

Cahn shrugs. "I think for a while he was trying too hard to leave his roots behind, to blend in. But look at his work on that wall: that's his true path. He came to embrace it more over the last few months. That abstract crap made him some money, sure, but it was a white man's poultice leaching into his soul."

Cahn sighs and continues. "I'll bet nobody who bought one of his abstract pieces even suspected he was Native. How could you tell from squiggles and blobs?"

I furrow my brow. "How could he afford to live where he did if his new paintings weren't selling?"

"I guess he was smart with his money. Last year, when he was the in-thing, he pulled down thousands per piece."

"And what about drugs?" I ask, remembering the coroner's report. "Did he use cocaine?"

"Doubtful. I don't think he could even if he wanted to. He was allergic to practically everything: penicillin, codeine, you name it. He was just lucky he wasn't allergic to his asthma medicine."

"How serious was it? The asthma, I mean."

"Serious enough. He took to wearing one of those Medic Alert bracelets."

I can't remember him wearing a bracelet in the time I knew him, nor can I remember seeing one on the body or during my search of his apartment. But then again, I didn't even know he was Navajo.

The kettle begins to whistle and Cahn fixes the tea.

"I've invented a new blend," he says, pouring boiling water through an opening in the hedgehog's skull. "Rosehips, honey, and dried orange peel. But where the layman would end the recipe there, I add a flowering bud of white tea from China. Mellows out the rosehips."

Cahn brings the teapot over to the table and I catch a whiff of steam as it spirals out the hedgehog's mouth. It smells awful.

"Diego had an Adamsky painting in his apartment. The police believe it was stolen. Any thoughts?"

"Stolen?" he repeats. "No way."

"Why not?"

"Diego was one of the most honest men I've ever met. He told me once about an incident at this factory where he was working. The pop machine stuck and spat out three Cokes. Diego had only paid for one. So like any other person, Diego gave the extra Cokes to his pals. But then …" he laughs lightly, remembering. "Then he mailed a check for two bucks directly to the servicing company. Now that's honest. There's no way he would steal a piece of art."

Cahn pours tea into two earthen mugs. He hands me one and I sip. It is weak and bitter and as awful as it smells.

"I notice you don't carry Adamsky's work," I say.

He smiles. "Not my scene."

"Did Diego ever mention Adamsky to you?"

"Not that I recall."

I glance down at my notes. "You said he worked at a factory. Do you know which one?"

"I don't know the name of it, but when a cousin of his moved to town, he managed to get a job for him there too. I think it was down near his art studio."

"His studio!" I kick myself for not thinking to ask about it earlier.

"Yeah, he worked out of an old warehouse on the Central Basin docks. It's kind of an artist's commune thing, you know? Community owned, cheap rent, lots of space. A modern hippie happening." Cahn laughs again.

"Do you have an address?"

"Warehouse two twenty-two. He told me he liked the number, but that's all I know."

Cahn pours more tea for himself. I decline a top-up, but dunk half a wholesome cookie into my cup to soften it before stuffing the whole thing in my mouth. Cahn laughs and offers to make lunch, saying he is hungry himself. I accept and we spend a good hour eating egg salad and sprouts on whole grain, discussing art.

With the background information from Cahn, I'm feeling that I know Diego better in the grave than I ever did when he was alive. The realization is regrettable.

When the clock strikes one, I stand to leave.

Cahn looks over the rim of his mug. "Err, there's something I want to ask before you go."

"Sure."

"Well, I don't want to sound morbid, but do you know when the police will release Diego's final work?"

"The blood painting?"

"I suppose you can call it that." He struggles for the words, obviously uncomfortable. "I know this does sound morbid, but I've had a six-figure offer, sight unseen. I am still his agent ..."

"*You're* his agent?" I interrupt.

"Yeah, for all his new stuff. He had another arrangement when he was doing the abstracts, but I represent everything he's done since last September."

I pause. "There's another man claiming to be his agent who was at the scene of his death. Casper Blymouth. He said Diego left him detailed instructions to pick up the blood painting."

"Well, that's not right," Cahn says. "Diego hated that little creep. He's an errand boy for Roger Kingston, not someone who cares about the artists. No way Diego would trust him with something so important."

"If you have a contract, maybe—"

Cahn winces. "Paperwork was never my strong suit, I'm afraid. We did everything on a handshake."

He tries to smile, but it hangs there like limp celery.

I don't know what to say.

———

Back at the *NOW* offices, I dig out the files on Diego and Adamsky and go through my messages.

There is sticky note from John, the copy runner, apologizing for not finding a single dealer who recognized the Adamsky. He enclosed the Polaroid, which I slip into my pocket.

I scribble a quick thanks, enclose an IOU for a beer, and pop it into the runner's mail slot.

A second message comes in the form of a blinking red light on my phone that informs me I have voice mail. I punch in my personal passcode and hit the button for play. The voice belongs to Rip Van Winkle.

"Yeah, hello. This is Paul Gibson, you asked me to call. Err, anyway, the hospital said I'm OK, probably just overworked or overstressed or something. Sounds like a good excuse for a vacation. Well, thanks again for waking me. Bye."

I've never cared much for voice mail; people always sound stupid. Personally, I prefer e-mail. Like a letter, you have time to think about your reply before sending it. Of course there will always be people like Clooney who want to spoil it for the rest of us and insist on placing obnoxious happy faces at the end of each sentence. :-)

I would have preferred to hear that Gibson was drugged with some unique form of chloroform only found in a remote village where an eccentric collector of Adamskys lived, but as it is, I file his message in the trash can folder of my mind to be emptied later.

The newspaper archives on Diego are painfully thin. One clipping from two years back is a piece on happening young artists with a thermometer-style graphic showing each one's unique hotness factor. Diego's name tops the list with a thermometer rating of "sizzle." A second story only mentions him in passing with the sentence "noticeably absent from the showing was new work from last year's top seller, Diego Chino." Neither story mentions that he is Native.

The file on Adamsky is slightly fuller, and one of the stories even contains a color photo of one of his paintings. Strangely, there are no profiles on either artist, just stories about their work.

I close the files and dial Frank. He answers on the third ring.

"Did you check Casper's phone?" I ask without preamble.

"Yeah, but I gave it back. Why? You want to call him? Could be a good catch."

"Ha, ha," I say without humor. "You read the text message from Diego?"

"Yep."

"Genuine?"

"It was sent from his phone. That's about as genuine as we can be sure of."

"So someone else could have sent it?"

"If they had access to his phone."

"Which means legal ownership of the blood painting could be in doubt."

"Sure, if someone wanted to take it to court, the text message wouldn't stand up as a last will and testament. Why? You think he wanted to leave something to you?"

I grin. "We parted on amicable but volatile terms. I don't think he gave me any thought."

"You might be surprised," Frank says. "You're a tough dame to forget."

I laugh. "Thanks, Frank, you're all heart. I'll talk to you later."

I hang up.

After dropping the archives in the library's return basket, I slink my way over to Clooney's desk. She isn't around, which is good, as I need to rummage through her desk. I find her social registry in the bottom drawer underneath something skimpy and silky.

I don't want to know.

It takes some detective work to find Roger Kingston's name. Curiously, it is listed under M, which I'm guessing stands for money, making me curious about the names listed under S.

I dial Kingston's private number on Clooney's phone.

"Good afternoon," answers a very polite English accent. "You have reached the residence of Sir Roger Kingston. How may I be of service?"

I can just imagine the man on the other end of the line: tall, stiff-backed, and perfectly attired in tuxedo tails and starched bowtie. What the English gentry call a gentleman's gentleman.

I try to bleach some of the blue collar out of my voice.

"I would like to speak with Sir Roger, please."

"Could I have your name and intended business, miss?" Efficient too. I can imagine a touch of silver at his temples to contrast short, lightly oiled black hair.

"It's Dixie Flynn. I work for *NOW* magazine and I'm interested in a painting."

"Please hold the line."

I rummage through Clooney's book while I wait, noticing that Kingston is also listed under P. Power? I flip forward to S, but don't recognize any of the names. I hear footsteps approaching over the phone and try to guess the butler's name. My money is on either James or Albert.

"Miss?"

"Still here, James."

There is a slight pause. "My name is Oliver."

"Of course. Cool name."

"Thank you, my mother will be pleased that you approve, but as to Sir Roger. He has asked me to inform you that he shall be free to meet with you tomorrow at twelve-fifteen on his ranch here in the valley. He apologizes for the delay, but he has a full schedule today."

"That's fine," I blurt, surprised by the invitation.

"Will you be needing a car to bring you by?"

Impressive, but I've read too many Mickey Spillane novels to accept a ride out to the country from someone I've never met.

"No, thanks, Oliver," I reply, then add on a whim, "the Jag could really use the exercise."

"I understand perfectly, miss. And if you would be so kind, what is your favorite refreshment? I'll be sure to have some on hand."

"What does Roger drink?"

"Sir Roger has been known to enjoy an Australian beer with lunch."

"Make it two."

"Excellent. I shall place the bottles on ice."

When Oliver hangs up, I can imagine him dusting off the receiver before returning to his regular duties.

I copy Kingston's address out of Clooney's little black book before tucking it back in its proper hiding place under the unknown silky item.

TWENTY-ONE

CAB DRIVERS RARELY TAKE fares to the Central Basin dockyards where Diego has his studio.

For one, it's the perfect spot to jam a gun into the sweet spot of their skull, take their cash, and leave them for dead. And two, if a passenger gets mugged after leaving the cab, there's a chance the company could be held liable for being careless enough to leave him or her in such a desolate area.

Welcome to the land of endless opportunity: sue thy neighbor, get rich, and use the money to sue someone else. No wonder we're all paranoid.

Mo isn't on duty when I call Veteran's Cabs, but the day dispatcher knows who I am and agrees to find a driver.

Twenty minutes later, I hand a taxi slip with Stoogan's signature scrawled on the bottom to a nervous Charlie Parker. I slide out of the cab to the crunch of gravel underfoot, my nose rebelling against the stench of fermenting seaweed and spilled diesel.

With a wink, Charlie hightails it back to civilization, leaving me alone between two rows of dilapidated wood-framed warehouses, their tails dipping into the black water like bloated whales washed ashore to die. Creosote-stained walls and sun-bleached tin roofs huddle together, collecting wind-scattered garbage at their feet like spilled offal.

I kick a crushed beer can down an alley just to break the silence, watching as it skids across the droppings of a thousand gulls. In five years, revitalization will probably turn the whole area into a fashionable fisherman's market or—if the current mayor has his way—a city-licensed, Amsterdam-inspired red light district. But for now it's just a ghetto for abandoned wares; the perfect spot for teen gangs to play dare.

I find Warehouse 222 and search for a recognizable way inside. After wasting fifteen minutes, I resort to pulling on some loose boards attached to a set of rusted hinges. A makeshift door bends open just enough for me to squeeze through.

The inside of the warehouse is dimly illuminated, natural light spilling from twin rows of windows two stories up that stretch uniformly below waist-thick rafters and a sagging roof. The air is stale and tastes of paint, turpentine, and salt. Waves crash against timbers beneath my feet and the floor groans in protest. One wrong step and I could probably break through.

To my left, the warehouse is a wide-mouthed cavern littered with old crates. Abandoned in its center stands a thirty-foot, ripe green avocado made from hammered steel and fiberglass. I reckon it's meant to be an outdoor installation, but Henry Moore can rest easy; I can't imagine someone ever buying it.

The rest of the space is empty, although thick shadows hide the farthest corners.

To my right, a plasterboard partition stretches across the full width of the building. The wall is at least twelve feet tall and the ceiling rafters are a good twenty feet above that. Cutting a gash through the middle is a narrow hallway illuminated by a single bare light bulb.

I walk to it and see that on each side of the hallway, five doors are spaced roughly ten feet apart. I guess they lead to individual studios, but no one has bothered to mark them with names.

I open the first door and peer into a pitch-black cave. After groping along the wall, I locate a light switch and flick it on.

The studio is painted in eggshell white and is clean enough to be an operating theater.

It belongs to a talented watercolor artist who is into postcard landscapes with perfect New England farmhouses sitting above velvet green valleys and fields of delicate wildflowers. Pretty standard fluff except for one half-finished painting that hangs off to the side.

This one shows a different, more inspired side of the artist. It's a portrait of a young farm worker with a deeply scarred face. He's chewing a stalk of wheat, his straw cowboy hat tilted back just enough to allow sunlight to filter across his eyes. One is blue, the other opaque.

Naked, the cause of the scars that mar his face still crisscrosses his body. He's wrapped in a tangled nest of barbed wire, every puncture of his skin releasing a droplet of blood. You can tell from his face that he bears too much pride, and it's that same pride that makes him struggle against the wire. But the harder he struggles, the tighter and deeper bite the barbs.

His flaccid penis is large, caught in that softening post-orgasmic state before it retreats back into itself. Its shaft wears the faded kiss of a woman's delicate pink lipstick. The color choice is not what I would have anticipated.

I shiver slightly, both moved and disturbed, before retreating to the next studio and the next.

Upon opening the fourth door, I am awestruck.

Glaring at me from the far end of the room is an unfinished Diego masterpiece. It's different from the work hanging in the Gimcrack, yet it embodies everything Cahn had been saying about him following a new path.

Strips of multicolored canvas have been brutally ripped, their edges in tatters, and then pasted haphazardly onto another whole canvas. At first, it looks like random shapes, but the more I study it the more I see. A rough, demonic outline is scribbled in black charcoal, and coating everything is a fine dusting of phosphorescent rock.

I can't tell what the outline sketch is going to be, but its anger and passion are undeniable. Even its unfinished quality strikes me as a reflection of the way its creator has died.

I'll need to tell Cahn about it. This piece, in my opinion, could one day be worth more than the blood painting.

I have to force my eyes from the canvas in order to begin a search of the studio, but even after turning away, the image continues to burn in my mind.

On a long wooden table pushed against the wall is the original canvas Diego had been ripping. It isn't multicolored scraps, as I first thought, but had once been a complete painting. In a rage, he must have ripped it with strong hands and maybe even sharp teeth. Then I spot the signature still intact on a piece of discarded canvas: Adamsky.

I hold the orphaned scrap in my hand, mind reeling. Somehow Diego came into possession of not one, but two Adamskys, and he was mutilating this one to create a new work of art. Why?

I return to the unfinished collage and note how he has added passion to the passionless by desecrating the work, but I can't understand what has built up enough anger within Diego to destroy another artist's work. Could it have been jealousy? Did he blame his own commercial downfall on Adamsky's rise?

"*What* were you, Diego?" I ask the shreds of canvas and paint.

"A tormented man," replies a soft, girlish voice from the doorway behind me.

Feeling déjà vu, I turn to see a slender, small-breasted woman covered from head to toe in layers of colorful paint that offer the illusion that her skin is transparent. I can see muscle and bone, but there's something odd about the joints—and her heart.

Noticing my stare, the woman looks down at her body curiously to see if something is wrong.

"Oops. I guess that's rude." Her voice is full of childish laughter. "You must be new here." She turns and skips out of the room, the soles of her feet sparkling in the light.

I catch the movement of her spine and notice what appear to be clockwork pieces connecting each vertebra.

When she reappears, she is wearing a white linen robe.

"I'm working on a new show," she explains. "It's going to be a performance piece. What do you think?"

"You, uh, look nice."

"Ugh, don't say that." She groans. "I don't want to be nice. I want to be battery acid dripping from the stars; your grandma, naked on a chair, leering; a wolf with no teeth; a spider trapped in a web; a clown on the end of a noose, hanged for making children cry."

She stares at me, hands on hips, legs apart in a strong stance, robe gaping.

"Really?" I ask. "My grandmother…naked?"

Her eyes crinkle into laugh lines below bright blue paint. Despite the sweet defiance of her voice, her eyes appear fragile, like a woman arriving on the doorstep of an emergency shelter for the first time.

I expand my focus beyond her eyes to note she possesses an odd prettiness: small, round face, marred only slightly by twin gold hoops hanging from her left nostril; large, doll-like eyes with long, thick eyelashes; and the triangular body of a gymnast—more shoulder than hip. If she had a tail or a third eye, she could be an extra in a George Lucas film.

"Can I see your heart again?" I ask.

She grins and opens her robe as I move forward for a closer look. The stencil of her heart is made up of gears and springs, like a clock.

"Be cool if I could make the gears move, but that would require Pico projectors—and where do I put those?"

I nod as if I understand what she is talking about. "It's cool. I like it."

"Thanks. You a friend of Diego's?"

"No…well, yes." As soon as the words leave my lips, they feel strange. I have become more involved in Diego's life since his death than I ever was when he was alive—even during our time as lovers—and now, inexplicably, something feels missing. "I'm investigating his death."

"You're not a cop." It's a statement.

"No, I'm Dixie. I work for *NOW* magazine."

"A writer, huh? I'm Aurora."

She holds out a speckled hand and I shake her glittery fingertips.

"Cool name."

"Thanks, picked it myself."

She smiles again, and the joyousness of it lightens my mood.

"Did you know Diego well?" I ask.

"Kind of. We would dream to each other now and then, but his bicycle wasn't really built for two."

"Bicycle?"

"His life," she explains. "He was too ... into himself, you know? But we shared some time together and we both had a common interest in art. I don't think he fully grasped my constant reinvention, but he enjoyed talking about ideas and stuff, you know?"

"What did you mean before about him being tormented?"

Aurora stares at me thoughtfully for a moment before leaping straight into the air. When she lands, she begins to skip around the room like a four-year-old.

"When I first met Diego," she says as she skips, "he was timid, jumping at every sound. He always had a smile for me, though. I like that." Her own smile slips slightly as she stops in front of the unfinished painting. "Over the last few months, his colors faded as though rain was falling all around him. He tried to bury his anger inside, but the devil wouldn't be quiet. I thought it would fly off in time, you know? But …" She pauses, closing her eyes for a second, fighting back tears. "But then I heard …" Her voice starts to quiver. "He was too talented to throw it away like that."

In silence, Aurora stares down at her green and yellow toes.

"Were you lovers?" I ask.

She smiles. "He turned me down."

"Hard to believe."

She smiles wider. "He said he was on a journey and that he needed to keep his mind and body pure so his soul could be free."

"A journey?"

"Art," she answers. "He was rebuilding himself as an artist, re-discovering his true path."

I point to the unfinished collage. "Did you know about this?"

Aurora shakes her head. "It's different, but it's still Diego. You can see his demons in it."

"Demons?"

"You know: anger, pity, betrayal, greed."

"What caused them?"

She shrugs. "Every path has its demons. Some are just more powerful than others."

"I'm not sure I follow."

She tilts her head and slowly rolls her eyes skyward as though attempting to see inside her own skull.

"If the path was easy," she says, "no one would ever step off. We would all be the same cookie-cutter apes in straitjackets. As we journey through life, we're presented challenges to make us falter. Some of us accept the deals early on, sacrificing happiness for wealth or position. Some hold on a little longer, trying to find that middle ground: white picket fence, family, a job you don't hate, you know?

"An artist needs to fight both angels and demons to stay on the true path. Diego made it a long way on his journey. A child's heart made fighting the demons as natural as breathing, but when the angels offered him wealth and recognition, how could he resist?"

She pauses, remembering. "Last time we talked, he was excited about a revelation he had. It was to be the basis of his next piece. I still don't know exactly what he meant ..." She turns to study the unfinished collage. "He told me: 'Man created God in his own image, but God usurped man.' He kept repeating it like a mantra, like he was trying to convince himself as much as convince me."

The words of the revelation puzzle me. If Diego believed God was created by man, rather than the other way around, then he wouldn't have any religious barriers against suicide. However, the second half, "God usurped man," could indicate a rebirth of spirituality: At first, God needed man; now man needs God. Or would it be the reverse?

The pieces spin around in my head, searching for interlocking partners. I release my breath slowly and force myself to refocus.

"Do you know if Diego worked at a factory nearby?" I ask.

Aurora wrinkles her forehead in thought before nodding. "I heard him mention some paint factory or something that's near here. Some relative of his, a cousin, I think, got hired there, but I don't know which building, sorry."

"Is it possible to find out?"

Aurora shrugs. "I can call a few people."

I hand her my business card.

"My home number is on there. Call anytime. It may be important."

"OK." She pauses and shyly kicks at the floor with her bare foot. "Uh, do you think somebody from the paper might want to review my show when it opens?"

"Sure. Call me when it's ready and I'll escort a critic there myself."

She beams. "Really?"

I laugh. "When I tell them how cute you are and … let's face it, how *naked*, they'll be fighting for the job."

Aurora grins and skips to the studio door. "I better get back. I still have a lot of work to do."

With a wave, she crosses the hall to her own studio. At the door, she turns back. "If I find anything, I'll call."

"Do."

She drops the robe off her shoulders and back-heels the door closed.

———

I return to my search of the studio, but don't find anything else out of the ordinary in the mess of paint, wood, canvas, and brush. I am just about to leave when the unfinished collage draws me in again. It is close to four feet in length, the canvas stretched and fastened to a rough wood frame.

The last time I took my eye off a valuable painting, it vanished. This time, I decide to take it with me. Once Diego's family shows up, I can either turn it over to them or to the Gimcrack.

With the painting under my arm, I glance around for a phone to call a cab. There isn't one.

I suppose it's time I join the digital age and sign up for an iPhone, but the idea of always being reachable seems like a large commitment.

I cross the hall, knock on Aurora's door, and enter.

Aurora stands against a backdrop of painted white brick, eight large floodlights illuminating the eeriness of her painted transparency. As I watch, she contorts and stretches for a snapping, medium-format Hasselblad. She controls the camera with a miniature remote, and I know a lot of professionals would be jealous that technology has deprived them of the job of photographing her.

The longer I watch, the less I notice her lithe nakedness. Instead, the waves of color that shimmer on her skin and the movement of her muscles enrapture my senses.

When she notices me, she reaches over to switch off a CD player that is pounding out dance hits from Prince and Pink. Strangely, until she turns it off, I hardly noticed it.

"Sorry to disturb you," I say. "But do you have a phone?"

"We use the last studio on this side at the end of the hall as a communal office. There's a phone in there."

"Thanks. Also, is there another door out of here? I don't think I used the right one coming in."

She laughs. "You found the right one. We haven't got around to fixing up that half of the warehouse yet."

I thank her again and let myself out. Someone releases a lustful cry as Aurora switches the music back on.

TWENTY-TWO

THE TAXI DROPS ME in front of the Dog House and I'm surprised to hear laughter behind the iron door. I skip down the short flight of steps and push my way inside with Diego's collage tucked awkwardly under my arm.

The usual assortment of pensioners and hard-drinking cops fills the hovel, but it's Frank who has been the main source of laughter. The after-effects have left him tilted dangerously on his stool, his face beet red, and coughing up a half-chewed peanut. Bill is standing behind the bar with a madman's grin, his massive belly still quivering with delight. He doesn't notice that the dripping wet dishrag in his hand has left an embarrassing stain on the front of his pants.

I prop the painting against the bar and take my usual stool beside Frank. He uses a napkin to wipe his eyes while Bill reaches into the fridge, pops the cap off a Warthog Ale, and places it in front of me.

Frank catches his breath and heads to the washroom as I take a long swallow from the bottle before the frosty vapor has a chance to leave its slender neck.

"Tough day?" Bill asks as I place the half-empty bottle back on the bar.

I shrug and tilt my chin toward Frank's retreating back. "What's he laughing at?"

"A story Al told me."

"Frank saw Capone?"

"No." Bill shakes his head as if I'm the crazy one. "You know how Al is. It was this morning before opening. I just told Frank."

I take another sip of beer and rise to the bait. "So what's the story?"

Bill grins wide and leans across the bar. He has recently finished smoking one of the cheap American-made cigars that he claims Al brings him, and his breath knocks my head back. He doesn't take offense, but the whiplash sends a stabbing pain through my neck.

He starts. "Al was telling me about this dame he was seeing, right?"

I nod and rub my neck.

Bill bares his yellow-brown teeth that always remind me of a post-apocalyptic skyline. In the ring, he had sported a sharp set of lethal, pearly white gnashers, complete with built-in spurting blood capsules for the full, ear-ripping effect. The trouble with real teeth, however, is you can't soak them in a jar while you sleep.

"Well, this dame was a looker, a *real* looker, you know? Long, tanned legs; big, firm tits, face like a cover model. A real wet dream, but high class too. This was no tug it for a fin, suck it for—"

"I get the picture, Bill," I interrupt.

He flashes anger, but it doesn't stick. A wild grin twists his mouth out of shape again. "So Al kinda likes this broad and he's treating her alright, you know? Flowers, furs, bangles, rings. But she's not happy. She keeps harping on Al for a commitment; she wants to know what their future is together. Finally, Al can't take it anymore—"

I lean forward and my elbow almost knocks my bottle off the bar. Bill flashes another annoyed look.

"Are you listening?" he barks, slapping the bar with one of his huge hands. A puddle of spilled beer sprays in a hundred directions, one of which finds my eye.

"I'm listening!" I yell back and grab a napkin to wipe my stinging eye.

"Well, sit still, then," Bill orders.

I continue to dab at my eye until the grin returns to Bill's face.

He continues. "So Al sits the girl down and begins to tell her his philosophy on life. About how he rewards his friends and slays his enemies. Then he gets on one knee, a goosedown pillow underneath it first of course, takes hold of her hand and looks up with doe-eyed innocence."

Bill tries to imitate the look, but his face is too much like Boris Karloff to get the proper image across. "Then," he continues, "Al says to her: 'I want to make you a promise.' So this dame is a puddle. She's thinking this is it. The big proposal, you know? And Al, who does a much better Humphrey Bogart impersonation than I ever could, takes a deep breath and says, 'Stick with me, kid, and you'll be farting through silk.'"

I thought a B-52 bomber had just flown a low-level pass above the bar as Bill's laughter reverberates around the room for a second time. The look on his face, rather than the story, makes me join in.

As the laughter subsides, Frank comes back and orders another O'Doul's. Bill immediately pours one before heading down the bar to serve other customers.

Frank turns to face me and sticks a limp, S-shaped cigarette between his lips.

"When are they going to invent waterproof cigarettes?" he grumbles after unsuccessfully trying to light it.

I shrug as he throws the ruined pack onto the bar. The question is on my lips, but I manage to bite it back, deciding I really don't want to know how the pack has come to be in such a sorry state.

"You're in early," I say.

"All quiet on the homicide front." He sighs. "I just know there's going to be a triple murder-suicide and the accidental death of a politician while humping his secretary as soon as I get settled in front of the TV tonight. It's in the air, kid." Frank takes a swig of nonalcoholic beer. "How's your day going?"

"I found a few things."

"Any more trouble with cars?"

I shake my head as Frank's face creases with concern.

"I'm being careful, Frank, OK? But there's not much I can do. I told you, I didn't catch a plate. I also haven't received any threats, so it might not even be about me. Kids go joyriding through Chinatown and spot a couple of white faces, think it would be hilarious to scare the crap out of them. It happens."

"It happens," Frank agrees. "But when it happens to you … let's just say I don't believe in coincidence."

We both take long pulls from our beers.

"Anyway," I start again. "What did you find out about our Sleeping Beauty?"

"Not much." Frank digs into his pocket and produces a thin notebook. He flips through the pages until he finds the right patch of chicken scratch.

"Paul Gibson. Criminal record for possession of marijuana in college. Paid a $250 fine. Must have scared him straight because that was the end of his run-ins with the law. He's worked at the same place, an accounting firm, for the last eight years. No outstanding tickets. Nice and boring, just how I like them."

I smirk. "You hate boring."

"Says who?"

"You do, with every breath. You need the action. It's what gets you up in the morning and puts you to bed at night."

"You sure that's me you're talking about?"

I slide my empty bottle across the bar and nod for another one. "Yeah," I say. "I'm sure."

Frank's mouth twitches. "So what else you got?"

"You know the cocaine found in Diego's autopsy?"

Frank nods.

"I asked his agent about it. Not the weasel trying to get his mitts on the blood painting, by the way, but his *current* agent at the Gimcrack Gallery. According to him, Diego's asthma would have prevented him from taking drugs. Cocaine could have killed him."

"It did," Frank points out.

"No," I say, "a shotgun blast to the face killed him. And if you're going to kill yourself, you don't want to have an asthma attack in the middle of squeezing the trigger. Bad aim could mean walking around alive, but with only half a face. Nasty. Why take the chance?"

Frank scratches his nose and rubs at wide, hairy nostrils with a thick knuckle. "You worry me, kid," he says softly. "I don't like to be worried."

"And?" I prod.

"The coroner's report came out this afternoon. I took a look before firing it to Northern."

"And?"

"Traces of cocaine were found in the stiff's lungs, but there's no signs of asthma mentioned. And I know those butchers. They love to look for that kind of stuff."

"So somebody's lying."

Frank sighs and scans the room. "I didn't say that. Right now, the file says a depressed artist got high and blew his brains out. Anything else is circumstantial at best."

"I'm not arguing," I say. "I'm just—"

"Arguing."

"Questioning. There are loose ends here that nobody wants to tie up."

"Except you."

I take a swallow from my fresh bottle of beer. The mist has evaporated from the glass, but it's still cool on the back of my throat.

"My editor hates stories with holes. As a large man with failing eyesight, loose ends represent tripwires. And if I make him trip, he'll make sure all his weight lands on me."

"So you're just covering your ass?"

"With Kevlar."

Frank laughs aloud, lifts his bottle of O'Doul's in a salute, and clinks it against mine before putting it to his lips.

"OK," he says after he swallows. "I'll talk to the coroner about asthma."

"Great. Now, what can you tell me about Chief McInty?"

Frank is surprised. "Why?"

"I had a talk with him this morning about the painting you found in Diego's apartment."

"And?"

"He told me Diego stole it."

"From where?"

"He wouldn't say."

Frank studies his beer. "McInty's the kind of man you don't want on your ass. And if he thinks you're sticking your nose into police business, he just might have it chopped off and framed behind his desk."

"It's a nice view."

"What?" Frank says, confused.

"McInty's desk. It's got a nice view."

Frank shakes his head and orders another O'Doul's. I decide I need a little warmth in my belly and order a scotch.

"Oh, by the way." I pull Diego's collage out from its resting space against the bar. "What do you make of this?"

Frank leans back on his stool and studies it carefully. "What is it?"

"It's another Adamsky. Only this time, Diego shredded it to pieces and turned it into this."

"Where'd you get it?"

"From Diego's studio. Met a nice girl there, too, by the name of Aurora. She paints herself from head to toe and poses in the nude."

Frank's forehead crinkles into a series of deep furrows. "You broke into Diego's studio and took this?"

"Chill," I say. "The police have closed their investigation. No one has claimed the body. And a close friend of his knows I have the damn thing. I just didn't want this piece disappearing before I find out who legally owns it. Everything's a clue, Frank. You taught me that. Now I have to find out how all the clues fit together, right?"

"I wish you wouldn't quote me after you break the law." Frank's jaw is tight. "It doesn't sound good."

He turns to face the bar. "Give me a shot, Bill."

Bill grins wide, showing all his crooked teeth, and deliberately folds thick arms across a thicker chest. He barely moves his head, but the intent is clear.

Frank's eyes drop to my empty shot glass and then back up to meet my gaze.

"You piss me off, kid."

I almost choke. "Me?" I sputter. "Why?"

"You make my life too damn complicated."

"Hey, I took lessons on being difficult from you."

"Bullshit! You were a pain in the ass long before we met. I'm just been trying to make you a better journalist so you can get a job at a real newspaper and move out of my jurisdiction."

"Well, you've failed."

"Damn right I have."

We're silent for a few moments until we both begin to laugh. With the laughter, Bill relaxes and resumes his bartender duties.

"Oh, by the way, you owe me twenty bucks," I say.

"What for?"

"I had to pay off your gambling debt with a Sergeant Woods before he would give me the time of day."

Frank reaches deep into his pocket and throws a couple of bills on the table. I pick them up.

"Hey, this is only ten," I complain.

"That's all I owed."

TWENTY-THREE

WHEN THE CLOCK STRIKES seven, Frank helps me on with what is left of my overcoat, tucks Diego's painting under my arm, and leads the way out of the Dog House.

From the doorway, I wave to Bill and for a hazy moment think I see Capone in his reserved seat at the end of the bar. His face is thick with heavy jowls and a bulbous nose that sports the misshapen tenderness of bruised fruit. A fog-gray fedora with a black silk band is tilted back on his head, exposing a forehead creased with deep wrinkles and a single slash of bone white. The scar runs diagonally from his left eyebrow to vanish beneath the hat. Clamped between his teeth is a thick cigar, and tendrils of yellow smoke curl above his head like the frayed ends of a hangman's rope.

Damn the luck, I think as the heavy door swings shut. *I finally see him and I'm too drunk for an interview.*

Dixie's Tips #11: *Before drinking heavily at a haunted pub, make sure to eat more than an egg-salad sandwich and horrible tea.*

Frank and I walk, singing old Sinatra songs in off-key splendor. When we reach my building, Frank points in the right direction and watches as I climb the stairs.

"'Night, ol' Building and Loan pal o' mine," I call down.

"I hate that movie," Frank calls back.

"No, you don't."

Frank grins with sparkling eyes.

"No, I don't," he admits and heads home.

———

Inside the lobby, I glance over at my mailbox and wonder if it's worth checking.

The tin slot isn't big enough to hold a "Let's do it again—soon" box of chocolates or an "I've been thinking about you all day" bouquet of flowers. As such, it seems to subsist on a simple diet of bills, unwanted flyers, and missed payment notices. It seems particularly fond of the notices, as they come in varying shades of red and taste just fractionally like licorice.

I sometimes suspect the box destroys the real bills, just so it can treat itself to another tasty notice. But try telling that to a bill collector.

Deciding against disappointment, I leave the mailbox alone for another day and head for the stairs. Despite the short distance, I don't make it. My feet trip over a solid, unyielding, and extremely furry object.

With a yelp, I find myself falling. One corner of Diego's painting hits the floor first and skids out of my grasp. It slides under the stairs as I throw my arms in front of my face a microsecond before I smack the ground with a solid whap.

My injuries from the night before return in jabbing shards and my alcohol-brittle toughness threatens to burst into a blubbering of tears. Before the walls come down, however, an unexpected sound makes me roll onto my back and glance at my feet.

King William of Orange is rubbing himself against my legs and purring. When he senses my perplexed attention, he strolls toward my face, purrs rumbling louder with every step, and places one paw against my cheek.

The pads on the bottom of his feet are much softer than I expect. I frown at him, my eyes still welling with the possibility of tears.

King William gently bonks his furry head against mine and then proceeds to lick my nose. His tongue is as rough as his fur is soft, but the affection it imparts is unmistakable.

"How did you get out?" I ask as I stroke his cheek.

King William continues to lick my nose and though I appreciate the exfoliation, I worry that I won't have many more layers of skin before he hits bone. Sitting up, I lift the large cat onto my lap. Instantly, he curls into a ball, covers his face with his paw, and falls asleep.

"Don't worry about me," I say. "I'll just sit here. It's not like I have plans to go up to my own bed or anything."

Apparently the idea of my being stuck in the lobby all night doesn't bother him. He is perfectly content in my lap.

Cradling the cat in my arms, I struggle to my feet and knock on Mrs. Pennell's door with my toe.

After the fourth knock, she answers. And when she spots King William in my arms, her face lights up with heavenly delight.

"You silly, silly boy," she scolds in baby talk as she transfers the sleeping cat into her arms.

King William yawns, but stays curled, completely undisturbed.

"How did he get out?" I ask.

Mrs. Pennell tuts her tongue. "He ran out when I was bringing in the groceries, and then he hid somewhere so I couldn't find him. I don't know what gets into him, but sometimes he just needs to go for a wander. I wish he understood how it worries me."

"Well, he looks happy to be home now."

Mrs. Pennell smiles. "Yes," she says. "Yes, he does."

She lifts her gaze from the cat and scrutinizes my face.

"And what about you, dear?" she asks. "How are you doing?"

"A little tipsy, Mrs. Pennell," I admit. "And a little sore. But nothing I can't handle."

"Just remember, you don't have to carry it all, dear. You have friends."

I nod, grateful for the concern.

"And speaking of which," Mrs. Pennell continues, "Mr. French was looking for you earlier. He was acting rather odd, but then when is he not? Him and that silly bird of his. He said he had news for you."

I thank her as she closes the door to give King William his evening feast. I contemplate leaving Mr. French until morning, since my stomach is rumbling and my scrapes and bruises could use a warm bath. Unfortunately, Mr. French must have been waiting behind his peephole.

No sooner does Mrs. Pennell's door close than his opens.

———

Mr. French's face lights up as he opens the door, but it instantly falls again when he sees the state of me.

"Oh, dear, Ms. Flynn, whatever happened?"

Having not looked in a mirror for hours, I'm not sure what part of me looks worst. I shrug.

"Well, come in, come in," Mr. French urges. "I'll make some tea and we can chat."

I follow the diminutive man inside the apartment, inhaling a smoky fragrance of vanilla bean, cane sugar, and something muskier—like black tobacco leaf grown in a peaty Cuban swamp.

The living room is lit by an array of candles and a gas fireplace set on a low flame. I make sure to gently touch Baccarat's cage in greeting before settling into an overstuffed armchair close to the fire. The heat is wonderful and I gratefully slip out of my boots and torn overcoat.

"I'll make us that tea," says Mr. French. "Make yourself at home."

I must have closed my eyes. When I open them again, Mr. French is sitting on the couch beside me and nibbling a triangular sandwich. Arranged on the coffee table is a large glass teapot filled with amber liquid. Floating inside the liquid is a large and rather beautiful flower.

Mr. French notices my interest.

"It's white tea from China," he says. "The Chinese pick the leaves and buds when the tea is quite young and bind it by hand into these beautiful arrangements before drying. When you steep it, the flower blossoms and the full fragrance of the tea is released. White tea possesses great healing properties. Shall I pour?"

I'm feeling great affection for this kindly little man, though I wonder why everyone I've met lately appears to be so into tea. I thought

213

we were a nation of coffee drinkers. Then I spot the plate of tiny sandwiches beside the teapot and remember how famished I am.

I wolf down four of the triangular delicacies before my cup of tea is poured, but Mr. French seems delighted by my appetite rather than disgusted by my lack of manners.

"These are wonderful," I say as I lift a fifth.

"I'm glad you approve. They're nothing special. Just a little potted meat, thinly sliced scallion, and a hint of hand-churned butter that I get from a local farm."

"We have farms?" I lift my cup and take a tentative sip of the unusual tea.

Mr. French laughs. "Don't tell anyone," he whispers conspiratorially, "but there is a whole world beyond these concrete towers."

"You're having me on," I say playfully.

"*Au contraire, mademoiselle*. I have seen it with my own two eyes. Tracks of land so vast one can stand on a hill, look across lush valleys, and not see another soul."

"Hmmm, you must be thinking of the Midwest. They say in Kansas, your dog can run away and two days later you can still see him."

"Ahhh." Mr. French's eyes glisten with delight. "Perhaps you are correct."

I giggle into my tea and help myself to another tiny sandwich.

When the sandwiches are gone, Mr. French produces a plate of finger-length shortbread cookies. After I have consumed two and am on my second cup of tea, Mr. French opens a small leather-bound notebook to a page filled with neat but incredibly tiny handwriting.

"Thank you for the second note," he begins. "The author used the same paper as the first, which lets us know the paper trail has a good chance of bearing fruit."

"What did you make of the wording?" I ask.

Mr. French sips his tea before answering. "I'm no cryptanalyst, and I hate to oversimplify, but the couplet struck me as the words of a jilted lover."

"Angry?"

"Most definitely," Mr. French agrees. "The opening line of verse states that loss of love is acceptable. Here, the author is putting on a brave face. The breakup of the relationship isn't something that was desired, but the author is willing to accept it. The second line, however, admonishes the recipient for abandoning responsibility. This gives the author an excuse to cling to the relationship, which means she won't move on until the matter is settled."

"So," I join in. "I don't love you anymore either, but you've hurt me, so you have to pay?"

Mr. French claps his chubby hands together in delight. "Isn't poetry fun?"

I smirk. "I'll stick with Tom Waits."

"I don't believe …" Mr. French pauses. "Ah, the singer. Hookers and gin. Quite, quite."

"So where did the paper lead us?" I ask before he veers off on Waits's fondness for singing about loneliness and patricide.

"Now this is rather interesting. Clifford—erm … Mr. Clements, he owns the stationery store—well, he and I had a wonderful day together going through his records. You know, paper is almost as fascinating as stamps. A touch more rudimentary in terms of history, perhaps, but—"

I yawn, my mouth opening so wide it eclipses my entire head.

"Sorry," I say once I regain control of my jaw muscles. "It's been a long day."

"Shall I cut to the chase?" He sounds only slightly annoyed.

"That would be great."

"I have five addresses of five women all within a five block radius of the stationer's."

"Wow, that's great. And ... tidy, with all the fives."

"Yes, we were rather pleased."

"Can I have the names and addresses?"

"Naturally. However, I was wondering if you would allow me to continue the investigation until I can deliver the sole name?"

"Well, sure, but you've already done more than I could have hoped. This is terrific."

Mr. French blushes. "This may sound a touch egocentric in light of the threatening nature of the correspondence, but I am rather enjoying myself. Digging into the meat of a mystery like this is the most exciting thing to cross my desk since the Okotoks kingfisher incident of 2004."

Fearing that he's about to launch into another stamp-related story, I rise to my feet and slip back into my shoes.

"In that case," I say, "I welcome the help."

Mr. French beams over at Baccarat. The bird chirps as if to show she is equally excited.

———

Back in the hallway, Mr. French has just closed his door when Mrs. Pennell's door swings open.

I am rather proud of myself that I don't curse.

"Oh, Dixie," Mrs. Pennell calls quietly.

I fasten a smile on my face and turn.

"Yes, Mrs. Pennell. Everything OK?"

"Yes, yes, everything is fine. King William is fast asleep in his bed, but I wanted to get your coat before you went upstairs."

I exhale quietly, relieved it is something I can accomplish with a shrug of shoulder.

I hand her the torn coat. "Thanks again."

"Not at all, dear. Have a good night."

I return to the stairs and climb, propelled upward by little more than sheer will.

TWENTY-FOUR

THE STAIRS GO ON forever, but finally I rest forehead against apartment door and fish for my key. Before I can hook it, however, the door falls open and the unexpected loss of cranial support sends me lurching clumsily off balance.

Being (much to my mother's chagrin) a ballet school dropout at the age of four, I naturally fail to find my footing and end up sprawled on the floor; cute ass in the air, embarrassing rug burn on my chin.

If I had a personal video crew—or a stalker with a camera phone—I could become an Internet superstar: *Presenting Dixie Flynn, the klutz* on YouTube.

After the initial shock, I can't help but laugh. It's either that or cry; at the moment I'm feeling too stupid to register one more bruise on top of the others.

Pulling myself to my feet, I flick on the lights.

Someone is sleeping on my couch.

A blonde tuft of hair is curled on the sofa with a pillow covering her face. She is dressed in a low-cut, close-fitting lemon-yellow silk dress with matching shoes that makes my couch look even shabbier than normal.

The shallow rise and fall of breast tells me she isn't dead. But if she's Goldilocks, what does that make me?

I clear my throat.

She doesn't budge.

I walk over and remove the pillow.

Yup, Kristy.

Silly girl must have decided to visit after another big night on the town. Her face is full of make-'em-drool war paint and her normally straight hair is curled so expertly that it would make all three Charlie's Angels jealous.

I stifle a yawn and try to shake the sleep out of my eyes. I wonder if she and Sam had a spat. Dressed like she is, Kristy couldn't help but attract attention, and she loves attention.

"Wake up, Kristy," I say, fighting off another yawn.

She doesn't move.

I shake her shoulder. Nothing.

The yawns keep coming and my eyes are growing heavy. I look down at the soft cushions and Kristy's warm body, my muddled brain convincing me I should curl up next to her on the couch and let the day come to an end.

I begin to give in, but the room is too warm, the air tastes stale, and my bladder is too full from cups of tea on top of the beer. I spin toward the bathroom, but my brain doesn't stop when my head does. It continues to spin.

Fighting the urge to vomit all over Sleeping Beauty, I stagger to the window beside the computer that overlooks the alley.

I push up on the frame, but it doesn't budge. The damn thing is stuck.

Frustrated, dizzy, and feeling bile rise in my stomach, I hammer the heel of my hand into the top of the wooden frame and feel it give—slightly. I hammer it twice more and push with all my strength, hoping the glass doesn't shatter in my face in the process.

Finally, the window slides all the way up.

I lean out to inhale deep breaths. The outside air is cool, moist, and oxygen-rich, not like the apartment at all. My queasiness begins to ease.

Brushing the thin curtain aside to see why the window was stuck, I notice a small rubber hose wedged into a crack in the sill. Following its trail out the window, I see the hose is attached to the drainpipe with a plastic clamp. A foot below it, clamped in an identical way, is a shiny metal cylinder.

"What the—"

Suddenly, I sense movement behind me and my stomach lurches again. This time it isn't from bad air.

My feet leave the ground, ankles gripped by a pair of strong hands, and I am propelled out the window.

Screaming loud enough to wake the dead, I instinctively clamp on to the ledge, my fingers clawing at the wood to fight off the forward momentum. Half in, half out the window and balanced on my stomach, I kick my legs, but my attacker has a strong, unyielding grip. Sharp fingernails dig into my flesh.

"Where is it?" a male voice barks. The voice is trying to be hard, but there is more than a touch of panic in it.

"If you think I have anything of value—"

He shoves harder and my aching fingers begin to weaken. But they aren't the only things losing strength. My over-filled and under-pressure bladder gives out first.

As hot urine pours down my legs, my attacker reacts in disgust and I kick again. This time his grip has slackened and I break free.

Grunts of pain echo as I flail my legs wildly, connecting solid blows with anything in their way. Before he can regain the upper hand, I push back from the ledge and slide across the floor.

Rising quickly to my feet, I discover I'm blind.

The apartment has returned to darkness: front door closed, lights off. Before I can process the fact that I am silhouetted against the open window, he attacks.

———

The rush of air warns me milliseconds before his hands reach my throat. Instinctively, I drop to the floor again, leaving murderous fingers to skim through my hair, followed by the crunch of knuckles against glass.

My attacker roars in both pain and frustration.

When I hit the floor, I roll, but not fast enough to escape a stunning blow to the kidneys from a sharp-toed shoe. I grunt in pain as another kick—a heel this time—slams into my chest, and lose my breath when a third digs under my rib cage, surely bruising my heart.

When another brutal heel lands. I stop rolling and cry out. Vision blurred, eyes rolling into my skull, I fear I'm going to lose consciousness and any hope of staying alive.

Iron fingers reach down to become entangled in my hair. I cry out again as I am yanked to my feet, legs wobbly beneath me, my lungs barely able to suck in enough oxygen to keep my brain working, never mind my muscles.

The invisible bastard has me at his mercy with barely three words of explanation.

His grip tightens on my scalp, twisting deeper into my hair, pulling my head back and exposing my throat. Strangely, the move reminds me of a boy I had a crush on in elementary school. While the other kids played cowboys and Indians, cops and robbers, or the Three Musketeers, little Stevie Simpson and I played werewolves and vampires. I had my first hickey in fourth grade—a vampire bite—and my reputation never recovered.

When Stevie had me by the throat, one move always threw him off. Dead weight.

I go limp, allowing gravity to do the work. Clumps of hair rip in his hands, sending more jolts of pain into my overloaded brain, but as soon as my butt hits the floor, I pay it back by spinning in place and kicking my right foot skyward as hard as I can.

The heel of my boot hits home to punch dangling organs deep within the body until they slam against the pelvis bone. Something meaty pops and my attacker squeals like a stuck pig.

Releasing my hair, he staggers backwards, breath wheezing like a deflated balloon.

With renewed strength, I get to my feet and advance.

But I'm too cocky.

My attacker pulls a hunting knife from behind his back and slashes the air. I jump back just in time to miss having my face sliced open like a ripe tomato, but there is nowhere left to go. The open window is at my back, and the knife-wielding psycho is bearing down.

Lights snap on, blinding us both.

"Dixie!"

Sam's voice. Terrified.

I am barely able to catch a glimpse of her as she bursts through the door.

My attacker stands before me, his face covered in a black woolen ski mask and eyes blazing through narrow twin slits. Blood drips from his mouth, where I must have either landed a lucky blow or made him bite his tongue when I crushed his manhood. He is off balance and in noticeable pain; his body is bent as one hand cradles an area to the left of his stomach where a kidney would be.

My attention moves to the knife just as he jabs it directly at my face.

Time seems to slow as the knife cuts through the air and my hands move into a position I haven't used since the reclaim-the-night women's defense training I underwent for a story the previous year.

In training, you were meant to simultaneously push the knife away with one hand while the other came up behind for a scissor move that could break your attacker's wrist.

I was very good in training, but reality is a different test.

I move too quickly, my hand arriving in front of the knife and missing the block completely. Before I realize what I have done, the knife pierces my exposed palm, slicing through flesh, muscle, and bone to exit the other side.

I scream as my right hand abandons its scissor move and instead slashes out, karate-chop style, to seek my attacker's throat.

Surprised eyes bulge as the dull edge of my hand slams into his Adam's apple. As he gags, he releases the knife, the blade still sticking through my left hand. He reaches for his throat, legs buckling, and then his full off-balanced weight slams against me.

I tumble back, head smacking the windowsill, legs and arms forcing him up and away ... shattering glass is followed by a scream ... and he is gone.

———

Through tears of pain and shock, I see Sam's pale face, her hands outstretched.

"I pushed him," she says in a distant voice. "I ... he went ... oh, God."

I glance over my shoulder at the broken window, realizing my attacker continued to hurtle forward after I hit the wall.

I turn back to Sam and hold up my bloody hand with the knife sticking through it.

"Ouch," I say dryly, attempting to sound brave and witty.

Sam's eyes are drawn to the knife and, after a moment, my comment breaks through her shock.

She bursts into laughter, but then covers her mouth, embarrassed by her reaction.

I attempt a grin and don't quite make it as the pain twists my lips in a different direction, but hopefully this conveys the message that Sam has done the right thing.

"You saved my life," I say. "This son of a bitch meant business."

Sam nods and wipes at her eyes and runny nose.

"I ... I'll get ..."

"Check on Kristy," I say. "I'll be fine."

Sam pulls her eyes away from my bleeding hand and rushes to Kristy's side. Goldilocks hasn't budged.

With Sam occupied, I cradle my wounded hand against my chest, clench my teeth against the throbbing pain, and carefully rise to my feet.

Upright, I have to lean my shoulder against the wall, feeling weak. My head spins once again.

I take several deep breaths, drawing cold air into my lungs from the broken window. On the narrow, crushed-gravel lane below, a dark form lies on the roof of a coffee brown, or possibly maroon, '70s Chevy.

Without warning, I lose an internal war and my stomach empties. Sour contents splash unceremoniously on the unmoving body below.

Shivering from shock and feeling near death, I grab the phone from beside the computer with my good hand and punch in Frank's number.

He answers on the first ring.

TWENTY-FIVE

TENDRILS OF YELLOW MIX with smoky gray to dance upon fleshy screens. I blink the ghosts away, head pounding with each flutter. My left hand throbs, my body aches, and my skull is a bruised honeydew of tender spots.

I'm not on the floor anymore. Instead, my neck and back are cushioned with pillows. I feel the fabric with my hand. I am on the couch. The couch where Goldilocks slept through the angry bear attack.

I open my eyes. A wilted cabbage, thick leaves flapping like loose skin, looks down at me. I wonder if I have fallen down the rabbit hole again.

"Drink this," says the cabbage, holding out a small glass of clear liquid.

"Is that to make me grow or shrink?" I mumble. "I forget what comes first."

The cabbage looks away, its green leaves flapping at something beyond my line of sight.

When its face returns, it begins to look familiar.

"Wake up, kid," says the cabbage. "You're gonna be OK."

I blink again, trying to focus. The cabbage slowly fades and Frank's concerned face blossoms into view. He looks like hell: baggy eyes, tousled hair, out-of-control eyebrows, and a dusting of gray stubble darkening his chin as though he sneezed in an ashtray.

"Did I wake you?" My voice is hoarse.

Frank laughs. It sounds wonderful and despite my pain, I try to join in. My own laugh is weak and broken, but still, it's good to be alive.

"Can't leave you alone for a second," he says. "What the hell happened?"

"Ask the idiot who dove out the window."

"The window?"

"Yeah. Dumb move. No fire escape on that side."

Frank's brow knits in a frown.

"You sure he went out the window?"

"You didn't see the body? He landed on top of a car in the alley. An old Chevy, I think. Made a real mess of the roof."

Frank moves to the broken window and peers out. I follow him with my eyes. Everything else hurts too much.

"Nobody down there, Dix," he says. "No dented car, either."

"You sure?"

Frank's mouth twitches. "I've had some practice spotting these things."

"I thought he was dead. Bastard stabbed me in the—"

I hold up my left hand. The knife is gone and my hand is wrapped in a thick white bandage. I can't move my fingers.

"That's just a patch job," says a woman's voice from the kitchenette.

I turn my head to see a broad-shouldered woman in her early fifties with a tanned, oval face that, although we all need a little help, doesn't require much makeup to be pretty. She is wearing a loose-fitting jogging outfit in a cheerful shade of purple. It's the kind of thing you throw on when you need to dash to the corner shop for a chocolate bar before your favorite TV show starts. A matching lavender scrunchie keeps shoulder-length hazelnut hair pulled back from her face. With her hair down, she probably looks younger.

Sitting beside her on the kitchen counter is a small leather doctor's bag. It's monogrammed in silver.

"Dix, meet Ruth," Frank says. "Ruth was kind enough to come over when I called. You had a knife sticking through your hand."

"Yeah," I say dryly. "I noticed that."

Ruth steps forward so I don't have to crane my neck so far, and I suddenly recall where I know her name from.

"You're the coroner!" I say.

Ruth smiles and nods.

"Frank's mentioned you," I add.

Ruth's smile grows brighter. "I cleaned and stitched the wound. You're fortunate. The knife was sharp and the blade went through the flesh without obstruction."

"And that's good?"

Ruth's chuckle is low and husky, like I imagine Marlene Dietrich's would be after a night smoking cheap German cigarettes and drinking twelve-year-old cognac.

"It means I can't see any reason for permanent damage. The knife appears to have sliced nicely between the metacarpus bones, which in itself is a minor miracle. The damaged muscle is very good at self-repair, given time. It's more difficult, however, to see tendons and nerves without really getting in there. I fabricated a splint to prevent you moving your fingers until you can get to the hospital and see a specialist. All in all, I would say you're a very lucky woman."

"Yeah, I feel it." My eyes drift to her medical bag again. "You don't happen to have anything in there for pain, do you?"

"Oh, I never thought of that," she says. "My regular clients never ask."

I stare at her open-mouthed. "That's because they're dead!"

Both Ruth and Frank burst out laughing.

"Oh, you guys are hilarious," I say. "What do you do for an encore? Sonny and Cher songs?"

"Nope," Ruth replies with a wink. "We're into line dancing."

My lips curl into a less than congenial sneer but soften again when Ruth brings over a small container of Percocet.

"Go easy on these," she says as I pop two. "They can be addictive."

I swallow, not caring if they're laced with heroin, just so long as they take the edge off the pain.

I close my eyes for a few moments to allow the drugs time to dissolve into my bloodstream. When I open them again, I ask, "How's Kristy?"

"She's fine," says Frank. "I carried her next door to her bed. Sam's with her."

"Was she injured?" I ask.

"No," Ruth joins in. "Her pulse is fine, but she's in a deep sleep. Possibly drug-induced. I couldn't wake her."

"It was some kind of gas," I say. "There's a small tank attached to a hose outside the window."

Frank returns to the broken window and looks outside again. "I don't see it."

"Shit!" I try to sit up. And fail. "Is Diego's painting still around? I dropped it in the lobby."

"I'll check later."

"Who in hell was I fighting, Frank?" I ask angrily. "Spider-Man? It's a two-story drop out that window. There was no way he was getting up and walking away. I saw him lying on that car after the fall. Hell, I puked on him, and he didn't budge."

"We'll find out, kid." Frank returns to the couch and sits on its edge. He takes my uninjured hand in his. "But for now, get some rest."

I want to argue with him, but the Percocet is kicking in and my eyelids are heavy. I decide to let them rest, just for a little while.

———

When I open my eyes again, it's morning.

A proud, red-breasted robin sits on the ledge of my broken window and chirps its delight at the absence of rain and an unexpectedly clear, fog-free sky. I would have chirped, too, but the Percocet has worn off and I am feeling too damn grumpy.

I grope around for the prescription bottle, pop the cap one-handed, and swallow two pills dry.

When I get to my feet, the robin takes flight. I can't blame it; I must look a fright.

Carefully, I stretch my muscles. Knots the size of Frank's fists lodge in my shoulders, legs, and back. I bend from the waist, touch my toes, and all the blood in my body rushes to my brain in a dizzying flood.

I must have blacked out. When I open my eyes again, I am back on the couch. But at least I'm sitting up. I stand again, wait a few breaths, and then head toward my bedroom. I unbutton my jeans as I go, desperate for a shower and fresh clothes.

I have just pulled my T-shirt over my head when—

"Hope you don't mind, Dix, but there was nowhere else to sleep."

I don't scream. I think about it, but my brain doesn't seem capable of even the basest instincts.

"Jeez, Frank!" I clutch my heart and awkwardly pull my t-shirt back down. "You trying to finish the bastard's job from last night?"

Frank's mouth twitches. "You know, maybe it's the light, but you don't look a thing like Whitney Houston."

"Hmmm, and you're Kevin Costner, I suppose?"

"Practically twins."

Frank throws his legs over the side of my bed and stretches his arms. He is still fully dressed in his wrinkled suit and tired trench coat. His thin, unkempt hair looks the same post-sleep as it does pre.

"You could have taken your coat off you know? I do wash the sheets."

Frank stands up. "That would be like asking Batman to remove his cape."

I grin. "Well, if you wouldn't mind slinging your bat-hook somewhere else, I desperately need a shower."

"No problem, you got anything to eat? I'm starved."

I glance over at Bubbles, the oldest goldfish in the world, swimming happily in her bowl.

"Anything that doesn't move, you can eat," I offer. Bubbles looks relieved.

Frank plods out of the room.

Grabbing a fresh towel, I head to the bathroom, strip, and step into the tub to shower. Before I can turn on the water, there's a knock on the door.

"What?" I call out.

"Got a present for you," Frank calls back.

"Can't it wait?"

"Nope."

I step out of the tub, wrap a towel around myself and open the door a crack.

Frank holds out an empty plastic grocery bag and a thick elastic band.

"Nice. Make it yourself?"

"It's for your hand," he says. "You don't want the bandage getting wet before you see the specialist."

I grab the bag and elastic with my good hand.

"I'll cherish it," I say and close the door.

———

After dressing in clean clothes and popping two more Percocet, I feel almost human until I look in the mirror. I don't need concealer; I need to book myself into the local autobody shop for major reconstruction. After doing my best with what I have on hand, the final ingredient necessary for complete transformation is coffee.

I exit the bedroom to the sound of Frank's laughter as he talks on the phone.

I flash him a goofy face and enter the kitchenette to the blessed aroma of fresh-perked No Sweat Peruvian. Expecting the worst—based on my experience with men who could only make coffee if you left instructions in the form of a Bil Keane *Family Circus* comic strip—I pour myself a small splash in a mug and taste.

To my surprise, it is excellent.

I fill the mug almost to the brim, add a drop of cream, and inhale.

"Dix!" Frank calls from the sofa. "Phone's for you."

"Who is it?"

"Your mother."

I stiffen. "You're talking to my mother?"

Frank nods.

"And laughing?"

"Yeah, she's—"

I hold up my hand to stop him. "Gimme the phone!"

Frank hands over the receiver with an expression that suggests I have just grown a second head.

"Hi, M—"

"Who is that nice man who answered the phone? He sounds older, much too old for you, but very nice. Is he single? How do you know him and why is he in your apartment? He didn't stay the night, did he?" She gasps. "Don't tell me you've become a prostitute."

"No, Mom! I'm not a prostitute."

Frank grins wide and crosses his arms. I sit on the couch and turn my back to him.

"Well, who is he then?"

"He's a cop. A detective."

"What have you done?"

"I haven't done anything. He's help—"

"I've always said the city is too dangerous. Remember that time your father and I visited and that man urinated on our car wheels? Who does that?"

"I remember, Mom. How could I possibly forget? You kee—"

"You should come home."

"I am home. San Francisco is my home."

"No, you should come back to your family."

"I have family. My friends are—"

"Hmmm. I was watching Dr. Phil and I think your friends across the hall might be more than roommates."

"Really?" My mind flashes to the image of Sam handcuffed to the bed and wearing a dog mask.

"Yes. Dr. Phil says it's becoming more and more common now for women to—"

"How's Dad?" I interrupt, knowing it is a cruel question, but seeing little alternative.

"Don't get me started. I think he's on Viagra."

"Mom!"

"Well, I mean, at his age, and then suddenly there's talk he's been at the Barn and dancing with everything in a skirt. Young, old, he's not picky."

"He's allowed to have a life."

"You always loved h—"

"You're allowed to have a life too."

"Hmmmm." She sniffles. "Who would want me?"

"You don't need a man to enjoy yourself."

"No," she says softly. "But it helps. I like to be treated right."

"I gotta go. I have a meeting. Was there anything you needed?"

"No, dear, I'm fine. You go on, don't worry about me. Marcy's coming over later and we're going to hit the thrift stores and then maybe catch afternoon bingo."

"OK, have fun. I love you."

"Love you too, little bird."

She hangs up.

I turn to Frank.

"Don't say a freakin' word."

Frank's mouth twitches—a lot.

———

"So you want me to drop you at the hospital?" Frank asks as we reach the bottom of the coffee pot.

I shake my head. "I appreciate the offer, but I have an appointment first."

Frank frowns. "The Percs may dull the pain, but you need to make sure—"

"I will, Frank, but Roger Kingston isn't an easy man to see and from what I hear, he holds a grudge if you disappoint. I'll go to the hospital later. Promise."

"What are you hoping to get from Kingston?"

I shrug. "A reason why Diego hated Adamsky would be good. Was he obsessed? Jealous? Is there a woman involved? Is that why he topped himself in such dramatic fashion—or why someone helped speed his demise along? Also, why does Kingston want the blood painting so badly that he had his rep arrive at the apartment before the body was even cold? And how did he know about it so soon, especially if Casper was no longer legally representing Diego's work?"

"And you don't think it's dangerous?"

"Dangerous?"

"You've been attacked twice, Dix. Once while you were with a gallery owner who's in Kingston's pocket and then—"

I interrupt. "How many headlights does a Chevelle have?"

"Depends on the year. Why?"

"Say an early to mid-70s model."

Frank scratches his head. "A lot of the old Chevys sported four. Again. Why?"

"You got me thinking about the alley in Chinatown. The car had four headlights."

"And your flying attacker—"

"Landed on the roof of an old Chevy," I finish.

"That's what I'm saying. You've obviously pissed someone off, and I don't think—"

"Where is it?" I interrupt again.

Frank rolls his eyes. "Where's what?"

"That's what my attacker said: 'Where is it?' I wonder if he meant Diego's painting. The one I had with me last night."

"You said you dropped it."

"Yeah, I tripped over King William in the lobby when I came in."

"Hold on, I'll go look."

With Frank gone, I turn to the computer and check my e-mail. Aside from a few medical advisories on how to lengthen my penis so I won't be embarrassed in the locker room ever again, there are two e-mails from Stoogan. I don't need to read them to know what he wants, since the headers give away his intent: "Where's my story, Dix?" and "Cover or not? Need to know ASAP."

I fire back a quick reply: "Will know more today. Interviewing Kingston. Few loose ends."

Loose ends? When I boil down what little information I have, I'll be lucky to pull together a short obit, never mind the cover feature. Of course, that's where **Dixie's Tips #12** comes in: *Never let them see you sweat—even if you're wearing wool underwear in a sauna.*

Frank returns with the painting.

"It was under the stairs," he says. "Where do you want it?"

I think about it. "How about your place? I was planning to give it to Diego's family when they show up, or to his agent at the Gimcrack to sell for them."

"And in case this is what the break-in was about…"

I'm stone-faced. "I would rather it be with someone who sleeps with a gun and isn't afraid to use it."

"Ah, so if I'm attacked?"

"Aim for his balls, then the kneecaps, and if that doesn't stop the bastard, two to the head."

"A bullet to the balls usually gets their attention," says Frank.

"True, but I wouldn't take any chances with this one."

———

"Anything happens or you just don't feel safe, you'll call, right?" says Frank.

"Don't I always?"

"Yeah, but I don't want you thinking you're taking advantage and should maybe let it slide this time. I would rather be pissed at you for calling than pissed at you for dying."

"Sweet."

Frank's mouth twitches. "I'll look into that car. Dented roof and four headlights, right?"

I nod. "And if there's a dead creep on the roof, chances are good it's the right one."

TWENTY-SIX

SAM OPENS THE APARTMENT door and invites me inside. She looks older: pale and creased, nail marks cutting into her stubbled scalp. Her normally bright eyes are lost beneath swollen lids. A night of tears has left hollow cheeks stained with salty tracks.

"How is she?" I ask.

"Still sleeping." Her voice is unusually weak. "Ruth said she'd wake up sometime this morning. She'll be hungry, thirsty, and in desperate need of the toilet. Apart from that, Ruth says she'll be fine. She took a blood sample to run some tests."

"You should get some rest too."

"I'm OK, just worried and a little scared." She tries to smile, but her eyes fill with tears. She clenches her teeth, angry with herself. "We had a fight. At the club. When she wasn't here when I got home, I didn't know what ... then I heard screaming at your ..." She sighs heavily. "I don't want to cry anymore."

I step closer, wrap my arms around her, and hug tight. Although stiff at first, Sam slowly relaxes until she melts into me, her face buried in my shoulder.

"I'm so sorry, Sam," I say. "You'll never know how sorry."

Her body trembles as more tears flow. But like the fighter she is, her strength soon returns. She loosens her grip to wipe her eyes with a tightly bundled tissue.

"I don't blame you, Dix," she says quietly. "I'm just thankful it wasn't worse."

Sam reaches down and lifts my bandaged hand.

"When I saw that knife sticking through your hand ... I just ... rushed him, I guess."

"Good thing too. I was out of options."

"I don't believe that," Sam says. "You even cracked a joke."

I smile. "Too many John Wayne movies with my dad."

Sam's eyes lock on mine, her eyebrows knitting into a serious black line, while her piercings accent the storm within. "What did he want?"

"Not sure. He may have been after a painting."

"A painting?"

"One of the final ones by the dead artist I'm writing about. I found it at his studio and brought it home for safekeeping. Bad decision, I guess."

"How did he know you had it?"

The question gives me pause; the answer uncomfortable.

"Only one person saw me at his studio."

"That narrows the list."

"Considerably."

"Is it valuable?"

I nod. "Diego's new collection hasn't been selling, but his death will change that. This last painting is different. It's more unique in that he took another, more successful artist's work and tore it to shreds to create a new piece. That gives it controversy."

"And controversy sells," Sam interjects dryly.

"Every time."

"So this is about money?"

I shrug. "It usually is."

Sam clenches her teeth. "Fucker deserved to die."

"I agree, but"—I hesitate again—"it doesn't look like he did."

"What?"

"The body is gone. So is the car he landed on."

"But that's a—"

"Two-story fall, I know. Frank wondered if I was hallucinating."

"*I* wasn't."

"No. He was real."

Silence falls between us and I callously begin to worry about time.

"Can I see her?" I ask.

Sam leads me to the bedroom. Kristy is curled in a ball on the queen-size bed, her breathing calm and regular. Her face has been washed and her slinky dress replaced with comfortable pajamas. Sam and I smile like proud parents looking in on their young before closing the door and walking back to the front room.

Awkwardly, I clear my throat and try to find the best words to fit my upcoming request.

"I can read you like a book," Sam says, a touch of brightness returning to her eyes. "What do you need?"

I feel like a heel. "I was going to ask Kristy before all this trouble, but now I ..."

"Just spit it out."

"I need to borrow the Bug."

I look down at my feet in embarrassment, but when I look back up, Sam simply hands me the keys.

"Just don't smash it," she warns. "Or Kristy will kill us both."

TWENTY-SEVEN

THE DRIVE TO NAPA Valley is hot and sticky, but with the top down on Kristy's classic '79 VW Bug and my face buried beneath an industrial layer of makeup to disguise just how badly beat-up I look, I don't care.

I even found a pair of sunglasses stuffed in the glove box to prevent the sun from blinding me as it glares off the buffed electric-yellow hood. The only downside is the glasses are a vibrant shade of butterfly pink with tiny red hearts on each corner. If I meet any studly porn-star hitchhikers along the way, my cool is blown.

Leaving the city behind, I pop a Barenaked Ladies CD into the six-speaker deck, press down on the gas, and try to relax. The warmth of the morning combines with the Percs to soothe my aching muscles as I exit Highway 29 and turn onto the lazy, winding roads of wine country.

The sweet mossy scent of wildflowers and oxygen-rich foliage fills me with a sudden desire to pull over for a lazy picnic of liver paté, crusty sourdough bread, and a bottle of chilled Chardonnay. I could lie back in the grass and let the birds chirp my troubles away.

As it is, I keep driving, the words of "It's All Been Done" strumming in my ear.

Sir Roger Kingston lives in the mouth of the valley on a winery that *Forbes* claims rivals both Robert Mondavi and the Christian Brothers. Unlike those two, however, Kingston doesn't allow tourists the opportunity of a fruitful mid-afternoon tour. Instead, he is known to invite only the golden parachute crowd of business elite and political dignitaries—among them four former presidents—for weekend excursions.

The tastiest rumor I heard about those weekends is that Kingston ships in wild boar and leads his own hunting expeditions in a fenced-off game reserve.

Apart from rumors, little is known about the man's private life. He pops up at charity events throughout the city, donating money, shaking hands, and slapping the mayor on the back, but once he steps off the stage, the media is *persona non grata*. Try and take his picture or ask a question unrelated to the event and his handlers shut you down faster than a jogger with the runs.

Personally, that's never bothered me as much as it does the mainstream press. Everybody has the right to not talk to the media, so long as you don't bitch about how that makes you look when reporters have to get their information from other sources.

After two hours of self-absorbed, wind-in-my-hair bliss, I come to an electronic gate guarding a private road that I recognize from an Annie Leibovitz photo shoot for American Express. Made from crushed mother of pearl shell and imported New Zealand sand, the glistening white road is rumored to need constant maintenance and grooming at a cost of $50,000 per year.

A camera on top of the ornate steel gate focuses its glass eye on me. I take off the sunglasses and smile demurely, since I don't want to crack the false face I've painted on. Though if I was the guard, there's no way I'd allow a sorry-looking wretch like me inside.

The gate opens silently and I feel a bit like Dorothy's anal-retentive cousin. Instead of the swirling, curling yellow-brick road, I drive down a path so straight and white it could have been designed by a dentist. On each side of the bleached road stretches row upon row of such perfectly uniform vines that I am a little surprised the grapes don't wear blaze orange jumpsuits with serial numbers stenciled on the back.

As the Bug's near-bald tires crunch along, the vineyards give way to acres of lush green lawn and I catch my first glimpse of Kingston's summer home. The building is no ordinary mansion—it's a genuine castle.

Piecing together the details from newspaper files, the story goes that a once-powerful aristocratic landowner in Britain—cousin to Queen Elizabeth II, twenty-second in line for the throne, and (if a certain NYT-bestselling mystery writer is to be believed) a possible direct descendant of Jack the Ripper—fell on hard times. Kingston supposedly offered a price for the supremely British castle that couldn't be turned down. Coincidentally, that was also the year that English-born Kingston was knighted for his charitable contributions to preserving British heritage.

With his knighthood secured, Kingston returned to America and brought the castle with him, shipped brick by brick across the Atlantic.

In the New World, however, he must have felt the medieval architecture was a touch on the drab side. To brighten it, he had every ancient stone sandblasted smooth and dusted in a spray of white sand and crushed seashell until it sparkled like something born in the cryogenic depths of Walt Disney's imagination. All sense of history was erased in one smooth stroke, leaving nothing in its path but a garish monstrosity.

The driveway ends in a large parking area in front of a crystalline moat. The moat is spanned by an ancient drawbridge that appears, from the well-oiled links of chain attached to each corner, to still function.

I park and walk to the drawbridge. I take my time to give my throbbing muscles time to warm and stretch. The moat looks inviting. Instead of sharks, alligators, or sharpened metal spikes beneath the surface, it's filled with huge carp the color of tropical fruit. Of course, there's no guarantee that Kingston hasn't trained the giant goldfish to eat human flesh. I move on, not wanting Bubbles to be jealous that I am admiring other fish.

Once across the drawbridge, I stand before two huge slabs of oak, twenty feet tall and studded with brass and iron. A pizza-sized knocker in the shape of a lion's head yawns at me. Warily, I lift the heavy iron bar clutched in the lion's mouth and release it. It hits the door with a heavy thud rather than the roar I am hoping for.

Somewhere within the hallowed halls, a gentle chime echoes.

The massive doors slide open on greased tracks with the gentle purr of a hidden generator. Waiting inside, a tall, regal gentleman stands stiffly. He is just as I imagined on the phone: impregnable British face; milk-white complexion; short, perfectly trimmed black hair; neatly pressed charcoal tuxedo. A poster child for the vanishing craft of butlery.

"Oliver, how are you?" I boom enthusiastically.

"I am afraid that I am not Oliver, Miss Flynn," he says without emotion.

"But I talked to you yesterday."

"That would have been my brother. My name is Oxford."

"As in the dictionary?"

"Quite."

I whistle. "Two butlers. Impressive."

"No, miss. I am the lone butler. Oliver is Sir Roger's gentleman's gentleman and private secretary."

"Ahh," I say, as though I understand the difference.

Walking into the bright and spacious cobblestoned courtyard, I glance skyward. A glass roof, anchored at each of the four turrets, offers the impression that I am still outside, but without the worry of having to suffer nature's mood swings. Again, every stone is drained of its original texture and color. Even the hand-carved water fountain in the center of the courtyard, where the lord's men once watered their horses after battle, hasn't escaped the painter's brush.

I wonder what it must have been like centuries ago when all the inhabitants of the castle, soldier and servant alike, gathered around the fountain to wash clothes and exchange the gossip of the day.

The thought opens my eyes as to why Kingston wanted a castle of his own. It's the dream of every six-year-old who ever read about King Arthur and the Knights of the Round Table.

"This way, miss," Oxford says, indicating a fortified door to the right of the fountain.

I follow, running my hand along the wall in the faint hope I might feel a long-dead pulse.

Behind the door, Kingston stops pretending it's a castle. Luxury assails at every turn. Indian carpets, Italian tile, every door a hand-carved masterpiece. Most of all, I notice the art.

Paintings and sculpture fill every crevice. My lower jaw un-hinges as I pass paintings by famous impressionists hanging along-side modern abstracts.

"In here, miss." Oxford indicates a carved set of double doors that are made to resemble a giant book.

I head in that direction, but just before entering I notice a tiny black chalk sketch that appears to be a self-portrait of Leonardo da Vinci. It sits on the mantel of an unused fireplace in a tiny study off the hall, like an old family photograph you've forgotten to put away.

"Is that genuine?" My voice is a whisper.

"I believe it is, miss."

"Wow. Can I take a closer look?"

"Certainly. I shall await your return."

Up close, the sketch is even more magnificent, but not just in an artistic sense. To actually own something by such an historic visionary is so far beyond my comprehension that I have a hard time absorbing it. And it's just sitting there, like an afterthought.

I shake my head in both disbelief and a touch of disgust at the dark side of a society that celebrates such greed. I return to Oxford in front of what I assume must be the library.

"If you would care to wait inside, Sir Roger will be with you shortly." The butler pauses and his tone becomes less stuffy. "Forgive my asking, miss, but do you need anything for your hand?"

I lift my bandaged left hand to see the palm is stained with blood as though in stigmata.

"I'll be fine," I say. "Driving must have loosened a few stitches. The Bug's a standard, so I needed both hands."

Oxford's face does a little dance between perplexed and confused before he decides to simply nod.

"Please make yourself comfortable." He closes the door and leaves me alone.

———

The room is the size of a dance hall, surrounded on all sides by floor-to-ceiling bookshelves. The colored spines of the books create a wonderful abstract that reminds me of pixel art, elongated rectangles taking the place of perfect squares. Yet aside from the books, the rest of the room is practically bare.

An ice-white marble fireplace dominates the center of the outside wall. Its hearth is large enough to roast a whole pig or a belligerent servant. In front of it, arranged on a thick Persian rug, the only furniture is two white armchairs and an ice bucket on a silver stand. Near the chairs, I spy the brass legs of a large easel; the rest of it, including the painting it must be holding, is hidden beneath a spotlessly white sheet. It appears my host has a flair for the dramatic.

Intrigued, I walk to the easel but am stopped by the contents of the ice bucket. Inside are four bottles of beer. Two are an imported Australian brand I have never heard of, but the other two are Warthog Ale.

How in hell does he know my favorite beer?

"Help yourself, Dixie," says a warm, deep voice. "You've had a long drive."

I turn to see a handsome, lantern-jawed man with a battery-cable spark in his ocean-blue eyes. The eyes are set deep in an un-lined, tanned face and crowned by soft blond eyebrows that are too perfectly shaped not to have been waxed.

Looking much younger up close than from across a crowded room, Kingston is wearing a white explorer's outfit: fitted shorts cut high on the thigh to show off muscular legs, short-sleeved shirt cutting tight on toned biceps, white socks, and hiking boots. He also carries a handgun in a canvas holster strapped to his waist. All he needs is a pith helmet and I would have replied, "Dr. Kingston, I presume."

I pluck a bottle of Warthog from the bucket. "Thanks," I say. "Don't mind if I do."

Oxford had the foresight to supply a silver bottle opener; unfortunately, with the fingers of my left hand immobilized, it doesn't do me much good.

"Would you mind?" I hold out the bottle.

Kingston strides forward in a masculine gait and obliges.

He gestures to the chairs. "Please, sit down."

As I sit, Kingston grabs one of the Australian beers from the bucket and twists off its cap. He takes a long swallow.

"Ahhhh," he sighs. "There's nothing like Aussie brew."

"I thought you were English," I say.

"I was born there," he says matter-of-factly. "But I prefer to split my time between Oz and the States. More *simpatico*."

"In what way?" I ask.

"Every way that counts."

It's a dead-end answer. I either have to back up and try another route or let it go.

"You're younger than I expected," I say, trying a new approach.

Kingston grins. "Wealth doesn't come with age, Dixie. It takes brains and balls."

"Unless you inherit it," I argue.

His eyes narrow. "Inheritance is for the weak."

"You never got any?"

"The only thing my old man gave me was a cuff on the ear and a thirst for beer. The rest, I earned."

"Or stole," I say, before quickly adding, "according to some reports."

Kingston's face hardens, but only for a second. "It's rare nowadays to find an opponent who isn't afraid to speak her mind."

"I didn't know we were competing."

"Always. In this game, everyone you meet wants what you have. Some are carrion and some are hawks. Remember that."

We both finish our beers at the same time.

"Another?" He makes it sound like a challenge.

With the Percs running through my blood stream, I really shouldn't. I drop my empty into the bucket. "Sure."

Kingston uses the opener on a Warthog for me before twisting the top off his Aussie brew. Oddly, he never bothers asking about my bandage.

"So what's under the sheet?" I ask, guessing it's probably Adamsky's latest masterpiece with which he hopes to impress.

"My latest acquisition. Would you like a peek?"

"Sure."

"First, I have to tell you its pedigree."

With dramatic flair, Kingston rises to his feet and stands beside the draped canvas. His voice is smooth and melodious—the gift of a natural showman, politician, or con artist.

He begins. "This artist was a man who painted from his very soul. A tortured being who believed every canvas he filled contained a piece of himself. But, as is the way of the world, he was forced to sell each piece in order to buy food, shelter, more paint, and canvas. With a stroke of luck, the artist soon became noticed and then became wealthy, but still he continued to pour his heart into his paintings. Each new piece commanded a price twice that of the one previous."

He takes a breath, the sound of his own voice and the story he's inventing pleasing him. He continues.

"One day, the artist woke to find his heart was empty and his soul had become so frail it was barely a wisp of air. Desperate to regain both, the artist ventured into the world in search of his peddled art. He believed that by reclaiming his old paintings, he could also rebuild his heart and reclaim his joy. But every time he found a painting, its new owners refused to sell such a wise investment and slammed the door. The artist was lost. How could he go on in the world without the happiness he once felt? Then, a final bolt of inspiration struck. If he couldn't recover his lost art, he could join it."

My skin turns cold and every hair stands on end. I know what hides under the sheet.

"The result," Kingston says, his voice rising with excitement, "is this."

The sheet is pulled back and Diego's blood painting screams at me.

Even in the bright expanse of the room, I feel its darkness throbbing on the canvas.

"It's one of a kind," Kingston brags. "Art and artist merged together on canvas. You can actually see pieces of bone and brain matter."

I want to speak, but my mouth refuses to work.

"Are you hungry?" Kingston downs the rest of his beer. "I feel like steak."

Numbly, I follow Kingston out of the room and up a narrow staircase to the peak of one of the castle's four turrets. A cozy, circular room offers a spectacular view of the valley. Oddly, there is no glass in the narrow, rectangular windows and the soft breeze is cool on my skin.

In the center of the room awaits a small table with just enough room for two. It is set with china plates, white linen cloth, silver cutlery, and crystal wine glasses. It makes me wonder if I am being seduced.

Crossing to one of the open windows, I gulp in a lungful of air with the hope of disguising how shaken the unveiling has left me. The vineyards below stretch for miles, their stringy trunks looking like fortified fields of barbed-wire fence. It reminds me of *Sleeping Beauty,* where the creeping vines and dagger-sharp thorns closed in around the castle to hide the spellbound princess until she was all but forgotten.

Oxford enters the room, carrying a bottle of wine on a silver tray. When he looks at me, no emotion escapes his face. With a false calm, I follow him to the table and take my place.

"How do you like your steak?" Kingston asks, watching eagerly as Oxford pours a thimbleful of wine into his glass.

"Medium rare is fine."

Kingston swirls the wine around in his glass, watching for impurities as it catches the light. He inhales its bouquet, dumps it into his mouth, and does everything except gargle.

"Excellent."

Oxford nods appreciatively and fills both our glasses before placing the bottle in a new silver ice bucket. He retreats out the door, only to return a minute later with a chilled pewter platter heaped with large pink prawns, beheaded but still in their shells.

After setting the prawns in the middle of the table, Oxford produces two bowls of cocktail sauce and two of spicy peanut. He places one of each in front of our plates.

"Hope you like shrimp."

"Will there be anything more, sir?" Oxford asks.

"Yeah," Kingston barks. "Stand someplace where I don't have to look at you."

"Certainly, sir." Oxford moves to the wall directly behind his employer and stands as stiff and silent as a statue.

Kingston winks at me; I am rather pleased that I don't shudder.

"Dig in," he commands and grabs a prawn by the tail to noisily suck the meat from its shell.

I fill my plate, suddenly realizing how hungry I am.

"Do you like caviar?" Kingston asks between bites.

"I haven't—"

"I despise the stuff," he interrupts. "It's the only thing the Commies have worth exporting, and they've tricked the West into thinking it's something great. Well, I say screw 'em. If I want to eat fish eggs, I'll squeeze 'em out of an American trout."

The thought makes me feel sick.

"I wanted to ask about Adamsky," I say to get the conversation on track.

"Ask away." Kingston brushes spent shrimp shells off his shirt.

"First, where did you get Diego's blood painting?"

"I bought it."

"From his agent?"

"No, his family."

"They're in town?"

"Doubt it. I had a representative in New Mexico make the deal there."

"You don't waste time."

"Never do."

"How much did you pay?"

"None of your damn business."

"What are you going to do with it?"

"Ah!" Kingston's face lights up. "Do you know much about computers?"

And I've blown it. Once your subject starts asking the questions, the only thing to do is ride the wave for a while until you can get back on track.

"Computers connect everything," he says with enthusiasm. "Fridges talking to clocks talking to stores talking to schools talking to banks. Everything. And the money to be made is damn near criminal. The trick is to corner a market and squeeze everyone else out of your way. Look at those two bozos that set up a video site, got the users to upload their own content, and then sold the damn thing—plus all the copyright headaches—to Google for millions. And do you know why it succeeded?"

I shake my head.

"Because America is a dangerous place. Who wants to get carjacked on the drive to work? Who wants to send their daughter out at night to rent a video? The streets are filled with rapists, druggies, and murderers. So why go out when you can get everything you need delivered at home? We're becoming a nation of hermits, imprisoned within the walls of our own homes."

His teeth tear the shrimp apart like a lawnmower blade across grass.

He continues, "The future means the closing of libraries, art galleries, museums. But people still need to feel civilized, right? They need to know they're part of a larger community, one with history and beauty. Cyberspace, virtual reality, *those* are the galleries of the future."

I interrupt. "But what does this have to do with Diego?"

Kingston glares at me. "Everything," he hisses. "I'm going to bring the galleries and libraries into your home. I'm going to supply the culture America craves. Imagine sitting in your favorite chair and being transported to the greatest museums in the world. And I'm not talking about interactive DVD on a forty-two-inch screen. I'm talking *virtual reality*. You'll actually walk along the corridors, smell the musty air, and virtually stroke every painting. And you know what that means?"

I shake my head again.

"Copyright. Just like YouTube and iTunes and all the rest. Whoever owns the art gets a piece of every dollar. That's where

Chino and other artists like him come in. Before long, people will be bored with plain old museum tours. They'll crave more.

"Imagine now, instead of clicking on the TV, you slip on a VR headset and you're transported to an artist's studio. You watch him paint, you listen to his story, you feel his pain. Now you watch as he stands in front of a raw canvas and puts a shotgun in his mouth."

"Jesus!" I feel sick.

Kingston laughs. "Don't be squeamish, girl. You've already seen the blood; your curiosity is quenched. Let everyone else have a go."

"It sounds like the worst of tabloid TV to me," I say.

"That's because your imagination is limited. You have to think beyond today. Once people know the story of an artist, they'll want his art. Imagine another scenario where a painting in your own home could be of anything you wanted. Just hang a paper-thin digital frame on your wall and with the touch of a finger it's Van Gogh's 'Sunflowers.' Bored with Van Gogh? Touch it again and it's Chino's blood painting. Don't want horizontal? Hang it vertically and touch it once more. Mona Lisa smiles at you, six times larger than life, if you want."

I've heard enough.

"What about Adamsky?" I ask. "When Diego's body was found, he had an Adamsky under his bed. Do you know anything about it?"

Kingston looks annoyed that I've changed the subject, but he answers. "Sure, it was mine."

I pause. "He stole it from you?"

"Yes."

"When?"

"When he worked for me."

"When did he work for you?"

Kingston mindlessly plucks the legs off a headless shrimp one by one before peeling back the carapace and shoving the rubbery meat into his mouth.

I try again. "Where did he work?"

"A warehouse I own on the docks."

"Doing what?"

"How the hell should I know? I don't have time to keep track of all the people who work for me. He probably unloaded crates or something."

"Why would he steal an Adamsky?"

"Money."

"It would be difficult to sell."

Kingston shrugs. "Not if you already have a buyer."

"Did he have a buyer?"

"How should I know? But *I* wouldn't steal a painting unless I did."

"Why didn't you report it?"

"What?" He frowns, warning me off the question.

"The police didn't know it was stolen until after they took possession," I press. "Why didn't you report it?"

Kingston pushes away from the table and walks to the window. He stands with his back to me, not bothering to hide his impatience.

"I can't keep track of everything," he says. "I own a lot of paintings."

"When did you notice it missing?"

"I didn't. A friend called."

"Chief McInty?" A guess.

"I don't recall."

"Do you know the police chief?"

"I know everyone who is important to know."

"Where was the painting stolen from?"

A blue vein pulses in his neck. "The warehouse probably."

"Probably?"

Kingston spins, his face flushed. "Look," he huffs. "I invite you into my home, break bread and share wine, and all you can do is fire unintelligent questions like a … a … dung beetle."

"I explained on the phone why I wanted to meet."

"Yes, to ask about Adamsky. As his agent, one of my duties is to meet with the press no matter how lowly. But all you've done is blab on about Chino, some second-rate artist—"

"Whose final painting you rushed out to buy and unveil to me," I interrupt. "They're connected."

He snorts. "How? Chino was a thief; Adamsky is an artist. Where's your connection?"

"Diego didn't need to steal."

"Oh. Friend of yours, was he? Lover, perhaps?"

I stumble, caught off guard by the change of direction. "He—"

"Let me tell you something before I have you thrown out," Kingston snaps. "Chino was a good-for-nothing, backwater Indian with a history of trouble, but I gave him a job that paid his rent and afforded him time to work on his art after his fifteen minutes were up. He rewarded my generosity by stealing from me. The man was worth nothing, but thanks to his dramatic exit, at least his death should be profitable. I like to profit."

"You're all heart," I say.

"Get out now, Miss Flynn, while you still can."

"I still have questions."

"You should have thought of that earlier." Kingston's voice has returned to an icy calm. It worries me more than his rage.

TWENTY-EIGHT

BACK IN THE BUG, I slam my good hand against the steering wheel and curse. I did that all wrong. Kingston is obviously a chauvinist who likes his women meek and accommodating. I should have used my feminine wiles to flirt with the jerk instead of coming across like… well, like myself. Some bats of the eyelashes and a padded push-up bra and I might even have lasted long enough to try the steak I ordered.

Then again, I wasn't naive enough to believe he hadn't planned the whole damn thing—especially the unveiling of the painting.

That was a nice touch.

To calm myself, I take a deep breath, hold it until my bruises ache, and release it slowly through my nose. It doesn't work, so I put the car in gear, stuff the Police's reunion tour CD into the deck, and try to burn a little rubber on the annoyingly pristine white road.

The Bug squeaks more than roars, and instead of rubber we may have left a dribble of oil, but what the hell. It's the thought that counts.

Two hours later, I'm crossing the bridge back to the city and singing "Every Little Thing She Does Is Magic" for the fourth time at the top of my lungs. I'm feeling relaxed and hungry. I only managed to eat a couple of prawns at Kingston's, and I hadn't been smart enough to grab a handful before I left. The thought of take-out from Pegasus brings a grin to my face.

I press down on the accelerator, but no sooner does the Bug begin to respond when flashing red and blue lights fill my rearview mirror.

With a resigned groan, I finish crossing the bridge and pull off to the side of the road. The cruiser pulls in behind with two blank-faced officers, eyes hidden behind mirrored sunglasses.

Using the rearview mirror, I watch as the driver radios in my license plate. I take the opportunity to slip Lily, my pearl-handled switchblade, out of my boot. Just in case I end up being searched, I toss it under the seat. Cops tend to have a bad reaction to concealed weapons.

After a minute, the driver nods to his partner and steps out. To my surprise, he's drawn his handgun. Just as that gun is registering, I am doubly shocked to see his partner pull the shotgun from its cradle between the front seats and crouch behind his open door. He aims the shotgun directly at the back of my don't-give-a-damn haircut, which instantly makes me give a damn.

"Is there a problem, officer?" I call nervously, being careful not to move.

"Keep your hands on the steering wheel," the driver shouts back.

"No problem."

I stay perfectly still until I feel the hard muzzle of a Glock automatic pressing into my left ear. Swallowing the lump in my throat, I steal a glance toward the passenger door to see the other officer approaching, his shotgun still aimed at my head. From this distance, and without a roof or rear window to deflect any of the shot, he can rip me in half.

"Search the trunk, Cort," the driver says.

His partner moves to the rear of the Bug.

"That's not—" I try, but am silenced as the gun's muzzle digs deeper into my ear.

"What you got?" the driver calls.

"Uh, nothing, Harley," Cort replies. "Looks like the engine's back here."

"That's what—"

Harley hisses menacingly. "Best you shut it."

Good advice.

Cort moves to the front and opens the hood.

"It's here," Cort calls out as he removes a brown paper bag from the Bug's interior.

"Care to explain?" Harley asks.

"What's to explain?" I ask. "You found somebody's old lunch bag?"

"Show her."

Cort reaches into the bag and pulls out a small black chalk sketch in a hermetically sealed glass frame. I have recently seen one exactly like it on the mantel of an unused fireplace in Sir Roger Kingston's whitewashed castle.

"Well, well." Harley pushes the gun deeper into my aching ear. "I suppose you have a receipt for that?"

Fuck.

"Honestly, I don't know how it got there."

Harley laughs. "You wouldn't believe how often we hear that line."

"It's the truth."

"That one too."

TWENTY-NINE

As we pull up outside Northern Station, I notice the painter is busy again with his bucket of gray, repairing another midnight graffiti attack. The symbol of choice seems to be Nazi swastikas, but whether that is a comment on the occupants or the taggers, I can't speculate.

I wait in the back of the cruiser, my hands cuffed in front since I'm too girly for the big men in uniform to be overly concerned for their safety, and wonder what Kingston is playing at.

Harley and Cort have been no help at all. I told them I was hungry and would treat them to drive-thru burgers, but either they'd already eaten or just didn't care to share a meal with me.

The rear door is finally opened. I'm pulled out by my elbows and escorted inside the station to stand before the bored countenance of Sergeant Woods. Harley and Cort stand on either side of me like bird dogs waiting to have their ears scratched.

"He owes me ten dollars," I inform my escorts.

"Put her in a cell," Woods barks, barely glancing up from his computer.

"Don't I get a phone call?" I protest as my arresting officers drag me toward the elevator.

"Didn't you have one already?" Harley asks.

"How could I—"

"Yeah, I'm sure she did," pipes up Cort.

"Listen—"

"Cheeky bitch called a 900 number," Harley adds.

"Yeah," Cort sniggers, "it was a lesbo sex line too."

I decide to shut up. Eventually, they'll have to give me access to a lawyer, I hope. Although ever since former President George Bush Jr. broke out the Patriot Act, you can't rely on a lot of things you think you know from TV anymore, no matter your race, religion, or sex.

The main holding cells are in the basement. Most are empty, but a few are filled with the regulars. One cell holds the drunks, the stink of urine wafting in a haze around their soiled bunks. Another cell holds two men waiting for transport to either jail or court, the surly looks on their faces making it difficult to tell which. At the end of the row, three cells are reserved for the sex workers. One for boys, one for women, and one for those the cops aren't too sure about.

Harley and Cort drag me to the end of the row.

"Which cell you want?" Harley asks. "Whores, fags, or freaks?"

"Any place is better than out here with you."

"Open three."

Cort unlocks the cell where a group of three transvestites stare at me with bored expressions through a blue haze of cigarette smoke.

Harley removes the cuffs and shoves me through the door. When the cell is locked behind me, Harley leans close to the bars.

"You should ask these fellas if they like art," he says with a laugh. "Give you something to chat about while you rot."

I raise the middle finger of my good hand and turn away before he can see the false bravado fade from my eyes.

———

"They do that to your hand, sweetie?" asks a muscular black man who introduces himself as Dorothy.

"Trouble earlier," I explain.

Unlike the other two, Dorothy doesn't appear to identify as a woman. The sprinkle of coarse dander on his chiseled chest says he isn't on hormone pills, his close-cropped scalp is cut to a smooth carpet, and the Kama Sutra–inspired tattoos on his impressive biceps are enough to make a longshoreman blush.

The only giveaway of his feminine side is the purple dress with matching shoes and a pair of shaved, silky smooth legs to show them off.

"Wouldn't have surprised me," Dorothy says. "They smashed my hand in a desk drawer once. Broke four nails. They was natural too. Had to switch to fake after that."

He shows me his long nails, painted to match his dress, but with white French tips. Both thumbs have the added touch of tiny Swarovski crystals in the shape of a flower.

"You a regular, then?" I ask with a smile.

Dorothy grins back. "Used to be more often before the chief took a fancy. Now they mostly leave me alone unless Chiefy wants a little play time."

"Chief McInty?" I ask.

All three women nod.

"You see that desk he has?" Dorothy asks.

"On the raised platform."

"Uh-huh. Well, he likes me to climb on top and—"

I hold up my hand. "I don't need the details."

Dorothy laughs. "Life is *in* the details, honey."

"Then maybe we can arrange to get some photos one day," I say. "Give you a little leverage."

"And you a hell of a story," Dorothy says smugly.

I'm surprised. "You know who I am?"

"Hell, Ms. Dixie Flynn of the San Francisco *NOW*." Dorothy flashes a beautiful set of white teeth. "I'm your biggest fan."

———

When Frank arrives, I'm hunkered on a steel-frame bunk, listening intently to my three companions share their life stories and the daily struggle they still face. I thought growing up as a woman was tough, but it's nothing compared to growing up knowing you're a woman and yet trapped in a man's body.

"You play nice?" Frank asks gruffly as he steps up to the bars.

"It's been refreshing," I say, crossing to meet him. "I don't think I'll take the simple fact of sitting down to pee for granted anymore."

My cellmates smile at that.

"You don't look great," Frank says. "Show me your hand."

I hold up my hand. The bandages are completely soaked through with blood.

"I've made you an appointment at the hospital," Frank continues. "No arguments."

"Ooh, la, la," Dorothy mocks from the bunk. "Who's your gorgeous sugar daddy, honey?"

I grin.

Frank doesn't.

A uniformed officer arrives and unlocks the cage.

Frank takes my arm.

"Let's get out of here," he says.

I oblige.

―――――

The walk to freedom is a short one. Chief Caleb McInty stops us at the top of the stairs with hands on hips and a meaty face flushed with anger.

"What are you doing with that prisoner, sergeant?" McInty bellows.

"She made bail, sir," Frank replies in a calm and courteous voice. "I'm making sure she doesn't cause more trouble on the way out."

"You have no authority at this station, sergeant."

I notice that McInty likes to emphasize Frank's rank, while dismissing the detective side of things.

"I'm not on the clock, sir."

A sharp-faced Asian gentleman in a $2,000 silk suit walks up behind McInty and flashes Frank and me a brilliant Tom Cruise smile.

"Detective Sergeant Fury is looking out for your department's best interests, Chief," the man says.

McInty turns and his face instantly loses some of its angry hue. "What do you mean, Mr. Yee?" he asks.

I glance at Frank, confused.

"That's your lawyer, kid," Frank whispers. "Quinlan Yee. He's won more lawsuits against corporations and police departments than anyone in the state. His opponents call him the Sunset Kid: When he shows up, your days in the sun are over."

Yee smiles graciously and hands McInty a neatly typed affidavit.

As McInty reads it, the blood drains from his face.

"As you can see," Yee says calmly, "your department refuses to divulge the identity of its source in this matter, which means your officers had no right to pull over my client, nor to search her vehicle."

McInty flushes. "What about the stolen painting?"

Yee smiles again. "My client claims the painting was planted by one of your officers. And due to the brutality of her arrest, which will require her to be immediately rushed to a waiting surgeon, not to mention the denial of her right to contact a lawyer, it would be in your best interest to make sure all charges are dropped posthaste. If you choose to persist, the lawsuit my client is prepared to file, along with the corresponding media coverage, will result in a public outcry for the resignation of whomever was responsible for allowing such an abuse of authority to take place."

"Are you threatening me, Mr. Yee?" The tops of McInty's ears blaze red.

"Of course not," Yee replies, the smile still on his face. "My client is."

I look at Frank, dumbfounded.

He whispers, "Woods called after you were brought in to say he's keeping your ten spot. He intimated I should bring Yee along for company."

Son of a bitch. I misjudged the desk sergeant.

The lawyer and the chief face each other in silence until McInty finally puffs out his cheeks and walks away.

Yee looks over and winks. "What are you waiting for? Go to the hospital and then get some rest."

"That's it?" I ask, still having a difficult time believing my change of luck. "They'll drop the charges?"

Yee nods.

"You're good," I say.

Yee grins wider and hands me a card. "Tell your friends," he says. "I love pissing off McInty."

"In that case," I say slyly, "you should talk to my new friend Dorothy in the holding cells. She has an interesting story to tell."

THIRTY

FRANK PULLS INTO A McDonald's drive-thru, buys a Big Mac value meal, and watches in wonder as I greedily wolf it down. The hospital surgeon used a local anesthetic, so I was kicked to the curb immediately after he re-stitched and re-bandaged my hand.

The funky digital scans didn't show any nerve damage and the surgeon praised Ruth's tight, neat stitching—which I obviously didn't appreciate since I ripped half of them out. I told him I would be sure to pass along the compliment since Ruth's usual clients were very close-mouthed and a bit stiff about showing their appreciation.

The surgeon was cute, which made me think of Declan, but when he didn't laugh at my joke and wrote a prescription for Tylenol 3s rather than Percocet, he dropped to one-night-only status. If Declan doesn't call soon, he is quickly heading in the same direction.

When Frank parks, it's on a quiet street in front of a picturesque turn-of-the-century house, painted lemon yellow with white and lilac accents. A stone pathway leads from the front gate to wind between flowerbeds before reaching a roomy front porch.

"Is this your house?" I ask.

Frank nods and walks around to my side of the car to help me climb out. We follow the path onto the porch.

"I never pictured your place like this."

It's strange; in all the time I've known him, Frank never once invited me here.

"Where did you think I lived? An army cot in the file room at the station?"

"Yeah, that sounds more your style."

Frank's mouth twitches. "It probably is."

Inside, the house is clean and perfect. Frank shows me into a cozy living room filled with antiques and paisley-patterned furniture. Sunlight streams in through a bay window to bounce off the polished brass of an old gas fireplace. Sitting on the mantel is a lone photograph in an ornate frame.

I walk to it and see a hand-colored black and white of a handsome young man and his new bride. Both of them are laughing, their faces full of life.

"I haven't really changed anything since she died," Frank says behind me. "Just finished up the list of chores she always left on the fridge: Fix the back step, it creaks; new light bulb in the root cellar; turn over the soil in the vegetable garden."

"It's nice, Frank. She must have been happy here."

"Yeah," he sighs. "Marion was always happy, always singing, always…" He laughs lightly. "Always cooking. If she was here, you would be stuffing yourself with homemade pie while she made a care package to send home." He pats his belly. "Never liked to see anyone too skinny."

I smile. "I wish I could have met her."

"Yeah, me too." Frank turns his gaze away from the mantel and walks out of the room. When he returns, he is carrying a small bottle and two tumblers of ice.

"So tell me," he says, splashing Dr. Pepper in the glasses. "Art theft?"

I accept the glass and take a sip. It tastes so good that I follow it with a healthy swallow. It takes away the medical tang of the Tylenol.

"Well, you know, journalism has its kicks, but…" I shake off the lame joke and take another sip. "I don't know what to make of it," I begin again. "Kingston wants to teach me a lesson, I guess."

"You piss him off?"

"Not on purpose," I protest. "Well, not exactly on purpose."

"Hmmm, you have a knack for that."

I ignore him. "With what little proof I have of murder or a cover-up or whatever, the story can't hurt Kingston. In fact, the way things are looking, the piece will end up helping him. The more I discover about Diego, the more tragic his life becomes. People will be interested."

"But?"

Frank is forcing me to think.

"But…" The gears turn slowly. "If I miss this week's deadline, the story loses its immediacy and ends up buried in the magazine.

If there is anything potentially dangerous in the story, it gets downplayed simply by the nature of placement."

"And getting tossed in jail makes it more difficult for you to meet your deadline."

I nod.

"So something in your story must frighten him?"

"I guess."

"Give me a theory."

I think about it.

"We know," I begin, "that Kingston has ties to Diego's original agent. Casper, the wormy creep who showed up at the death scene, works for Stellar Galleries. Stellar Galleries is funded by Kingston, so chances are he says who gets the biggest push in the art world. With the snap of his fingers, Kingston drops Diego in favor of Adamsky. Soon, Diego isn't selling and Adamsky is the rising star."

I take a breath before continuing.

"Now, what if Diego decided to teach them both a lesson by stealing a couple of valuable paintings. Kingston gets pissed and hires some muscle to make Diego give him his art back. The muscle gets creative and ends up blowing Diego's brains out."

"Not bad," Frank says. "But why attack you?"

"Because I decided to dig and Kingston didn't like it. He either has to buy me or frighten me. Unfortunately, he chose the latter."

"There must be easier ways to shut you up."

I grin. "Can't imagine what."

Frank shakes his head slowly.

"How have you survived in this business, Dix? You have more enemies than friends. That's not healthy."

"I didn't get into the biz to make friends."

"Well, you're lucky you made a few by mistake."

My grin widens. "And I appreciate it."

"You better," he says. "Because some days I wonder if you're worth the trouble."

I clink his glass with my own.

THIRTY-ONE

I WAKE WITH A start, the muscles in my neck cramped, back stiff, my left hand feeling as though someone has stuck a knife through it.

A hollow chime echoes somewhere in the distance and it takes a moment to realize where I am. I can't recall falling asleep, but I do remember the warm sun shining through the bay window and the comfortable, overstuffed couch where I still lay. The window is in shade now, but Frank has thrown a blanket over me to keep off any chill.

Rising slowly to my feet, I attempt to stretch my muscles. Every limb protests and the exercise only makes them feel worse. Giving up, I wander into the hallway in search of the hollow chime.

I find the source easily enough. A grandfather clock stands at rigid attention as though guarding passage to the kitchen. Its crystal face is cracked; a loose, glittering web crawling from a bullet-sized hole near the number six, but the polished wood of its cabinet sings with history and a preserved, loving care. The hands on its face inform me it's just after five o'clock.

In the kitchen, I splash water on my face and drag the wet fingers of my working hand through my hair. It's while I'm dripping water onto the linoleum and squinting half-blind in my quest for a dishcloth to dry myself that I spot the note stuck on the fridge door. There are only two hastily scrawled words on it—"work called"—and Frank's indecipherable signature.

I pick up a brass phone sitting on an elegant child-size desk in the hall and dial the Hall of Justice. It takes a five-minute game of telephone tag around the building before I'm told Frank's away from his desk. No one knows when he'll be back.

Without Frank's help it takes twenty minutes to make my way through the bureaucratic phone maze and find anyone who knew anything about Kristy's Bug. Finally, I'm informed it has been towed and that I can have it back just as soon as I cough up the $175 charge.

My wallet groans.

———

By the time I park the Bug in front of my building, I'm cranky and depressed over my impending deadline. Stoogan will be chomping at the bit for a story, but apart from annoying prominent businessmen and putting my personal safety in peril, I don't have an opening hook. Stoogan gave me two days, and that was two days ago.

Every theory I have is based on conjecture, but I'm not in the business of opinion. I need cold hard facts and indisputable proof.

The moment I enter the lobby, my dark cloud dissipates as Mr. French throws open his door and beams up at me like a teenage boy who's just touched his first breast.

"I believe," he says excitedly, "I have found the author of our notes."

He holds the door open as I walk into his apartment, the air smelling of cherry and moist cedar. Baccarat is sitting on her perch, pecking at a tiny mirror and chirping away.

"She has such big stories to tell at times," Mr. French says wistfully as he follows me into the living room. "Pity I've yet to master the language."

Mr. French whistles at his pet before producing his leather notebook and opening it to a marked page.

"Before I begin," he says softly, "may I inquire as to your health?"

"I look that bad, huh?"

"It's not that." The corners of his mouth turn up in a soft smile. "It's just I notice your hand, and the commotion last night. You are on the other side of the building and yet..."

"And yet throwing someone out a window tends to make a little noise?"

"Ahh, yes. Forgive my intrusion—"

I laugh. "You're not being nosy. I appreciate the concern. We...I had a burglar last night, but it's under control. The police are on it."

"A burglar?" His face pales. "Oh, dear."

"Don't worry," I say reassuringly. "He was after a specific item, a painting. It has since been moved to a safe location."

"Ahh." His face relaxes. "Well, thank you for the update."

"You're welcome. Now tell me what you've uncovered."

Mr. French goes into great detail about how he and the owner of the stationery store, Mr. Clifford Clements, approached each of the five women on their short list.

"Clifford was kind enough to load me up with paper samples," explains Mr. French. "As a way of gaining entry to the suspects' homes. I played the part of salesman."

"Very clever," I say.

Mr. French beams.

"I've always been a fan of Arthur Miller," he says excitedly. "So I imagined myself as Willy Loman, but back when he was younger, before the events of the play."

"Imaginative."

Mr. French beams wider still.

"All of the women were very friendly toward me, except for one, a Mrs. Irene Pennyworth, who said I smelled of a tobacconist and she could not in good conscience purchase paper from, as she politely put it, 'a walking corpse.' "

"Charming."

"Quite. However, I quickly ruled her out as our letter writer."

"Oh?"

"Yes, you see, upon closer examination, Clifford and I discovered something new inside the envelope of the second letter you delivered."

"Go on."

"A single, long white hair not of human origin."

"I'll call David Duchovny," I say.

"I'm not sure I—"

"*The X-Files*," I explain. "He played an FBI agent who investigated alien conspiracies."

"Ahh, I see," says Mr. French, although it is clear from the confused look that he doesn't see at all. "But, no, the hair isn't alien, it's feline."

"Feline?"

"Persian, to be exact."

"How do you know that?"

"Because we found the matching cat." Mr. French beams. "Long, flowing white coat; large, round head with a blunt, pug-like face; small, rounded ears; large eyes; and a short tail. Definitely Persian."

"Well, case solved, then. I should talk to her and see why she's sending the notes."

"You could do that."

"But?" I ask, sensing his hesitation.

"But matching paper and a stray cat hair does not an unbreakable case make."

"It doesn't?"

"No. It does give us enough to warrant an approach, but if she denies the fact, we have nothing to counter with."

"True, but—"

"Clifford and I are happy to continue our surveillance until such time as she delivers a third note."

"Catch her in the act," I say.

"Precisely!"

I smile and wonder how men ever manage to rule the world when all they really want to be are boys playing in puddles and tree forts as spacemen, cowboys, and detectives.

"OK," I agree, seeing little harm in allowing their game to continue. "So long as you don't perceive this woman to be a threat to Mrs. Pennell, we'll wait and catch her in the act."

"Excellent!" Mr. French claps his chubby little hands together in delight. "I'll finish making sandwiches and tell Clifford the good news."

"Sandwiches?"

"Why, yes!" Mr. French beams. "We're on stakeout."

———

In my apartment, I slide off my shoes, pour a stiff rum and ginger on ice, pop a frozen sausage pizza in the oven, and survey the room.

Someone, probably Frank or Sam, has nailed a piece of plywood over the broken windowpane, which makes the apartment darker.

I want my mind to switch off, to find that perfect balance of comfortably numb. To that end, I pop the last two Percs and head to the computer to see what is playing on TV.

Unfortunately, within the ten strides it takes to cross the room, I spot a rare blinking light on the answering machine. I hit play.

"Umm, hi, Dixie, it's Declan. Sorry I haven't been in touch. Work got a little crazy, and I was running around trying to organize a new showing. A lot of interest in Diego Chino now that he's, well, you know. Well, umm, I was wondering if you had plans this weekend. Maybe Sunday? We could get together for lunch or an early supper. Take in an art show or a play. So um, call me. Bye."

Not exactly wine and roses or "I haven't been able to stop thinking about you." His cuteness factor might sway the vote, but I have to admit he isn't making a strong case to avoid being flicked.

As my father often told me: Never settle for a man who won't treat you like the princess you are. So far, however, I have discovered that bagging a prince is not as simple as kissing a lot of frogs and licking a few toads.

The machine kicks over to a second message.

"Hey, Dixie. Aurora here from the co-op. I hate these machines, don't you? They turn us into Pavlov's dog, hear a beep, start to blab, blah blah drool blah. Hey that might make for a cool piece. You think? Everything freezes until the beep. Then two minutes later, freezes again, waiting for another fucking beep. Could be cool, no? Anyhow, I talked to some of the artists and they said Diego worked at the paint factory just a few buildings down. Number 201. It's patrolled by a couple of pervy young guys with guns, so best go during the day. Hope that helps. *Ciao*."

And there it is. Another misjudgment.

If Kingston is hiding anything about his relationship with Diego, it must have its roots in that factory. And there is no Goddamn way I'm waiting until morning.

THIRTY-TWO

WISPS OF FOG DRIFT off the cold water beneath the docks to wrap a gossamer cloak around a ghetto of dilapidated warehouses. The buildings are barely visible beneath a dull crescent moon and the potholed alleys between them are filled with impenetrable darkness.

In other words, this place gives me the creeps.

With the headlights of Kristy's Bug switched off, I maneuver blindly between wooden carcasses to park in a deep pool of inky night a few buildings away from 201.

There's no sign of the security guards, but I can't blame them for hiding away in some warm building with TV noise for company. If I were smarter, I'd be doing the same thing.

Softly clicking the car door closed behind me, I step into the night. My breath floats as my nostrils pinch against the stench of rotting wood, dead fish, and raw sewage. Focusing on the task ahead, I check my equipment: flashlight, Swiss Army pocketknife (in addition to my trusty boot blade), and my digital point-and-shoot in a padded case attached to my belt.

It isn't much, but hopefully it will do.

Dressed in black—jeans, T-shirt, socks, boots, and cable-knit sweater—I feel kinda sexy; a combination of Halle Berry from *Die Another Day* and Catherine Zeta-Jones in that cat-burglar flick with Sean Connery. I even found a woolen fisherman's cap to pull tight over my don't-give-a-damn-but-glows-in-the-dark red hair, and dulled my bruised and glowing complexion with a smudge of dirt.

The only thing missing is my lucky trench coat, which Mrs. Pennell's seamstress is still attempting to mend.

With the flashlight in my good hand, I trek to Kingston's warehouse. Darting from doorway to doorway, I keep my eyes peeled and ears open for the guards. It isn't until I'm almost on top of them that I hear laughter. Crouching low in the pungent darkness of a urine-splashed doorway, I wait and watch.

A metal door slams somewhere nearby and the laughter grows louder. The night twists the sound, making its direction unknown. I hold my breath, body tense.

Gravel crunches.

Too close.

Shit!

I stay perfectly still, trying to play that childish game of "If I can't see you, you can't see me."

There are two of them and they're moving closer.

Wincing slightly from the uncomfortable position, I slink deeper into the shadows.

Two guards turn the corner and stop directly in front of the doorway. I squint, not wanting to expose the whites of my eyes, so all I see are navy blue pants and heavy-soled boots.

"What did you say the record was again?" one of the guards asks as he lights a hand-rolled cigarette.

"Twenty-two."

"In one shift?"

"Yep."

"Musta found a nest."

"Prob'ly."

The smoke is overly sweet. Not tobacco at all. The guard hands the joint to his partner.

"Don't they count bullets?"

"Buy your own. Company'll never know."

"Good thinking."

"Yep."

"You got any?"

"Bullets?"

"Yeah. Extras like?"

"'Course."

"Wanna kill some?"

"You bet."

The slap of leather is unmistakable as the guards race each other to a quick draw contest. Both men giggle until one of them begins to cough. His friend slaps him on the back and lifts the joint from his fingers.

"Wish they'd give us semi-autos," one guard says as he lifts the joint to his lips and sucks in the pungent smoke.

"Buy your own."

"Really! They'd let us?"

"'Course not, but who's gonna tell?"

"Right. You got one?"

"Not yet, but next week. Damn Brady Bill. Found it on eBay."

"Sweeeeet."

"Yep."

"Let's hunt."

Both guards laugh and walk away, their loaded revolvers pointed in front of them.

I release my breath and suck in a mouthful of oxygen. It is tainted with marijuana smoke. I'm so nervous that sweat has trickled down my back and is beginning to freeze uncomfortably around the base of my spine. I hope the secondhand smoke won't make me paranoid, as I can already imagine tomorrow's headline:

NOSY REPORTER SHOT DEAD ON DOCKS

"WE THOUGHT SHE WAS A RAT," SAY TRIGGER-HAPPY GUARDS

I give the guards five minutes to move away from the area before creeping out of my hole and crossing the alley to the warehouse. I figure the doors will be locked, but from my earlier tour of the artists' commune, I also know the buildings are lucky to still be standing and large sections of the wood is rotten and weak.

In the distance I hear two shots ring out, followed by a celebratory whoop.

Licking my lips, I check a large, truck-sized delivery door without any luck before moving on, my flashlight checking the walls for accessible gaps.

I almost walk by the guards' door but try the handle on a whim. It isn't locked.

With a cautious grin, I open the door and poke my head inside. The cramped, windowless room is empty except for two metal folding chairs, a round card table, and a portable propane heater that gives off just enough heat to make the interior tolerable. A single 40-watt bulb in the ceiling provides light. There is no TV, phone, radio, or monitored security cameras.

No wonder they're out shooting rats. This is the kind of job that could make someone shoot himself just to ease the boredom.

Two more shots ring out.

They sound closer.

A narrow access door in one corner leads into the warehouse. Its hinges are coated in so much rust, I wonder if it has ever been used. Fearing the worst, I twist the locking bolt into the proper position and shove. The metal screeches as rust flakes off in my hand, but the bolt slides just enough to escape its latch.

Nervous sweat beads from every pore as I yank on the handle. The door slides open stiffly for the first six inches, but then begins to protest as the bottom of the door meets an uneven floor. Despite my abused muscles screaming at me to stop, I put my shoulder into it to try and squeeze another couple of inches. It refuses to budge, leaving barely a one-foot gap between it and the jamb.

Thankful that I hadn't taken the time to eat my microwaveable sausage pizza, I suck in my stomach and begin to squeeze through the gap. My bruised breasts and buttocks don't appreciate the sandpaper massage, which I know I'll pay dearly for tomorrow, but with determination I manage to get through the tight space and pull the door closed just seconds before the guards return.

"You see the size of that last hairy fucker?" one guard says, his voice muffled by the thick wall.

"It was a badger, man."

"Badger? It was a freakin' cougar."

"That why you shit yourself?"

"Fuck you."

Inside the warehouse, I flick on the flashlight to find myself on the top landing of a short flight of stairs. Unfortunately, the steps had collapsed into a rotten pile of worm-eaten compost some time over the last quarter-century.

Just what my poor body needs: an obstacle course.

With a groan, I lower myself over the edge and drop to the ground. Despite a soft landing, the massive floor creaks and groans under my scant weight. I pan the flashlight across the floor to see why this end of the warehouse isn't being used. Salt water and years of neglect have eaten away at the boards, leaving patches of rot that look as if they can barely hold a man's weight.

Hoping the trek hasn't been a waste of time, I direct the flashlight's beam to the far side. Against that wall are three long rows of low-walled cubicles with unlit industrial lights dangling from wires above. Without natural light, it seems a hellish place to work, but at least I now know somebody must.

Being careful to pick the strongest-looking beams, I make my way across the floor, alert to the possibility that I might need to leap at an instant's notice. It takes a few minutes, but soon the boards become stronger and I am able to walk without trouble. The closer I come to the cubicles, the stronger the smell of paint and turpentine.

Behind the cubicles, I spot a glass-enclosed office and a newer set of large steel doors. To the far left are stacks of cardboard boxes and large wooden crates.

I walk to the boxes first and find they're all clearly marked as oil paint, each color stamped in capital letters on the front. Using my pocketknife, I slice one open to find a hundred tubes of Cobalt blue. It's even a decent brand. Turning my attention to the crates, I spot a crowbar lying on the floor and use it to pry the top off one. Inside are bolts of high-quality canvas.

Bored with that discovery, I return to the cubicles. Each one is fitted with two metal easels, a professional light box for displaying 35mm slides, a padded stool, and a selection of brushes. Bright splashes of paint spot the floors, but oddly it seems that only one color dominates each table. The one directly in front of me is spattered with green, the one beside it in orange, and the next in blue.

Walking up and down the rows, I'm even more puzzled. Some of the workstations hold a strange assortment of stencils and laser-etched stamps. The last cubicle, closest to the office, is also the largest. It's roughly four times the size of the others, and it's the only one with a floor spattered in a multitude of colors.

I spot several dollops of paint leading in the direction of the shiny metal doors. Following the trail, I reach the doors and pull. A welcome gust of warm air flows over me and my spirits rise as the treasure is exposed.

Adamsky.

A whole room full of his signature abstract art.

Stepping inside, I reach out to touch one of the nearest paintings. The paint is still tacky and instantly I know it was created in the rows of cubicles behind me.

The scenario becomes clear: Adamsky doesn't exist. He's nothing more than the invention of a corrupt marketer who brings in cheap labor to slap colored stencils on canvas and trick the idle rich out of their weekly allowance.

The whole thing is a scam, and Diego must have discovered it. Only instead of going to the police, he decided to make a statement in art. And it cost him his life.

Fighting to control my excitement, I stick the flashlight between my knees and pull my camera out of its bag. I widen the light's beam to bathe the paintings in a soft glow and snap away.

When I'm done, I re-seal the doors and snap some flash shots of the cubicles. With enough evidence stored in digital format to add visual spice to my planned exposé, I turn my attention to the glass office. The interior is your basic foreman's mess with an angled architect's table, several file cabinets, and a cluttered wood desk.

The table is covered with a detailed outline for the next Adamskys to be mass-produced and shipped to galleries around the world. There, the rich would snap them up, all the time believing $50,000 to $100,000 is a bargain for an original from a much-publicized master.

Turning to the desk, I rummage through the drawers. There is nothing to find in the first three, but the fourth is locked. I pull out my pocketknife and attempt to pick the lock. After five minutes, I curse my Zeta-Jones–lacking burglary skills and storm across the warehouse to the crates. There, I tuck the knife in my back pocket and pick up the crowbar.

The locked drawer splinters open easily to reveal a small metal box. Inside is a metal stamp of Adamsky's signature. It makes me sick to think how easily I have been fooled.

Leaving the box open on top of the desk, I move to the file cabinets. Lucky for them, they're unlocked.

A quick search uncovers a lease agreement between the owners of the warehouse, Fish Mac Retailers, and Kingston Enterprises. The signature at the bottom of the document belongs to Casper Blymouth.

I stuff the agreement in my pocket and continue to search. This time my fingers stop at a folder with Chino's name on the label. Inside is a laminated ID tag with a thumbnail photograph. It isn't Diego.

Taken aback, I double-check the folder and see this file belongs to a Pascal Chino.

I check the file cabinet again and find Diego's folder. I compare his photo to Pascal's. Despite the similarities in bronzed skin and sharp nose, it's clear that Diego was blessed with better looks. Where Pascal's eyes are watery and shy, Diego's were seductive bourbon brown made even more arresting by thick black eyebrows and a teasing mop of naturally curly hair. The two men are definitely not brothers, but it's easy to see they're from the same gene pool.

I return the folders and look out the window at the warehouse, wondering what table Diego worked at and how long he did Kingston's bidding before deciding he couldn't stomach it anymore.

The floor creaks behind me.

Damn.

I raise my hands and slowly turn around, hoping the gun-happy guards won't shoot.

But it isn't the guards.

Before my eyes can focus on the lone figure, a stinging mist assaults my eyes and a leather boot slams between my legs.

I crumple to my knees with eyes on fire and my tender parts not much happier. I lift my head to deliver a profane tongue lashing, but a sharp blow to my right temple ends it before I can begin.

Everything goes black.

———

When I open my eyes, I can barely move. Every muscle in my body has united and immediately declared a general strike. I can't blame them; my mind isn't far behind. Unfortunately, the strike needs to be busted and quickly:

Wherever I am, it's on fire and heavy smoke is already making it difficult to breathe.

I try to move my hands; the bandaged left is useless, and the right barely budges. Panicking, I struggle harder and feel the coarse bite of a rope just above my elbows. I am tied to a thick wooden post that stretches to the rafters. Cursing, I attempt to stand and fail. My feet are bound together, making it difficult to find a purchase on the slick floor.

The smoke is becoming too thick to see and my eyes still sting from whatever the bastard sprayed me with.

Heavy footsteps walk past me, but all I can see is the tall silhouette of a faceless ghost. The footsteps vanish with the slamming of a steel door somewhere behind me. I twist my neck to peer after him only to find myself blinded by a flash and the eruption of a second fire.

Tears abruptly fill my eyes and I am frightened. I have always imagined fire to be the worst way to die. I've even had nightmares about it.

A new headline forms in my mind, but I force it away. Panic will kill me quicker than smoke. I need to think.

Desperate, I twist my hip closer to my hands and use my fingers to claw at my pants, hoping against hope that my attacker only took my camera. Pain shoots up my arms and I feel the new stitches in my hand begin to rip again, but every time I think about giving up, a burst of fire erupts somewhere in the warehouse for added inspiration.

My lungs burn from the smoke and sweat pours from my body. I use the sweat and the fresh blood from my hand to grease the ropes and slide my fingers deeper into my pocket. Finally, I touch metal, and with one last agonizing push I feel my pinkie grab on to the tiny loop on the end of my pocketknife.

With the knife in my hand, I have to concentrate to dig my thumbnail into the tiny notch on the large blade and ease it open while keeping a slippery grip on the knife's handle. Once I get past the halfway mark, the rest is easy. With gritted teeth, I saw at the ropes around my wrists, feeling the sharp blade slice through the dry hemp with relative ease.

As soon as I'm free, I lie flat on the ground and press my lips to a crack in the floor, gulping in mouthfuls of salty air. With a clear head, I scan the warehouse to find I'm standing on an island of rotten wood, surrounded by an ocean of hungry flame.

Panic sets in once more as I see no option for escape.

The fire draws closer, sucking in the last of the oxygen and growing so hot that even the damp wood can't resist its all-consuming hunger.

Around me wood splinters and cracks as the warehouse consumes itself. Trapped on my diminishing island, I study the fire, attempting to interpret the raging colors before me.

Finally, I don't have a choice. I pick a direction where I hope the floor is weakest and tense my legs. The muscle strike has been silenced by the stupidity of the host. Even the pain has retreated into a locked room.

To my own surprise, I hear myself utter a prayer before standing up tall and running straight into the inferno.

I want to yell and scream and curse Kingston's name as I leap as high and as far as I can, but I can't bear to give up my last breath until I know there is only death ahead.

Flames lick around me, setting fire to my clothing. I am blind and alight as I fall back to earth.

I land hard, crashing into the gates of hell without a key, feeling my flesh sizzle as I scream.

A sharp crack drowns me out as the wooden slats snap under my weight, dropping me into the bitter cold depths of the sea.

THIRTY-THREE

I SHIVER ON THE rocky shore; crusty shreds of clothing are seared onto my burnt skin. I don't want to open my eyes. I'm frightened that if I look I'll discover that I haven't survived the fire. At the same time, I'm scared that I have survived, but at a cost to my flesh that I won't be able to bear.

Eventually, as waves crash against my legs and my bloodied hands go numb from clinging to the rocks, I dare to look up.

Above me is a starless sky, undulating with reflected light. Beside me, two warehouses over, a fire roars out of control, searing light and smoke climbing into the abyss.

I look at my body, ghostly white from the cold, fresh scars of pink and black from burns, cuts, and bruises. I touch my face, tender but whole apart from burnt eyebrows and lashes.

I want to laugh. I am alive and freezing my ass off in Frisco Bay.

Fighting off shock, I drag myself from the water, across the jagged rocks to collapse on dry gravel. A spew of dust slowly settles in my hundred bleeding cuts. At least I'm still breathing, and the ground is warmer than the icy waves that saved me from certain cremation.

I don't know how long I lie there before pulling myself to my feet and hobbling back to the docks.

The two security guards stand in front of the burning warehouse, guns drawn, mouths agape. They turn toward me as I approach.

"Bitch of a night, huh?" I say.

Their bloodshot eyes roam my body, taking in my wet and badly burnt clothing but not knowing what to do with the information.

"Somebody was probably shooting at rats and punctured a gas tank or something," I suggest.

Their eyes grow wider, and in the distance I hear the howl of approaching sirens.

"I would holster the guns, boys," I continue. "Before the pros mistake you for vermin."

Both guards gulp and immediately holster their guns.

"I need to get into some dry clothes," I say and continue walking.

Neither guard attempts to stop me.

At the Bug, I reach under the back bumper for the spare key (I'd tucked the original in the pocket of my camera case) and climb inside. The engine sputters to life and the heater groans.

A shadow moves behind my shoulder and I flinch in fright.

"You OK?" asks a childlike voice.

I look into Aurora's mixed-up eyes and everything comes rushing up to the surface at once. I begin to weep.

She opens the car door and reaches in to hug me.

"It's OK," she says. "You're OK."

Snot bubbles leak from my nose, but I no longer care.

I begin to blubber. "W–w–who did you tell about the warehouse?"

"No one, I swear. I just called a few people to ask where it was. I left a message for Diego's cousin to call me back, 'cause I knew he worked there, but I don't think I said why I wanted the information. You think that fire is because of me?"

"No," I sniffle. "It's my fault. I wasn't careful enough." I laugh hoarsely. "Frank is gonna be pissed."

"Frank?" asks Aurora.

"Just a friend." I wipe my nose on my sleeve. "An overprotective friend."

"Oh." Aurora pats my hand. "You want me to drive you home? I know stick."

I shake my head. "I'll be OK. You'll want to make sure the fire doesn't reach your studio."

"You sure?" Aurora's voice is filled with genuine concern.

I nod, grab a box of tissues off the back seat, and blow my nose. Aurora steps back and I close the door.

Driving away from the docks, I wonder if whoever left me in the warehouse believes I'm dead. If so, he'll no longer be hunting. So the last thing he could imagine would be to find his throat in my hands, his feet kicking helplessly as I squeeze and squeeze.

This time, I tell myself, *I'll have the upper hand*.

THIRTY-FOUR

I WAKE UP IN my own bed when a startled gasp filters into a dream to force open my crusty eyelids. I spy a slim silhouette and wonder if the dead ever dream they're alive.

"Dix, are you all right?" Kristy's ashen face moves closer to my bloodshot eyes.

I try to answer, but my chest spasms into a rough cough until I can taste smoke caking my lungs.

"I'll get Sam."

Kristy vanishes from sight.

When the coughing stops, I try to sit up. Pain flares from every nerve, but the more I move, the duller it becomes. When I finally make it into a sitting position, I explore my flesh with rough, dry hands. I shudder as dried flakes of skin and scabs of burnt clothing crumble under my touch.

Kristy returns with Sam and together they help me into the bathroom. They lay me gently in the tub and fill it with lukewarm water.

I'm not overly shy, but I won't say that being naked in front of two fully clothed women is something I'm used to. All the same, the bath feels wonderful. Lying back in the tub, eyes closed against the pain, gentle hands scrub my skin clean of its dead and blackened debris.

After emptying and filling the tub twice, I am pink and raw, wrapped in a warm robe and sitting in my favorite chair. A mug of strong coffee fits in one hand, a professionally wrapped bandage on the other, and an oatmeal chocolate-chip muffin on a plate in my lap. Even Bubbles seems happy to see me as she swims circles in her bowl.

Kristy perches on the arm of the chair, her fingers stroking my hair, her teeth nervously biting the inside of her cheek. Sam sits across from me on the overstuffed couch. I tell them what happened and their eyes are wide.

Sam is first to speak.

"How did anyone know you were going to the warehouse?"

My eyes are cold. I've given that question considerable thought and I don't like the answer.

"I talked to Aurora. If she did tip someone off, it wasn't on purpose. She told me to wait until morning, so maybe whoever torched the warehouse was trying to get rid of the evidence before I turned up."

"Even so," Kristy says. "Arson is a long way from murder. Why would Kingston want you dead?"

"To save face. If—no, *when*—I expose his art scam, no one will trust him again. His empire could crumble."

"But murder?" Sam interjects.

"I don't think his hands are clean to begin with," I reason. "I don't have anything I can take to court, but he's mixed up in Diego's death too."

"I thought Diego committed suicide?"

"That's what we're supposed to think."

"But?"

"The night Kristy wouldn't wake up," I continue, "there had to be some kind of gas used. I think the same thing happened to the neighbor who lives below Diego."

"The gas sifted into his apartment?" Sam asks. "How?"

"Any number of ways. A leak in the hose, or it could be heavier than air and drifted down through the vents. Then they turned on the AC full blast to clear the air and cover their tracks. But the point is, if Diego was gassed, his killer or killers could have positioned him any way they wanted before making it look like suicide. Hell, his signature on the canvas might not even be genuine. They could have used a stamp like they did with Adamsky."

"Pricks!" Kristy shouts angrily. "I slept away a whole Goddamn day."

Sam and I both grin.

"What are you going to do now?" Sam asks.

"Go to Kingston with what I have and shake some truth out of him."

"You think that'll work?"

I shrug. "I don't need a confession. I just need to see his face when he realizes I'm about to hang him on the front page and let the readers watch him shit himself."

"That doesn't sound like you, Dix," Sam reasons.

"I lost my objectivity in the fire."

"You almost lost your life too."

"But I didn't. Kingston screwed up."

"So now he pays?"

"Now he pays."

Sam takes my face in her hands and locks eyes.

"Be careful," she says gently. "You may have the lives of a cat, but even that number eventually runs out."

Sam stands up to leave and Kristy leans in close, her lips tickling my ear.

"What Sam said," she whispers, "goes double for me."

She kisses me on the cheek before joining Sam at the door.

————

Alone with my anger and self-pity, I pick up the phone and dial the Hall of Justice. When the receptionist answers, I hang up.

I don't know what to tell Frank. I know he'll be angry that I went to the warehouse without telling him, and then he'll be angry that I broke in. Above all, he'll be angry that I almost didn't make it out alive.

The phone rings as I fight with myself. Automatically, I reach out for the receiver, stopping just as my fingers curl around it. The phone continues to ring as I walk into the bedroom to dress.

I don't want to talk anymore.

THIRTY-FIVE

ON THE STREET, I allow the sun to bake my tender, virginal skin before picking a direction and walking.

My mind is in a fog thicker than the familiar ghosts that evaporate in the blinding light of morning. At the end of the block, I stop and stare through the window of a Mrs. Fields bakery. Not even the sight of fresh-baked, double-fudge-chocolate-chip cookies can lift the glower from my mood.

When I turn to continue my pointless walk, I notice a scrawny kid standing beside me. I recognize him. I've walked by him a thousand times, often tossing the odd bit of change into his hat but never once stopping to look into his face. He has become a fixture outside the shop, no more noticeable than the dented mailbox.

Looking at him now, I wonder: if he was struck by a car and lay bleeding on the sidewalk, would I be able to say I knew him or would his face haunt me like so many others?

He can't be more than thirteen, yet I swear he's more like an old man. Underneath shabby, mismatched clothes, I see a different story than the one every hypocritical journalist, including myself, has told over the years to the uncaring masses. This time, I see myself. His skin is a different color, the clothes a different make, but the boy is still a child and but for the grace of … for the grace of who? I'm no longer quite sure.

Reaching into my pocket, I pull out a twenty-dollar bill. Handing it to the boy, I watch his unblinking, milky eyes as his hand snatches it out of my fingers. His eyes never leave my face until the money vanishes inside a tight fist.

He nods. I nod back. He never smiles.

Inside the bakery, a skinny Chinese girl fusses with her clean, candy-striped apron. Her eyes narrow suspiciously when the boy presses himself against her glass counter to ogle the display of edible treasure.

It takes him a while, but finally the boy points toward the tray of double-fudge-chocolate-chip cookies and holds up two fingers. Sticking out from between the fingers is the twenty.

The girl scoops up two cookies and lays them on tiny wax-paper squares. As soon as they are within his reach, the boy crams a whole one into his mouth, his cheeks bulging as he chews. The girl takes the bill from his outstretched hand with an exaggerated look of disgust.

After receiving his change, the boy carefully wraps the second cookie in the wax paper and slips it into a pocket of his torn sweater. He vanishes out the rear door.

I walk around the corner to see where he is running to, but he's already vanished. I am left to wonder how long he has stared at those cookies, only imagining their taste.

Deep inside, I feel the same way he must.

For too long I have been tracking a killer always just out of reach. And like the boy, I need a key to open that door in order to get the goods inside.

I straighten my back and flex my shoulders. I know what I have to do.

———

Back in my apartment, I dial Kingston's number.

"Sir Roger Kingston's residence."

"This Oliver or Oxford?" I ask.

"It's Oliver, miss. How may I assist—"

"Your master in?"

"If you are referring to Sir Roger, I'm afraid he is visiting the city on business today."

"What business?"

"He didn't share that information."

"Visiting his galleries?"

"That is something he enjoys," Oliver says. "Perhaps I could take a—"

"One question."

A pause. "Yes?"

"Did you plant the da Vinci in my trunk, or was that your brother?"

Another pause. Longer this time and followed by a soft sigh.

"That would be my responsibility, Miss Flynn, not my brother's."

"He's the good one, huh?"

"Quite."

"You have anything to do with Diego's death?"

A third pause and the sound of shallow breathing.

"My responsibility ends at the castle gates, Miss Flynn. What happens outside these walls is something I am not privy to."

"I'll try to keep that in mind." I hang up.

My second call is on speed dial.

"Dix, baby, you sound terrible," says Mo, his familiar raspy voice filled with genuine concern.

"I took up smoking to sound more like you. You don't like?"

"Smokin's for fish, Dix. Not fragile creatures like you and me."

"You listen to your own advice?"

"Trying to."

"Stick with it," I say. " 'Cause if your lungs feel anything like mine, breathing must be a bitch."

"At my age, sweetheart, everything's a bitch."

I laugh, but it hurts too much and ends in a wracking cough.

"You OK?"

"Yeah," I gasp. "Fine. Really."

"OK. Cab's on its way."

"Thanks."

————

At Ghirardelli Square, I give the driver a two-dollar tip. It doesn't buy his silence. As soon as I head down the stairs to Stellar Gallery, I spy him grabbing his mic to report back to Mo.

Big Brother is watching, like it or not.

At the bottom of the stairs, I stop in front of the gallery and stare through the main display window at a garish Adamsky. Sitting on a steel easel, thick swirls of red and yellow flicker like otherworldly flame on a three-dimensional checkered background of cobalt blue.

My fingers twitch, my mouth is dry, and my lungs ache. Deep inside, a scream claws its way out from the charred pit of my belly. *They wanted to burn me alive for this assembly-line shit?*

Beside me, a rock-speckled garbage can stands patiently, its own mouth open wide for candy wrappers, paper coffee cups, and the remains of bagged lunches. I bend my knees, wrap my arms around it and, with a strength I didn't know I possessed, heave it high in the air.

A volcanic screech escapes my throat as I hurtle the can. Upon contact, the picture window shatters into a hoard of angry mosquitoes and the frame of the Adamsky snaps in half as the can crashes through it.

Even before the reverberations subside, I step through the jagged frame of glass. Declan stands frozen in shock in the middle of the showroom. When he recognizes me, confusion replaces shock.

Shards of glass crunch underfoot as I lift the broken Adamsky off the floor. I slip my father's gift from my boot and flick it open. A five-inch blade locks with a menacing click.

Declan's eyes transform in disbelief as the knife rips the painting into worthless scraps. He struggles to speak as I storm through his gallery, my blade slicing through a second Adamsky and carving into a third. The knife screeches as its tip scrapes on the wall behind each canvas. I cross to a fourth and slash it with a zigzag cut that makes it fall in strips at my feet.

"STOP!" Declan screams, finding his voice.

He moves toward me but halts when I turn the knife on him. "Why, Dix? For God's sake!"

The answer flows in another voice, faraway tones of a woman whose childish ideals have been burned away. "You set me up."

"What do you mean?" His eyes search the faces of startled on-lookers standing outside the shattered window, too scared to enter.

"They're fake, just like you."

I can hardly stand to look into his eyes. His face, which just a few days ago had flushed me with excitement, now fills me with loathing.

"I was in the factory while your partner burned it to the ground." I pause. "Why do you want me dead?"

"I ... don't ... don't know what you're talk—"

I explode again, my knife jabbing out like lightning to slash the face of another Adamsky.

Declan curses and runs into his office to snatch up the phone. I stomp after him, too angry to be stopped. As he slams the door, I lash out to hit the glass with a heavy boot. My heel catches it in the perfect spot and the glass shatters into a million chunky pellets.

Someone behind me screams for the police.

Declan freezes, one hand on the phone, his jaw hanging.

"How did he know?" I ask sharply.

"Know what? Who?" He sounds genuinely scared.

"You know damn well. Who told Kingston I was going to the warehouse? Did Aurora call you? Or Casper? I can't see Kingston wanting to sully his hands directly."

"Aurora? I don't know any—"

I slam the knife into the plaster wall beside me. When I pull it out, a shower of white drywall dust pours from the hole.

Actual tears spring to Declan's eyes. He struggles to hide them, but his fear is palpable and I feel the scream inside me weaken.

"Where's Kingston now?"

"I don't—"

"Where is he?" I snap, my patience too thin, my anger too hot.

"The Devonian Hotel. He keeps a room there for when he's in the city."

Declan looks at me with the eyes of a puppy that's just been kicked in the ribs by its master.

"We'll take your car," I say, tilting the knife so it catches the light. "Unless you want me to finish redecorating your gallery."

Forty faces stare at us, most of them sporting *I ♥ Frisco* t-shirts adorned with happy cartoon characters. Nobody attempts to stop us as we cross the gallery floor and exit through the rear.

———

Declan sits beside me in the soft leather passenger seat of his Mercedes. His tears have evaporated and his face is a ruddy mask of controlled rage.

The car idles against the curb, a pebble in a fast-moving river of cars and hand-tailored suits. Above us, smooth towers of glass reach for the sky; around us, a rushing mass of ants.

In the midst of this jungle stands the Devonian. A fat-assed, fourteen-story antique made of mortar and brick. It huddles there, mostly forgotten and ignored, so easy to pass without noticing that all the men who stroll through its doors are wealthy, white, and soft-bellied. These are the holders of old wealth; the people *behind* the people behind the power.

Leaning back in the driver's seat, I stare through the moon roof and wonder what I will do to the man who waits above. Kingston left me screaming in the middle of a burning building. No escape; no mercy.

How do you forgive that?

Maybe I should have talked to Frank, but what could he say? There had been a time when Frank needed revenge, and he quenched it in blood. He'd never once told me that he regretted pulling the trigger.

"What are you going to do?" Declan's voice trembles slightly, but whether it is from rage or fear, I don't know.

"I'm not sure."

"Kingston may be a lot of things, but I can't believe he's a killer."

"Would you say the same about me?"

His lips vanish in a thin, white line. He doesn't answer.

"Where does he stay?" I ask.

"Top floor. He has a private elevator."

"Do you need a key?"

His eyes give me the answer. I pull the keys out of the ignition and study the fob. There are two gold keys of differing size. Each has a decorative D etched on them.

I drop the keys in my pocket and slide my old video-rental card from my wallet. Declan looks away as I slice the card in half with my knife and force it deep into his seatbelt lock. I cut away the excess to make sure it will stay jammed, then toss his cell phone to the back seat. There is nothing I can say that will stop him from warning Kingston, but I know by the time he wriggles out of the belt it will be too late.

———

The hotel lobby is elegant with brown leather smoking chairs around knee-high card tables on plush red carpet. Genuine crystal goblets hang in rows above a stand-up bar, and a walk-in humidor sports a generous selection of cigars. How they get around the city's smoking bylaws is story fodder for another day.

I walk directly to the elevators, my eyes never wavering. Everyone ignores me. All eyes are glued to a ticker-tape display of the stock market that flashes across TV screens mounted on oak-paneled walls.

The smaller gold key is warm in my sweaty palm as I slide it into the elevator lock and turn. The doors open silently. When they close again, I brace myself against the cold, mirrored wall. Sweat beads on my brow and I can smell my anger and fear.

The elevator glides to a stop on the fourteenth floor, the doors opening onto a narrow hallway that stretches on either side of two floor-to-ceiling doors. On each end of the hallway is a window.

One window offers a view of the street, the other of the back alley. The alley window doubles as a fire escape and I'm not surprised to see the black metal staircase outside is just as worn and tired as the rest of the building. Perhaps money buys that kind of false security.

After a deep breath, I return to the giant doors and slip the second gold key into the lock. The doors swing open effortlessly to reveal Kingston's bleached-white lair.

No one is there to greet me as I walk into the inner sanctum and find myself blinded by Kingston's sterile eccentricity.

Everything is white. Even the fine, antique furniture has its grain bleached out and the walls are scrubbed a medicinal clean. The effect is overwhelming, like a Hollywood version of Heaven. But if this is Heaven, I'd rather be in Hell.

"What are you doing here?"

Kingston storms into the room, his trim body wrapped in a white silk kimono. His legs stick out like sapling trunks, smooth and hairless. He holds a crystal glass in one hand. The liquid inside is colorless.

"I have questions," I say coldly.

"How did you get up here?"

I shrug. "Both angels and demons have wings."

"Are you drunk?" He advances toward me. His chest and arms look larger and more defined than I remember.

"No." I stand my ground as my one good hand curls into a tight fist. "I'm dead."

Kingston stops a foot away, his face bewildered.

Before he can speak again, a scream rises from my belly and my hand reacts. Kingston's head snaps back as I land a solid right to his nose.

The punch catches him by surprise and he staggers back into the wall. The goblet falls from his hand to shatter on the floor.

Kingston's eyes come alive with a murderous rage as blood flows from his nose. He roars like a bull elephant and charges just as I swing a Louis XIV chair at his head. Kingston steps directly into the path of the chair and takes the brunt of its force on the side of his head. His eyes roll skyward as his body crumples and he hits the floor with a muffled thud.

———

When he regains consciousness, Kingston finds himself strapped to a wooden chair with a silk rope I found in his bedroom. His face turns purple when he notices me looking out the large picture window. The view of the city is so peaceful.

"You're going to pay for this," Kingston snarls.

"You've already tried to collect … a few times."

I turn around to show him the switchblade.

"What do you want? Money."

"Answers."

"To what?"

"Why you killed Diego Chino."

"I didn't."

"Then you ordered someone to do it."

"I don't know what you're talking about."

I advance slowly, the knife held firm.

"What about your forgery operation?"

"What forge—" He stops as my knuckles turn white on the handle of the knife. "So what?" he adds quickly. "I faked a few paintings. Big deal."

"Why?"

"Because I can."

"Does Adamsky even exist?" I already know the answer.

Kingston shakes his head and snorts crimson blood. He actually seems to be enjoying the confession.

"I hired Diego to paint a few canvasses and then got a crew to churn them out by the truckload. I was getting bored with it though."

"So you torched the warehouse?"

"Why would I torch it?" He sounds genuinely surprised. "I don't own the building. There would be no profit in destroying it."

"But you got rid of evidence, and you almost got rid of me."

"You? You're nothing."

Anger twists inside me as I begin to doubt my conclusions.

"My story would ruin your reputation," I say. "You tried to stop me earlier by sending someone to my house. The same person you sent to take care of Diego."

Kingston laughs.

"You've got a lot to learn about power," he says. "What makes you think your feeble-minded readers even care about a few knock-off paintings? Most of them celebrate theft. They download movies, they pirate software, they rip songs off their friends' CDs. So a few rich people got punked. Who cares?"

My shoulders slump and the anger drains from my face. I suddenly feel sick.

"Face it, Flynn," Kingston continues with a smile growing on his face. "Your story can't even mention me. The warehouse is leased in Casper's name. And if any rumors of my involvement do start, I can crush them underfoot with a wiggle of my pinky toe. Oh, I might lose a good man in the process. But scapegoats are easy to replace."

"Declan?"

"His usefulness is diminishing."

I'm an idiot. Everything he said is true.

"Why don't you let me go now?" Kingston's smile turns devilish. "Before you add kidnapping to the list of offenses I'm going to sue your ass over."

I've blown it and now I'm going to end up in jail for breaking and entering and willful damage of a gallery. I wonder if Yee will still act as my lawyer.

I reach out to cut the rope.

"Don't move, Dix," warns a familiar voice. A voice I never expected to hear again.

I turn to stare into the face of a ghost.

The man pointing a double-barreled shotgun at me is Diego Chino.

———

"You're supposed to be dead," I say.

"So are you."

I recognize madness in his smile.

"Untie me, damn it." Kingston's chair rocks under his protest.

Diego smiles even wider.

"You're the last one, Mr. Kingston." Diego's teeth are red with blood as he chews the lining of his mouth. "You're not an easy man to catch up with."

"What are you talking about?" Kingston barks.

"I'm talking about death. Specifically, yours." Diego balances the shotgun in one hand and unsheathes a large hunting knife with the other.

"What did I ever do to you?" Kingston demands.

"You murdered me, of course."

"What are you babbling about? You're both crazy."

Diego raises the shotgun and I notice his eyes drift across the room for a moment before snapping back into focus.

"You stole my art, desecrated it, forced me to lie for you."

Kingston sneers. "I gave you a job when you were nothing."

"Only to use me. To steal from me."

"I paid you."

Diego shakes his head and raises the knife to his own face. The blade slices into his cheek, drawing blood. I can't believe what I'm seeing.

"You sank your teeth into my throat and drank your fill."

"You're insane. You didn't have to work for me."

"I didn't?" Chino screams. "No, I could have starved on your streets or cowered on my reservation, too afraid to leave, to even try for a better life. I wanted to live like a human, not a dog in a kennel. You used that against me."

"You destroyed yourself."

"NO!" Diego cocks the twin hammers of the shotgun. "You used me! When I wanted to leave, when my art was selling and I had a chance to follow my dream, you threatened to tell the world I was Adamsky." His voice cracks. "It meant nothing to you. You wanted to laugh at the world. You wanted to tell everyone that Adamsky was nothing but an Indian at the front of an assembly line. You wanted to prove just how smart you were." His voice is a rasp, his eyes swollen with pain. "But why? Why destroy me?"

Kingston spits blood on the floor. "No one walks out on me unless I say so."

Christ, it's a madhouse and the inmates are running the show.

Diego steps closer, his finger caressing one of the triggers.

"Who died for you, Diego?" I blurt.

His finger stops moving on the trigger and he looks at me blankly.

I rephrase the question. "Whose blood is on the canvas you signed?"

"That was foolish," he answers distantly, his voice weak. "I thought I ruined everything when I signed it, but it was powerful and I had created it. I signed it with my name, my real name." He starts to laugh, quietly, achingly. "The police are such fools. They thought it was a suicide note when all along it was a confession."

"But who died in your place?" I press. "Your cousin?"

"Pascal wouldn't let me walk away. He"—Diego nods at Kingston—"seduced him with a promise of wealth. A promise that Pascal bought, like legions of our ancestors before him, from the mouth of a forked-tongue devil."

Diego's voice drifts off and for a moment his eyes shine white as they roll into his head. I take a step forward but stop as the shotgun whirls upon me. His eyes snap back into focus.

"Quiet!" Diego yells, though no one is speaking. He rips open his shirt to reveal a mass of self-inflicted wounds. Some are deep and still bleeding.

"This is the blood of my people," he hisses. "Crying for vengeance."

He levels the gun at Kingston's chest.

"You were in my apartment," I say in an effort to buy more time as I let my own knife slip so the thin blade is firmly between my fingers. "You went out the window."

Diego grins and nods.

"I am an eagle," he says.

His finger starts to squeeze the trigger, and with nothing to lose I cock my arm and throw the blade directly at his chest.

In the same instant, I dive on Kingston, knocking him and the chair to the ground as a shotgun blast explodes in front of us.

A shower of plaster sprays above our heads as we land. Without wasting time, I scramble to my feet but find myself staring down the barrels of the shotgun again. My knife lies harmlessly at his feet.

I missed.

I don't have any ideas left.

"Goodbye, Dixie. Again."

I close my eyes and am deafened by the roar.

Warm blood splashes across my face as I collapse to my knees. Strangely, there is no pain.

———

"Dixie!" A familiar voice. "You OK?"

I open one eye.

Frank stands in the doorway with his gun drawn and smoking.

Diego lies in front of me. Most of his head is missing.

"How'd you find me?" I croak.

"I got Ruth to take another look at the corpse to find out about this asthma puzzle. She ran the prints and—"

"It wasn't Diego," I say.

Frank nods. "When I couldn't reach you, I called Mo. Turns out he was worried about you too. He had a taxi tail you here and your angry boyfriend downstairs gave me the room number."

Wiping the blood from my face, I turn to see if Kingston is OK, but my gaze is diverted to the blood splattered across the virginal white walls.

The effect is as powerful as when it bore Diego's signature, but this time the intensity comes from the lives it has saved rather than destroyed.

THIRTY-SIX

THE DRUNKEN CAMARADERIE FILLING the Dog House almost makes me turn around and head back to my apartment. I have been hiding for the last two days with only my computer and Bubbles for company. But the crazy, crooked grin on Bill's face when he spots me peeking around the door brings me to my usual stool between Frank and Capone.

The dozen hard-drinking customers around us are yelling and screaming over everything from horse racing to the endless bloody heat, but as Bill fishes a Warthog Ale out of the fridge and places it in front of me, the noise seems to slowly fade into the walls.

Frank sits patiently beside me as I take a long swallow and wipe the rich froth from my lips with a sigh. Then, with his huge hands wrapped around a near-empty mug of nonalcoholic beer, he asks how I'm doing.

"I'm OK," I reply. "The tribal leaders arrived to take the two bodies back home. It gave me a nice ending to the story."

"You get the cover?" Bill asks.

"Yeah." I grin. "How could they resist murder and art fraud involving the city's wealthiest asshole?"

Bill slaps the bar and grins like a proud father. "Al said you'd get it. I think he likes you."

"Nice to know somebody does."

I take another long pull of beer.

"Kingston still suing?" Frank asks as Bill walks down the bar to break up a scuffle near the washroom.

I nod. "I'm not too worried though. The case will be stuck in the courts for a bit and I don't have enough money to make it worth his trouble. Plus, he has to consider that if I hadn't broken into his place, you wouldn't have shown up and he'd probably be dead. I'm sure he'll eventually settle for a public apology."

"You planning on giving it to him?"

"Not much choice, but he'll have to ask nicely."

I grin and polish off my beer. Bill instantly appears to place a fresh one in front of me before vanishing to throw a mouthy drunk out the door.

"What about Declan?" Frank asks.

"Well." My grin disappears as I recall our conversation when I tried to apologize. "At least he dropped the vandalism, car theft, and kidnapping charges. I guess I had him figured all wrong. Shame it didn't work out, we could have had some fun. I don't usually spoil things that quickly into a relationship, but he made it quite clear that I was more trouble than I'm worth."

I take a sip of Warthog, trying to clear my mind of its troubles. "Anything new on Chief McInty?"

Frank shrugs. "He's taking some heat over closing the case on Chino's suicide so quickly, but that won't stick. Diego had us all fooled."

"Speaking of which," I say. "I owe you for saving my life."

"Hell, I was just doing my job. The people you should thank are the cabbies Mo put on your tail."

"Let me buy you a beer anyway," I offer.

"You already have," Bill pipes in with a cockeyed grin. "I figured you owed him a couple, so I've been putting the odd one on your tab now and again. I wasn't expecting you to stay away so long though."

"Thanks, Bill. I think."

"Don't mention it." Bill puffs out his chest. "Just doing my job."

His imitation of Frank is pathetic, but the three of us burst out laughing just the same.

"What's your plans for tonight?" Frank asks when the laughter subsides. "Will I be carrying you home?"

I shake my head. "I'm actually expecting a phone call. There's still one more mystery to clear up."

"Oh? Anything I need to worry about?"

"I don't think so, but you're on speed dial, just in case."

"Now I am worried," says Frank.

———

When the bar phone rings for me, I rush home.

Mr. French is waiting in the lobby and quickly pulls me into his apartment. He is holding a two-way radio.

"Clifford says she's on her way," he says breathlessly. "She's carrying a large brown box and a third letter."

321

"What makes you think she's coming here?" I ask.

The radio squawks and Clifford's voice says, "Sparrow to Eagle's Nest. Cuckoo has turned the corner. Four houses from you and closing fast. I'm covering the rear. Out."

"Ten-four, Sparrow," Mr. French says into the handset. "Eagle's Nest ready. Out."

"Cuckoo?" I ask.

Mr. French shrugs. "It fit the bird theme."

We hear the lobby door open.

The radio squawks again.

"Trap is sprung," says Clifford.

Instantly, Mr. French yanks open his apartment door and rushes out.

The woman bent over in front of Mrs. Pennell's door screams so loud, I'm afraid of permanent hearing loss. Mr. French, however, barely bats an eye as he wraps his short arms around her generous backside and grabs on for dear life.

The woman spins, whipping Mr. French off his feet, and charges for the lobby door.

She screams again when Clifford bounds up the steps outside and grabs the doors with both hands, barring her exit.

"I've got her," yells Mr. French, his face buried in the woman's plump back. "I've got her."

In the chaos, the woman drops her brown box.

"Get off me!" the woman screams as she runs in circles around the lobby.

Mr. French, however, does not oblige.

I bend down to the box and open the lid. Inside, a fluffy orange face looks up at me and begins to purr.

"It's a kitten," I say, lifting the animal from the box. Purring even louder, the kitten climbs up my chest to sit on my shoulder and nuzzle against my ear.

Mrs. Pennell's door opens. "What is going on out here? King William and I can't hear our show."

"YOU!" The woman gasps for breath. "Are responsible."

"Me?" asks Mrs. Pennell.

"Not you," says the woman. "HIM!"

She is pointing directly at King William, who sits at Mrs. Pennell's feet washing his face with a paw.

"King William?" I ask.

"Yes!" The woman stops moving and Mr. French loses his grip. He slides to the floor. "That beast took advantage of my poor Pearl. Look at the size of that brutish kitten. It has completely ruined her showgirl figure."

"Showgirl?" I ask.

"Pearl is a queen champion," the woman says. "But the scandal of this illegitimate offspring will cost her the crown."

"Well, I don't know how this happened," says Mrs. Pennell. "King William never goes outside."

"Except when he escapes," I say, remembering my late-night encounter a few days earlier.

"Ahh, yes, well…" Mrs. Pennell straightens her shoulders. "What makes you believe King William is the father?"

"Look at the kitten," says the woman. "It's a monster, just like your—"

"I think," I interrupt, "that insults won't solve anything."

"No," sniffs the woman. "You're right. We must rise above it."

"What can we do?" I ask.

"The damage is already done, but I shall not raise that monster in my home."

Bored with nuzzling my ear, the kitten curls around my neck and yawns.

"Well, neither shall I," says Mrs. Pennell. "King William is enough company for me."

"I'll take him," I say, smiling. "Hell, I'm already in love."

"Fine," says the woman.

I reach up to stroke the kitten's fluffy head.

"I suppose," I add, "with a king for a father and a queen for a mother, that would make this little guy a true prince."

The woman harrumphs. "Now," she says, "if you could get this little man off my leg, I would like to leave."

I look down to see Mr. French lying on the floor, both hands wrapped tight around the woman's ankle.

"You can let go now," I say with laughter in my voice. "But you may want to get her number for later. I think you two could hit it off."

Mr. French leaps to his feet, his face flush with embarrassment.

"Ahhh," he stammers.

The woman peers down at him for a moment, her face a mask of stone. But then something unexpected happens and her features soften.

"You know where I live," she says in a slightly gentler tone.

Mr. French nods, his face bright red, as the woman turns to shoo Clifford away from the front doors and makes her exit.

Enjoying the warmth I feel in my soul, I wish everyone a good night and head upstairs to cuddle with my new prince charming.

-30-

© Don Denton, Black Press

ABOUT THE AUTHOR

M.C. Grant is the secret identity of international thriller writer Grant McKenzie. (Oops, there goes that secret.) Born in Scotland, living in Canada, and writing fast-paced fiction, Grant likes to wear a kilt and toque with his six-guns. Often compared to Harlan Coben and Linwood Barclay, Grant has three internationally published thrillers to his name—*Switch*, *No Cry for Help*, and *K.A.R.M.A.*—that have earned him an avalanche of positive reviews and loyal readership around the globe. As a journalist, he has won numerous awards across Canada and the United States, including one in 2012 from the Association of Alternative Newsmedia—the same organization that Dixie's fictitious *San Francisco NOW* belongs to. He is currently Editor-in-Chief of *Monday Magazine* in Victoria, B.C. You can find him online at: http://grantmckenzie.net.